Fickle Friends

Betsey & Desmond,

with lots of love
and thanks

Jane

Other titles by the author

A Marriage of Mixed Motives

The Apparent Heir

Fickle Friends

JANEY WATSON

Bosworth Books Ltd

For Mum and Dad

First published in 2006 by Bosworth Books Ltd.

Cataloguing in Publication Data is available from the British Library.

ISBN 0 9553289 0 X
ISBN 978 0 9553289 0 9

Bosworth Books Ltd, Whiteway Court,
Cirencester, Glos GL7 7BA

Design and typesetting by Liz Rudderham
Printed in Europe by the Alden Group, Oxfordshire

Thanks must go to the following people:
to Mary Fitzgerald, my secretary, who suffers turning my
handwriting into text; to Anne Rickard, my editor, and
Liz Rudderham, for then turning it into a published novel.

And finally a huge thank you to all at Bosworth
for jollying me along.

1

*T*here had been a spate of severe frosts over the previous two weeks and the trees around the common had responded by turning to shades of gold. A young woman standing on the lip of the hill gazed appreciatively down into the valley which was now basking in the brittle November sunlight.

Amongst the jewels of beech and larch were the mellow Cotswold stone buildings that made up the village of Buscombe. In the depths of the valley were the stolid rectangular mill buildings teetering on the edge of the race whose foaming water winked and glistened.

Davina Stanley pushed her hands deeper into her muff and sighed before turning along the escarpment in preparation for leaving her viewing point. She knew she must return home before dusk fell or her over-anxious mother would scold her but the common had a hold on her in its autumnal glory.

There were animals turned out for winter grazing, a few tethered house cows but mostly ponies, sheep, pigs and cattle mingled and jostled, searching for the best fodder on the sparse ground. One of the ponies came up to her, hopeful of a treat. She showed him an empty hand briefly released from her muff, so he threw up his head playfully and turned tail, the cold air making him skittish.

The wind, though bracing, did not penetrate Davina's warm pelisse and her feet, safely encased in strong leather boots, were not cold. She was a tall slender girl with well-defined features highlighted by dark brows and fine brown hair which was drawn back from her face and tucked securely under a serviceable bonnet. She had undertaken to walk to the hillside cottages well prepared and she was now returning home after executing her commission.

The sun was setting as she trod resolutely across the raked gravel to the front door. Fromeview Place was protected from the common by a thick, low wall of weathered Cotswold stone. The house was of modern design having been built some twenty years earlier in place of an Elizabethan manor that had become too difficult to maintain for two elderly spinsters. The Miss Leonards, Felicia and Leonora, had enjoyed considerable wealth and in a last act of exuberance before entering their dotage, they commissioned their friend, Anthony Keck, to design them a house modelled on Brownshill Court at Painswick. Because their needs were simple they had dispensed with the matching single storey wings to either side and had settled on the commodious square house on three floors. It was symmetrical about a central Venetian window on the first floor and its main doorway was augmented by a tall pedimented Ionic porch.

Davina loved this house with its bayed frontage; it seemed to envelop her in love and security. Letting herself in through the door she felt a wave of warmth assail her as she crossed the threshold. From the nether regions of the house her mother appeared as though she had been on the watch for her although she could not have seen Davina's approach from the back of the house.

Mrs Stanley was a graceful woman of medium height who disguised her still relative youth by wearing dark clothes and a lace cap. Her attire proclaimed the widow but when the light was on her beautifully-cut dresses it could be seen that they were not in fact true black but had a sheen of green or blue or bronze like the feathers of a bird. Her features were regular but her dark eyes held a hint of wistfulness for what might have been.

Inured to her mother's gentle anxiety, Davina parried her

breathless questions and allowed herself to be drawn to the hall fire that was burning enthusiastically.

Mrs Stanley tugged a bell in capitulation. It was very quickly answered by the brisk steps of a middle-aged housekeeper.

'Mrs Tulley, quickly please, we must remove Miss Davina's coat and get her warm again. Please send Nancy for a shawl.' Nancy, a round-faced country girl familiar with Mrs Stanley's ways, had already followed Mrs Tulley out of the staff premises. She now turned without being told and headed for the back stairs.

Mrs Tulley met Davina's eyes with a hint of a smile, her comely face full of sympathetic understanding.

'Now, don't you worry ma'am, we'll soon have the young lady warm again,' she said over her shoulder to Mrs Stanley.

Davina made no attempt to dispute that she was cold, as she knew from long experience that it was better to let her mother assuage her initial concern with a little fussing.

'I really don't know why you must walk everywhere, my dear,' her mother said as she dithered around while the housekeeper removed Davina's coat and took her hat. 'Carter would be only too happy to take you in the gig.'

'You know why I walk, Mama,' laughed Davina, shaking out her crumpled hair and receiving the shawl from Nancy who had returned in record speed. 'The road cuts across the common and the views are indifferent. If I walk I can see right across the valley.'

'But you have seen that view any time in the last sixteen years. Do you never weary of it?'

Davina mouthed her thanks to her attendants and, linking her arm through her mother's, led her through into an elegant saloon. Here too there was a roaring fire and many brightly burning candles compensated for the fading light outside.

'Never,' cried Davina, 'with every day it changes. Every day there is something new to see and enjoy.'

Mrs Stanley let out a deep sigh. 'You are a romantic, my dear; it would be well if others too could cultivate your contentment with simple pleasures.'

To an uninitiated auditor it might be thought that Mrs Stanley was dissatisfied with her own life. Yet it would be hard to imagine why she might be so. She had been very fortunate in latter years and was now surrounded by the trappings of wealth.

Mrs Stanley had arrived at Fromeview Place, some sixteen years previously, on the recommendation of her godmother to her friends the Miss Leonards. She was seen to be a young widow whose soldier husband had been lost at sea on his return from the war in America. Mrs Stanley had come to be companion to the old ladies and she had brought her tiny daughter with her.

The old ladies had been charmed by Mrs Stanley, whose willingness to serve them had been unbounded. They soon had her running the house and organising the daily routine. And, if they had been charmed by the mother, they had adored the daughter who, from the moment she had arrived, had entranced them with her sweetness of disposition.

As the Miss Leonards became more and more frail, they relied heavily on Mrs Stanley, who had risen to the challenge, employing an efficient housekeeper to augment the services of the very elderly butler. (His presence was never looked for from luncheon until four o'clock in the afternoon, as everyone knew he had retired for a nap.)

The house ran smoothly even as the old ladies became bedridden and then, as quietly as they had lived, they died, Miss Felicia only outlasting her younger sister by six weeks.

Mrs Stanley and her daughter had been devoted to them to the last. None of the anxiety that characterised her latterly had been evident then. She had been calm and busy, taking at face value the old ladies' assurances that they would not leave her destitute. She had not let worldly considerations overshadow her care of them, only expecting a small legacy that would allow her and her daughter to live frugally in a country cottage.

Mrs Stanley had not considered the possibility that she would inherit a substantial amount. She had neglected to take account of the fact that the Miss Leonards had been the last of their line.

There were no obvious heirs and the ladies had been free to pass their money to whom they wished. So besides a number of smaller bequests to their old retainers, they had left the newly built house and grounds and £35,000 to Mrs Stanley outright. The remainder of their funds had been left to Davina, in trust until she was twenty-one. The trustees were the local Rector and their solicitor, one Mr Pomford, based in Stroud. Miss Davina Stanley was now an heiress to a fortune in excess of £100,000.

None of these stirring events however had altered either of the beneficiaries very much. If Mrs Stanley indulged herself in the purchase of haute couture she did not flaunt this amongst her neighbours. Her daughter remained much cherished but there was no encouragement to her to give up old friends and aspire to new ones. The Rector's third daughter was still her closest friend and confidante. There was no attempt to climb society's ladder. The Stanleys remained, as they had always been; stalwart friends and neighbours.

One aspect of their existence had changed however. Mrs Stanley's active mind, with less real employment, occupied itself with anxiety and all of it centred on Davina. There had come a point when even the most patient of daughters would have rebelled at so much cosseting. However, luckily for Davina, the Rector's wife was a very sensible woman and on seeing some of Mrs Stanley's exquisite stitchery had commissioned her to produce some elegant embroidery for her second daughter's trousseau. Soon, Mrs Stanley, discovering in herself an aptitude for design, turned some of her excess attention to her handiwork. She would still fuss and flutter but it was no longer oppressive and Davina's sweet-tempered tolerance was assured.

The two ladies, having refreshed themselves with a dish of bohea and after exchanging details of their afternoon retired to change for an early dinner. Having no expectation of visitors that night, Davina dressed with the help of Nancy into a high-necked gown with thick underdress. She wrapped the warm shawl around her, for despite many fires warming the rooms it could still become chilly as the evening wore on and the fires were allowed to die down.

Downstairs in the saloon, Davina found her mother awaiting her. This good lady was much more composed now and had turned her attention to preparations for the staff Christmas party that had become a tradition long ago established by the Miss Leonards. Although neither mother nor daughter had a lady's dresser, they both were attended by maids. While Mrs Tulley oversaw a cook, two housemaids, two kitchen maids, and a tweeny, Mr Masterson, the butler, had a footman and an under-footman to run his errands. Outside the wiry old head groom ruled the stables with a rod of iron, supported by the coachman and a stable boy. There were also two gardeners. As it was a rural area most of these people had families, so the party Mrs Stanley was contemplating spanned four generations and included about fifty people.

The ladies continued the discussion throughout their meal, trying to recall successes and failures of previous years so that they could amend their plans to accommodate them.

It was after they had again returned to the saloon to set some stitchery that the doorbell was tugged vigorously. Mrs Stanley's eyes flew to Davina's face in swift enquiry but Davina shook her head. She had no idea whom it might be. They both waited in statue-like anticipation for Masterson's laboured footsteps to cross the open hall.

There was the babble of unintelligible voices, then the sound of hasty footsteps in their direction. The door burst open and Miss Ernestine Greenaway arrived in the room in a haze of frills and furbelows and delighted laughter. Her mother, sniffing with disapproval, followed more stolidly in her wake and waited for Masterson to announce her.

Casting aside their embroidery both Mrs and Miss Stanley rose to greet their unexpected guests.

'My dear Mrs Greenaway, what a charming surprise. I thought you were fixed in Bath for another week.'

Stripping off her gloves the Rector's wife gave Mrs Stanley's hand a perfunctory shake. 'You are in the right of it,' she agreed in her matter of fact way, 'but Mr Greenaway sent an urgent message that Cook is indisposed and that he could spare us from the Rectory no longer. He is always so busy as Advent approaches.'

'What a disappointment for you,' murmured her hostess who was always eclipsed by the force of Mrs Greenaway's personality.

'Oh but we have got something much, much more exciting to discuss,' exclaimed Ernestine unable to contain herself any longer, her mobile face alive with enthusiasm. She took Davina's hand and drew her to a settle near to the fire. 'Can you imagine, my Aunt Maria has invited us,' she said gesturing with her ever-moving hand to include both Stanleys, 'to a house party at her home in Averbury at Christmas time.'

Davina's eyes lit up. 'Oh Ernestine how delightful, how very kind of her.' She turned to her mother. 'Mama please do say we may go.'

Mrs Stanley's pallor deepened. She looked first at Mrs Greenaway's rather stern countenance framed by crimped grey curls and then at the daughter who was almost her antithesis in appearance. Where Mrs Greenaway's hair was rigidly secure, Ernestine's strawberry blond curls were escaping in all directions about her face. The girl was dressed in light apricot furbished with lace and down while Mrs Greenaway favoured clothes of a sober hue. The dusky murky purple she was currently wearing made her appear dowdy and unfashionable.

'It is most kind of your sister, Mrs Greenaway, most kind,' Mrs Stanley managed, 'but you must know that I do not go out into society. Since the loss of my husband....'

'Oh fiddle,' said Mrs Greenaway, cutting across her without apology, 'of course you must go. You cannot deny the girls their treat. You are aware of course that I must attend the parish during this time, so your presence would be required if they are to go.'

'No, I'm sorry.' Mrs Stanley, who had sat down when her guest had, now stood up with some decision. 'I really cannot accept this kind invitation, it would not be in keeping with my husband's memory.'

'Oh Mama.' Davina stood up to join her mother. 'Could we not go this once?'

'No my dear, it would not be suitable.'

Ernestine, whose mercurial temperament had swung from ecstasy to despair, bit her lip and winked away easy tears.

'Well,' said Mrs Greenaway, considerably put out by such unprecedented stubbornness from a lady whose will she could normally bend. 'I think you refine too much upon your widowhood. You owe it to your daughter to shake off your melancholy and present her to society.'

Mrs Stanley chose not to reply, so, admitting defeat, the Rector's formidable wife angrily pulled on her gloves again and swept herself and her daughter out of the room and out of the house.

They left behind them a profound silence as though a spell held the Stanleys motionless, until suddenly and without warning, Mrs Stanley pulled out a lace handkerchief and held it to her mouth. She gave a shuddering sob and ran out of the room.

Baffled by her mother's strange behaviour, Davina collected up the embroidery and returned the silks to their respective boxes, her mind seething with conjecture. Then, with a hesitancy that reflected her inward agitation she moved towards the stairway and made slow progress up its sweeping curve. Once on the first floor she knocked on her mother's bedroom door. The delay in her pursuit had allowed Mrs Stanley a moment to collect herself. She came to the door and indicated to her daughter to come in.

The room seemed to reflect its occupant's unhappiness. Normally, when well lit it gave the impression of a rose garden with its floral drapes both at the window and around the four-poster bed, the sweet-smelling pot-pourri pervading. Tonight, however, in the poor candle light and with only embers in the fireplace it seemed drab and chilly.

'You have no doubt come to apologise.' Mrs Stanley's words were frigidly uttered.

'Apologise?' stammered Davina, thrown off balance.

'I will not have insubordination in front of visitors however well we are acquainted with them,' her mother pronounced. 'You did not see Ernestine setting herself up in opposition to her mother's dictates.'

Davina was appalled; she had never heard such words from her kind and doting mother.

'I'm sorry...,' she faltered, 'I didn't mean...'

There was a lightening of Mrs Stanley's expression. 'No, very well,' she said hurriedly, 'we will put it behind us. We will not mention it again.'

'If you say so, Mama,' agreed Davina submissively.

Her mother leaned towards her and gave her a brief hug before turning away to call the maid. Davina withdrew, conscious of deep and crushing disappointment. She had previously had no expectation of visiting country houses of the sort owned by Mrs Greenaway's sister, Lady Thistledown and had thus never considered how she might feel about entering the upper echelons of society. The gaiety of her life was limited to small country parties where they knew all the guests. A situation where they might have to meet visiting aristocracy had never presented itself before. For although the two older Miss Greenaways had made their début into polite society they had done so whilst Davina was still in the schoolroom and her mother only the companion to the Miss Leonards. Davina went to bed bemused and confounded by her mother's behaviour.

A night of undisturbed slumber appeared to have restored Mrs Sansom to a more equitable mood. She skirted quite ably enough to her bewildered daughter over breakfast, but her sombre mood was replaced by the admiration of the terrace by the afternoon hours.

...she soaked in the softest comfort of what was to be endured a long time...

Davina peered up at her mother through her eyelashes, unwilling to look her directly in the face. The much-tried lady came fully into the room and manoeuvred one of the upright chairs so that she could sit immediately opposite her daughter. She then removed the embroidery from Davina's now slack hands and took hold of them, shaking them gently.

16

2

A night of undisturbed slumber appeared to have restored Mrs Stanley to a more equitable mood. She chatted amicably enough to her bewildered daughter over breakfast but her sunnier mood was eclipsed by the admittance of the Rector by the ancient butler.

He arrived at the earliest extreme of what was considered a polite time for morning callers and indicated a need to speak to Mrs Stanley alone. He was a powerful man both in frame and in his vocation and he generally carried all with him as he was well liked and true to his cloth. His booming voice and penetrating blue eyes only served to augment his armoury when dealing with recalcitrant parishioners.

Davina waited in the music room, trying in vain to concentrate on practising her sonata. She did not need to hear more than the resonance of the Rector's voice to know what it was about and it made her fingers wooden on the keys. In exasperation she gave up and retired to one of the smaller parlours at the back of the house, completely out of earshot, to take up her stitchery. It was here, some twenty minutes later, her mother discovered her.

Davina peered up at her mother through her eyelashes, unwilling to look her directly in the face. The much-tried lady came fully into the room and manoeuvred one of the upright chairs so that she could sit immediately opposite her daughter. She then removed the embroidery from Davina's now slack hands and took hold of them, shaking them gently.

Davina lifted her head and managed to meet her mother's eyes. The trouble she saw in their depths banished any lingering desire to pit her wants in opposition to those of her mother.

'Oh Mama, I crave your pardon,' she begged hurriedly. 'I do not wish to go if it causes you even a shred of disquiet. Please let us put the whole matter aside.'

'Regrettably, my love, we cannot now follow that course.' Mrs Stanley smiled warmly at her daughter but it was a lopsided smile. 'The Rector has seen fit as your trustee to remind me that my duty to you outweighs any considerations of mine own.'

Davina was perplexed. 'Duty? What duty to me does it include?'

Mrs Stanley sighed. 'You are encumbered with a large fortune, Davina. The Rector believes you should be given every opportunity to marry. His contention is that you will need a husband to manage your fortune.'

'But the Miss Leonards never did!' The words burst from Davina before she could check them.

Mrs Stanley put up a hand to forestall any further hasty words. 'It is an argument which does not weigh with him.' She stood up and took a turn around the small room. 'In many ways he has it correctly. The Miss Leonards' father was an austere man, who kept his daughters very close until after they were of marriageable age. You can be sure that if they had been offered the choice earlier in their lives they would have embraced it. A married lady has much more freedom than a single one, my dear. I cannot reasonably impose the restrictions of my life on you.'

After the one outburst Davina knew she must contain herself, so as she groped for the right words, there was a pause punctuated only by the crackling of the fire in the grate. 'You speak as though you have agreed to let me go alone,' she said eventually.

Mrs Stanley moved to straighten the heavy curtains at the window. 'I have so agreed,' she said as she looked out at the leaf-strewn lawn which the under-gardener had begun to rake for the third time that week. 'You are too young to appreciate the sentiments that bind me to your father's memory. To have to accept that I would never see him again was a bitter blow which I could only withstand by withdrawing from society. One day I hope to be able to make you understand but that time is not now.'

It was on the tip of Davina's tongue to question her mother further about her father but past experience had told her it would be futile. Instead she asked: 'But how can I go without you, Mama? Who will chaperone us?'

'That is all arranged.' Mrs Stanley did not turn to face her daughter. 'As you know Lady Thistledown is Mrs Greenaway's sister. It is her house and her presence is ample protection for both you and Ernestine.'

'If that is so, why are the Greenaways so determined on my going? Ernestine does not therefore require my presence.'

Mrs Stanley hesitated. 'Perhaps not,' she conceded.

Davina went to her side. 'Can you not tell me more, Mama? You can repose complete confidence in my discretion, of that I can assure you.'

Mrs Stanley turned to her daughter and put her hands up to cup the sweet face.

'I know, I know.' She dropped her hands and went to the fire to encourage it with a poker. 'It seems the Greenaways fear an attachment between Ernestine and an unsuitable young man, a nephew of Lord Thistledown. Ernestine and he have met many times over the years and have shown a consistent and decided partiality for each other's company. Now that she is nearing marriageable age, the Greenaways wish to ensure that that partiality does not become widely known.'

Davina, who was to some extent in her friend's confidence, was thunderstruck. The liaison had always seemed so suitable to her. Ernestine's Charlie was a well connected young man, who, as a second son, might reasonably have been able to choose a wife to please himself rather than his family. Nor had Davina ever heard ill of him. She was at a loss to understand why he should have been deemed unsuitable.

Her silence prompted a fuller response from her mother than another outburst might have done. Mrs Stanley began to elaborate. 'I understand from Mr Greenaway that Lord Thistledown's sister married into the family before it was known how deeply some members of the family were addicted to gaming. Her father-in-law had mortgaged the estates and her new husband frittered away her settlement on poker and the horses. The Greenaways' full intention is to prevent any increased connection to that family.'

'Poor Ernestine,' Davina said sadly, 'and they want me to be the leaven?'

'Yes,' said Mrs Stanley eagerly, 'it will not look so particular if you accompany Ernestine on expeditions of pleasure.'

'No indeed, I see that.' Davina also saw that the Rector had been guilty of using-self interest when insisting that it was Davina's future well being that demanded her attendance at the Thistledown's house party. Clearly he had another agenda. It surprised her that he could be so manipulative; she had always thought of him as straightforward. It left an ember of unease in the back of her mind. 'But what of you, Mama? What will you do while I am away?'

'Oh you need not concern yourself about me. The Greenaways are to include me in all the parish festivities. I shall be very well occupied, thank you.'

There appeared nothing left to discuss, but Davina's initial enthusiasm for the expedition had been thoroughly extinguished. The few private moments snatched with Ernestine before their departure left her feeling like a Judas. Her friend was full of happy expectation. Her last meeting with Charlie had been a formal morning call during her visit to Bath; she anticipated many more opportunities during the Averbury visit to enjoy his company.

'I am so glad you are to meet him, Davina,' she had told her friend, a pretty colour in her cheeks and her soft eyes misty with tears. 'You will soon learn for yourself how considerate he is, how good looking.'

'I'm sure I will,' Davina had responded flatly, trying to stem the flow. She was only too thankful that Mrs Greenaway had hurried her daughter away on that occasion and that subsequent meetings had been fleeting acknowledgements in the street in the local village of Minchinhampnett or a more formal bow across the aisle of the church on Sunday.

When the day to depart finally came, Davina was jittery and pale. Her anxious mother feared she was sickening for something and would have vetoed her removal if she had received any encouragement from her daughter. This she did not get, not because Davina would not have gladly stayed at home, but because Davina knew that if she could not go then neither would Ernestine be allowed to and she most certainly could not disappoint her friend.

The journey was accomplished without incident and completed well within the short winter day, Averbury being only a little over thirty miles away. The Rector, fearful that his delicate daughter might suffer from the cold, had sent the young ladies and their maids all in the one carriage surrounded by rugs and with their feet on hot bricks. Thus they arrived less chilled than might have been foreseen.

They were welcomed effusively by Lady Thistledown who appeared a larger and more indolent version of her sister. She was dressed opulently and her hair clearly had lost any contact with its natural roots many years ago. Davina could not be sure whether the lady still favoured the wearing of a wig or whether her hair had been dressed directly with some colour enhancer but, coupled with a prominent nose, it did not encourage Davina to warm to her.

As they had been announced Lady Thistledown had risen theatrically from her chair and proceeded to make far more of Davina than Davina felt her nominal role as companion warranted.

'I welcome you to Averbury Grange most warmly, Miss Stanley, I do entreat you to be free with my home and my servants. Do command of them what you will.'

'You are very kind, your ladyship,' Davina managed to murmur whilst shrinking behind Ernestine's effervescent form but Lady Thistledown would have none of it, drawing the girl into the vast room to present her to the other guests already assembled.

'Well, well, so this is the gel,' said an elderly lady dressed in the fuller fashion of the previous decade. Briefly she extended her hand to give Davina's a limp shake. She tilted her head which was dressed in a ring of glorious grey curls so that her beady black eyes could examine the girl more closely. 'We've heard much about you,' the old lady said with no consideration for Davina's finer feelings, 'but little of it to the point. Who is your father? From whence comes your family?'

Davina flushed at so unprecedented an assault. Unequal to the task of combating it she turned her eyes imploringly to Ernestine who stepped nobly to the breach.

'Now come, Great Aunt Sophia, you can't start on your cate-chism before we have even changed for dinner,' she tinkled. 'You must not mind her,' she whispered into her friend's ear, 'she does it to everyone.'

This was small comfort to Davina to whom the questions had exposed a glaring omission in her life. She realised that she did not know anything much about her father or any of her fore-bears. She turned thankfully to be introduced to Lady Thistledown's daughter, Amelia and her sons Gerard and Basil, all of whom welcomed her in a detached and rather perfunctory way.

The other occupants of the room included a drab little woman in a high-necked gown and scraped-back hair who appeared to be the great aunt's lackey, and the much vaunted Charlie. Davina took one look into the face of this young man and knew him to be all that Ernestine had described. He was good looking with a shock of wavy golden hair. His clothes were well fitting and fash-ionable and his snowy white cravat was tied in intricate folds. Davina knew him to be just twenty but he looked and behaved with more maturity. While his eyes fleetingly devoured his lady love, his good manners brought the majority of attention to focus on Davina.

'Delighted,' he said, smiling kindly as Ernestine introduced them.

'Indeed, so am I,' Davina braved with a twinkle, such was the charm and ease he displayed.

Charlie drew the two young ladies away from the rest of the party before murmuring to Ernestine, 'I am so glad you have come. There has been so much vacillating that I was sure you would be forced to stay away.'

'No, no.' Ernestine stretched out a hand and laid it on Davina's arm, drawing her in to include her. 'Davina has been most steadfast in agreeing to come despite all her mother's protestations.'

'You are most kind, Miss Stanley,' Charlie assured her. 'I fear you will find little to amuse you. My aunt does not exert herself to entertain her guests, imagining an invitation to her abode to be sufficient.'

'It is indeed rather fine,' Davina murmured, gazing around the huge room wide-eyed. The walls were of deep peach, the paint rag-rolled to the dado rail to create a marbled effect. Three vast chandeliers hung from the arched ceiling that was beautifully decorated with intricate plaster mouldings. On three walls were a profusion of paintings, some large, some small, mostly depicting members of the family, but a few were elegant landscapes. One of the longer walls had lean tall windows that reached the ground and were adorned with great looped drapes which fell in graceful cascades down each side.

'Fine, certainly,' Charlie laughed, humouring her, 'but it will not take you many days to tire of it. Familiarity, Miss Davina, will soon lead to the inevitable contempt.'

'Sh! Charlie, you should not say so,' scolded Ernestine tapping him with her painted fan, 'my aunt is coming over, do pray hush.'

'Now what secrets are you discussing, children?' demanded Lady Thistledown as she came towards them like a ship in full sail. ' I will not have you poisoning Miss Davina's ears with your tittle tattle. Come, join the assembled company.'

So like a royal command was it, that none of the young people sought to gainsay her. They travelled meekly across the room to the rest of the gathering. Luckily for them though, before they could be dragged unwillingly into some insipid conversation, Lady Thistledown announced that dinner would be served in less than an hour and everyone hastily quitted the room to make themselves ready.

An urbane butler delivered Davina to her room where she discovered the maid, Nancy, still unpacking her clothes.

'Is it not a fine place, Miss?' ventured Nancy as Davina went and stood beside the fire.

'Very fine. I hope they have made you welcome below stairs?'

Nancy shot her an enquiring look before turning Davina so that she could undo the back of the girl's dress. 'Welcome enough, Miss,' she said circumspectly.

An involuntary shiver ran down Davina's spine.

'Now Miss, what made you do that then?' asked Nancy in some surprise.

Davina did not immediately answer, as though she were searching for the words to illustrate her feeling. 'I feel ...' she said slowly, 'out of place,' she finished lamely.

'Well,' said Nancy, 'if that is all it is Miss, then we have nothing to fear. Neither one of us is used to a household of this nature, we will grow accustomed to their ways.'

'I do hope you are right,' Davina sighed, 'because four weeks here feels like a very long time.

3

*N*ancy had turned Davina out in fine trim. The girl had never adopted the fussy toilette that Ernestine favoured. The latest fashion of a slimmer dress suited her exactly and she arrived in the dining room looking more like a goddess from an ancient Roman temple than a nineteenth century debutante at her first major social event.

A liveried footman attended Davina at her place and she was dismayed to find that she was sat next to Lady Thistledown's eldest son, Gerard. She could not imagine what she might find to talk to him about. It was fortunate then that he had little expectation of being entertained by her. Other guests, not honoured by an overnight stay, had been bidden to come to dinner. On Gerard's right hand there was a lively young lady who had clearly known him since birth and kept up an endless flow of conversation about the horses in the Thistledowns' string of hunters with whom she seemed intimately acquainted. Not having ridden since the demise of her own darling pony six years ago, Davina could offer nothing to this conversation at all. The gentleman to her left was a pimply youth, hampered by acute shyness, so any conversation with him was stilted and forced. Davina was left to look across wistfully to the other side of the table where Ernestine was seated next to Charlie. Just once did Ernestine look rather guiltily in her direction and blow her a tiny kiss. Davina could not help but suspect that somehow Ernestine had rearranged the seating. In fact when the ladies withdrew after dinner this suspicion was borne out. Despite the presence of several unknown ladies, Great Aunt Sophia was loud in condemnation of Ernestine's behaviour.

'Oh do pray hush,' commanded Lady Thistledown with a weather eye on her patently interested guests, 'there is no reason why Ernestine should not sit next to her cousin. It is of no moment, they have been as brother and sister for years.'

'My point, exactly,' countered the elderly virago, determined to have her voice heard. 'You know very well, Maria, that it is to introduce Ernestine to a wider society and to...,' she stopped abruptly as her eyes settled on Davina, 'that she is here.' She swooped on to the next sentence, daring anyone to notice the non sequitur.

'But it is only her first night here, Aunt,' said Lady Thistledown, 'not all our guests have yet arrived. I have every confidence that Ernestine will do her duty when the time comes.' She worked her face into a series of contortions indicative of her determination to have the matter closed.

Davina could take no more of what appeared to be double entendre and innuendo, and she put a hand on Ernestine's arm to feel it trembling.

'If I play the piano, will you sing?' she asked her friend.

Grateful for the diversion, Ernestine nodded. So after first asking permission, which was graciously granted, Davina went and sat herself at the piano.

After a hesitant start Ernestine threw herself into the music and soon the huddle of gossip-hungry ladies drifted apart, some to come closer to the music, others to take up different conversations in smaller knots around the room. By the time the gentlemen appeared, the tension had eased. Looking up from the piano, Davina was just quick enough to intercept a look from Charlie, and she frowned and gave a small shake of the head. He had taken a step towards the piano but stopped at Davina's instruction and instead he walked across to the tea tray that had just arrived and allowed his aunt to direct him in carrying the teacups to the various guests.

Davina sank into her bed that night exhausted already by her role of duenna. Ernestine had accompanied her to her bedroom door and had embraced her emotionally.

'I know it was foolish of me, Davina,' she whispered, 'but I thought it was harmless. Oh how I wish Great Aunt Sophia was not here to make mischief.'

Davina could not but agree. The old lady seemed to home in on any weakness or flaw. She clearly had no compunction about embarrassing people in front of others and her rapier-like tongue reached the nub of any issue in less time than it took her victim to gather their wits.

It was therefore an increasingly nervous Davina who descended for breakfast the next morning. The day was bright and crisp and there was a hum of eager anticipation amongst the horsemen and women of the party. The hunt would be gathering at the next village and every able-bodied person was doing their utmost to secure a mount for the day.

Gerard parried demands and entreaties, unmoved by the pleas of his guests. There were a few who had brought their own horses and another clutch of those with whose riding ability he was cognisant. These favoured few were eventually promised accommodation. Davina found his manner forced, lacking in sincerity; she thought he was enjoying the attention and liked him less than the evening before. She took her seat at the breakfast table as far away from the baying throng as she could.

The babble which had clearly been going on for no little time ceased abruptly at the entrance of Lady Thistledown and the so far unsuccessful supplicants turned as one body, like a shoal of fish, to assail her ladyship.

'What is all this nonsense?' she cried, throwing up her hands to ward off the approach. 'Of course there are horses enough for all. What can you be thinking of Gerard?'

Gerard's already florid countenance became suffused with a ruby red. He had long since grown out of receiving his mother's censure with composure and objected strongly to having his word countermanded. He came across to his mother, who was just taking her seat, and such was his ire that he nearly jostled one or two of the more excitable ladies.

'Mother,' Davina heard him hiss, 'half your guests know not one end of a horse from another, I will not have our beasts ridden to a standstill or put at a wall so they break their knees. I beseech you, have a care, this is valuable stock.'

Davina had to hide her mouth in her linen napkin to disguise the smile which had involuntarily lit her face. It would appear that Gerard had no care for his human guests but only for his horses.

Lady Thistledown, as robust an egotist as her son, had no plans to back down. She pursed her lips and ignored him, turning to Davina to say, 'Will you be joining the hunt, Miss Stanley? I am sure my son can find you a suitable lady's mount.'

Davina dabbed her lips with her napkin, to give her a little time for recovery. 'No,' she managed, 'no, thank you, I have not had the advantage of my own horse for some years, so I think I would be unwise to include myself.'

She thought that she saw a flicker of approval in Gerard's eye but it could only have been brief, if there at all, as he was using her response to prove to his mother the justification for his earlier decision. Davina did not know where to turn and longed for breakfast to be over so she could make her escape. She had never experienced family dissension carried out so publicly as it was in this house and it left her feeling distinctly uncomfortable.

'Cheer up, Miss Stanley.' Suddenly Charlie was on her other side, his laughing face bent down close to hers. 'Now you know why Ernestine chooses to take chocolate and toast in her room!'

It would have been rude to agree with him with Lady Thistledown in earshot so Davina tried for a noncontroversial answer. 'Is that what she does?' she asked, 'I wondered why I hadn't seen her.'

'She does not like brangles,' he said in a voice Davina wished he would pitch rather quieter, 'her only experience thus far has been when it was just the family. However I believe she guessed how it would be this morning.'

Glad to take the opportunity to change the subject, Davina asked him whether he knew if Ernestine planned to ride out that morning.

'Of course,' Charlie assured her, 'Tina wouldn't miss it for the world. She is an excellent horsewoman.'

The use of the diminutive form of Ernestine's name caused a flutter of anxiety in Davina's breast. She cast a look under her lashes in Lady Thistledown's direction but that formidable lady was still matching people to horses in the teeth of her son's opposition.

'But I cannot go with her,' she said breathlessly, assailed by the fear that she might be expected to accompany her friend.

'Oh, there's nothing to that,' Charlie assured her, 'all the cousins are going, even long-faced Amelia enjoys the chase, so you need not agitate yourself.'

Although relieved by this reprieve, Davina could not help feeling rather forlorn. It seemed that nearly everyone would be taking part. Even Aunt Sophia and Lady Thistledown were going to the meet in an antiquated barouche, to see the pack leave. It had occurred to Lady Thistledown to invite her young guest to join them in the carriage forcing Davina to accept with as much gratitude as she could muster.

On quitting the breakfast table, Davina had had no expectation of being involved in the day's pursuit so she had returned to her room to fetch the score of a piece she was learning on the piano. On her return she had passed the door of what appeared to be her host's study. She heard her name mentioned and thought Charlie was calling to her so she went to the door, which was just ajar, ready to knock and go in, when she heard Lady Thistledown's immoderate voice saying words which were clearly not for her ears.

'I am glad you are attempting to make the gel's better acquaintance Charlie. The fortune would set your family aright. The lack of lineage is lamentable but such is the desperate nature of your uncle's finances that I think you must overlook the mysterious nature of her parentage.'

'Aunt, please.' Charlie's voice had none of the light-hearted tones of half an hour earlier, it was laden with care. 'You know that I am all but promised to Ernestine, our affections are engaged. I cannot in all honour transfer my attention to someone else, no matter how charming, to suit the family coffers.'

'Charles, I am surprised at you. You have always seemed so steady. This is your duty.'

'My duty,' the words seemed to explode from Charlie's lips, 'why should it be my duty? The debts were my father's and grandfather's and Lucien has compounded them. Why should I be the one to make the sacrifice, when my uncle has seen fit to remain single. He could as easily have taken a rich wife years ago. Yet it is I, who have done nothing to add to the total, who is being expected to give up my love and marry a fortune.'

At first frozen by the implication of the words she was over-hearing, Davina could not move, but a silent and bitter struggle was going on in her head. She knew she must walk away, hear no more - that it would only stab her with further shafts of pain. However, she could not make that move. She thought of the pain these people had inflicted on her mother, who had been induced to allow this visit by methods of emotional blackmail. The Rector was supposed to be their friend, her moral mentor, but instead he had involved himself in a desperate ruse to snare her into saving a section of his wife's family to whom she owed no allegiance. Davina found that a wave of nausea was surging up from the pit of her stomach, so real that at last she had to turn and flee to the sanctuary of her bedroom. She tugged the bell vigorously for Nancy and waited, a drooping statue with a cloth pressed tightly to her lips, for deliverance.

It took Nancy a little time to answer the summons. She flurried into the room and took in as many details as one can from the profile and stance of another human being.

'Good heavens, Miss, what has happened?'

Davina let the cloth slip. 'We must away from here, Nancy,' she cried, her stricken face alarming the maid considerably, 'I cannot stay here, not with these people.'

The maid, while never having confronted Davina in this state had seen Mrs Stanley similarly afflicted in the past, so she set about trying to restore some calm before getting to the root of the problem. She took Davina's hand and drew her to the bed and then, leaning the girl's head on her shoulder, she stroked the silky dark hair.

'Now then Miss,' she counselled, 'take a deep breath and tell me what has upset you.'

'I,' Davina faltered, conscious that speaking of what she had heard was tantamount to admitting to eavesdropping.

'Yes.'

'I...' She could not find the words, and her tongue cleaved to the roof of her mouth. 'I cannot,' she stuttered.

'Oh yes you can,' said the maid determinedly. She wanted to get to the bottom of this as she feared some ardent young man might have frightened her beautiful young charge.

Davina took the recommended deep breath. 'Very well then,' she said on a little sob, 'but I beg you not to think badly of me.'

Nancy tightened her hold. 'I could never do that Miss,' she assured her.

'Then I will tell you what I have overheard.'

Nancy could not quite stifle a sigh of relief.

'Yes, go on then,' she prompted.

So Davina recounted the conversation between Charlie and Lady Thistledown. 'So you see, I am betrayed by my friends,' she finished on a dramatic note.

Nancy took a moment to reply, then what she said was rather unexpected. 'Not by all your friends, Miss. By the older generation, I grant you. Mr Charlie and Miss Ernestine, mind, have no thoughts of betrayal. You must see that.'

Davina lifted her head from Nancy's shoulder and looked down at her hands as she began to fiddle with the loose braid on her dress. 'No thoughts but for each other.' The words had a slightly hollow ring.

'Now you are being unkind,' said Nancy firmly. 'They are young, very much in love, they know their family intends to thwart them. Even you, Miss Ernestine's friend, had already been primed to divide them.'

'No!' Davina stood up in a quick jerky movement. 'No, I would not betray them, never, never' she finished on a passionate note.

Nancy stood up too but she did not approach the girl. 'Perhaps not intentionally, Miss, but you young people are at the mercy of the whims of your elders. Those that pay the piper call the tune, that's for certain. Miss Ernestine will have to do what her parents dictate. Mr Charlie cannot marry her as he has no money. This much I have already learned from the servants hall.'

'Is there talk of me there?' Davina was momentarily diverted from her impassioned stance.

'Harmless tittle tattle, that's all, nothing to concern yourself about.'

'Tittle tattle. I know what that's about,' Davina snapped, 'who was my father, where was he from?' Her voice mimicked her critics and it carried with it acid undertones.

'Miss Davina!'

Davina's voice changed immediately. 'Take me home Nancy!' she wailed, 'please take me home.'

Nancy gave a gesture of hopelessness. 'And what would we say to your mother, Miss, what would we say to her?'

Davina's eyes met hers but could not maintain the hold. 'You are right, of course, I cannot go home, but it will be purgatory while I wait for the time to pass.'

4

*B*y the time Davina's agitation had subsided enough for her to quit her room, Lady Thistledown had left. The formidable hostess had seen no reason to await her guest's pleasure or to send a message up to her room requesting that she should make haste. Davina descended the stairs to find a strangely quiet house.

Resorting to her music, she went to the music room and started playing rather diffidently as she felt uncomfortable disturbing the peace. Gradually, however, the music took over and she gave in to it, allowing the ebb and flow of the melody to express and then soothe her lacerated feelings. She played for nearly an hour and finished on a delicate and complicated rondo. As the last notes of the instrument died away there was movement from behind her.

'Bravo, bravo, I say.'

Davina swivelled on her seat to confront her auditor and found herself being appraised by a tall man in his early forties. His dark hair was greying at the temples and his eyes, while twinkling at her now, were surrounded by the fine lines of deep sadness. For all that, his bearing was good and he was smartly dressed in a navy blue coat of superfine. His cravat, although not intricately tied, was evidently donned with care. Davina thought him very fine and blushed with embarrassment at his scrutiny.

'Thank you, Sir,' she managed to murmur.

'You play well, Miss Stanley, a joy to be heard.' Her surprise that he knew her identity momentarily overcame her shyness; her eyes flickered to his face and she rose from the stool.

The gentleman came forward and executed a fluent bow. 'I see I have advantage over you,' he smiled, 'my name is Restharrow, Lord Restharrow.'

Davina bobbed a curtsy; the name meant nothing to her but he seemed so well disposed towards her that she dared ask him how he knew her name.

'A process of deduction,' he laughed. 'I met Basil on my arrival, he had taken a toss and had to return with his horse. He told me the house was empty of guests except perhaps yourself whom he had not seen at the meet.'

'I see.' It was indeed a morning of revelation. Davina was surprised that Basil had noticed her absence as he had shown even less interest in her than his pompous elder brother Gerard.

There was a pause, an extended silence while neither moved to fill the gap. Davina felt that Lord Restharrow's gaze had not left her face but her eyes, after the initial activity, refused to raise above the ground. It was the gentleman who eventually found his voice.

'Come,' he said with decision, 'it is a fine, bright day so let us take a turn around the shrubbery while we await the others' return.' Davina acquiesced gratefully. She had had no very good idea of how she was going to pass the time now that she had done her music practice and she did not want to be alone with her thoughts. She went to the bell rope and asked the maid who answered the call to send Nancy down with her pelisse and bonnet. It may have been bright outside but it was cold and crisp as well.

The shrubbery was not far from the house but it was extensive with many paths criss-crossing it. There were ancient privet hedges, fashioned into archways and turrets and tunnels of wistaria, bare now while likely to be fabulous in late spring when its opulent pendants of flowers adorned it. The paths were wide and well gravelled ensuring that mud did not spatter up the ladies' dresses. Davina had to wonder why money was so freely spent here on the house and gardens yet there were such desperate efforts to ensnare her to save the fortune of other family members. She wondered if her new acquaintance might enlighten her. He was currently pointing out rare specimens of tree for her attention.

'It is quite a collection,' he was saying as he stopped to point out a narrow tree of deep evergreen.

'But who is responsible for its gathering together?' Davina asked as he had fallen silent.

'Why my Lord Thistledown, of course,' he responded, mildly surprised by her ignorance. 'In his younger days he travelled widely. Had his health not failed him, I believe he would have established a pinetum to rival any in the country. It is a pity that neither of his sons interest themselves in its continuation.'

'So what has become of Lord Thistledown? I did wonder because Gerard is not Lord Thistledown yet, is he?'

'Good heavens, no.' Lord Restharrow turned to her and directed a searching look into her upturned face. 'Have you not been introduced to him?'

Davina shook her head as her escort gave an exclamation of annoyance. 'Really this is too bad. Maria really ought to have more care of the proper observances. When we have finished our walk I will take you to him.'

They continued on together, chatting easily. Davina found him a good listener and found herself telling him much more about her home and circumstances than was her custom. They were soon discussing how she filled her time when she was not concentrating on her music. He was dismayed to hear that she had not ridden for so many years.

'I had hoped we might enjoy an expedition of pleasure to the ancient stones at Avebury,' he said.

'We could go by carriage, Sir,' Davina suggested, anxious not to miss out on a treat.

He was dubious. 'They are spread over a wide area inaccessible to a carriage. It is most unfortunate that you do not ride; what can your mother have been thinking of?'

Davina, taking the question at face value, began to defend her mother's decision. 'When my old pony died it was after the Miss Leonards had died. We had no gentleman to advise us except the Rector and my mother had to lean on him rather heavily already. You must know him, Sir, he has a large family and a busy parish. My mother did not like to burden him further. Our coachman is elderly and would not take on the responsibility. It seemed wrong to pursue it.'

The gentleman beside her gave a chuckle. 'You are too forgiving, Miss Stanley,' he said. 'What you should say is that your mother preferred to keep you close and did not want you galloping around the countryside exposing yourself to danger.'

For all her quickness, Davina had never examined it from that perspective and she felt a spurt of anger assail her. She bit her lip, knowing she should challenge what he said but it had too clear a ring of truth for her to do so. Luckily Lord Restharrow did not appear to want a response.

'I have it,' he said, pleased with himself, 'I shall teach you to ride while we are here. Amelia has more hacks and hunters than are good for her, we will beg the use of one from her.'

'But we cannot possibly,' cried Davina, torn between her delight at the scheme and her determination not to be beholden to this conniving family.

'Of course we can,' he said with decision. 'Lady Thistledown is after all my sister-in-law if one stretches the point.'

'I'm sorry,' gasped Davina.

He caught her under her elbow as she tripped. 'Miss Stanley are you all right, pray what is wrong, do you feel ill?'

'No, no, I am fine.' She brushed his concern aside and gently removed his hand from her arm. She stumbled forward to a conveniently situated garden chair and sank on to it thankfully.

Deeply troubled, Lord Restharrow came and sat down beside her. 'What can be the matter, Miss Stanley?'

'Nothing, nothing, pray forgive me. A moment, just give me a moment and I shall make a recovery,' she said breathlessly.

There was silence as she struggled with herself. He, on the other hand, sat attentively, deep perturbation showing on his lined face.

After a while Davina seemed to overcome her stupor, and she turned wide questioning eyes to his face.

'Am I to understand,' she faltered, 'that you are Mr Winstanleigh's uncle?'

'Yes, I am Charlie Winstanleigh's uncle, what of it?'

'This makes you brother-in-law to Lord Thistledown's sister?'

'Yes, yes, have I not said that Lady Thistledown is virtually my sister-in-law. What of it?'

Davina turned her head away to stare blindly up the avenue down which they had just come. She felt weak with the enormity of the conspiracy around her. She had taken to this man, she had responded confidingly to his charm and now it seemed he was just another player in the game to snare her fortune.

She knew she had all but given herself away to him. She could not see any clear path through it. She needed Nancy's counsel, and she tried to imagine what the maid might say. Foolish to rely so heavily on her but all this manoeuvring was so alien to Davina's previous experiences coming as she did from such a cosseted and cushioned environment. From somewhere an unlooked for inner strength stiffened her back and turned her away from defeat and despair. She stood up with decision.

'Forgive me,' she said in a voice firmer than she was accustomed to using, 'a momentary faintness, nothing more.'

The concern on his face lightened. 'Perhaps you are in need of sustenance,' he said quickly, 'let us repair to the house. I believe a light repast is to be laid out in the dining room. I have detained you here too long.'

They moved back to the house with one accord and were greeted in the hallway by Lady Thistledown, just recently returned from her outing.

'So you have met our young guest,' she said to his lordship. 'I trust you are pleased with her.'

Despite all her new resolve, Davina could not prevent herself from blushing.

'Yes indeed, charming, charming.' Lord Restharrow drew Davina's hand through his arm and patted it. 'We have been making each other's acquaintance in your absence.'

'Very sensible,' replied Lady Thistledown, dismissing the matter and sweeping on to the dining room. The others followed in her wake.

Here they found Basil nursing a bruised arm and a cut above his left eye. He had begun eating but broke off and stood up when the others entered. His mother threw up her hands in horror at the sight of him but he fended off her intrusive questions with a dexterity which made his brother's breakfast blustering seem boorish in comparison. Davina looked at him afresh. He had thick auburn hair which would have made him appear dashing if it had not been for the slightly puffy rounded appearance of his face. His features seemed to congregate too close together in the centre of it. Davina realised she was studying him too closely and averted her eyes to discover Lord Restharrow was watching her.

She made a little show of settling herself at the table determined not to allow herself to exhibit further embarrassment and awkwardness. Luckily Lady Thistledown, having exhausted her son's minor injuries set about demolishing her neighbours with slightly cruel descriptions of their antics at the meet and the quality of their horses. In this she was ably seconded by Great Aunt Sophia who had followed them into the dining room accompanied by her companion, whose name Davina could not recall.

The poor lady had positioned herself next to Davina and was eating heartily, making Davina wonder whether Great Aunt Sophia ever fed her. Fortuitously such was her concentration on her food Davina did not feel obliged to make conversation; it gave her a moment's pause for thought.

For half an hour, she had thought she had found a new friend only to have the tables turned on her. It came to her that Lord

Restharrow was the man who, debt-ridden, eschewed marriage for himself but was surely a party to the scheme to marry his younger nephew to a fortune. All his earlier protestations of amity and goodwill must needs be false. If she had been alone Davina would have shed a bitter tear. Her mouth felt dry and her appetite diminished. She forced herself to eat in order to escape comment. Suddenly she was dragged from her reverie by the sound of someone using her name.

'On Miss Davina's behalf, Maria, I have cause to beg you a favour,' she heard Lord Restharrow say.

'And what might that be, pray?' Lady Thistledown threatened to look affronted.

'It seems she has not had the benefit of tuition on a horse.'

'Yes, yes, I know that well enough,' Lady Thistledown interrupted him without compunction, 'what of it?'

'I was going to suggest that if you could put a quiet lady's hack at her disposal then I would gladly do my utmost to provide the necessary tuition.' Lord Restharrow seemed unperturbed by her unmannerly interruption.

Davina murmured a disclaimer but was ignored. Great Aunt Sophia had given a knowing chuckle which, given her propensity to meddle, almost sounded like a cackle to Davina's sensitive ears.

'Now you are behaving like a sensible man, Carmichael,' she said, 'better catch the bird yourself than flush it into the sights of another.'

Lord Restharrow did not deign even to look in the old woman's direction, but merely repeated his request to his hostess.

'Oh very well,' Lady Thistledown conceded ungraciously, 'but you must consult with Amelia as to which of her horses she can most easily spare.'

Davina did not discover whether Amelia was any less reluctant than her mother to provide her with a mount as Lord Restharrow applied to Amelia later in the day when Davina was absent. She found it all very contradictory, on one hand that Lady Thistledown had been determined that everyone should be provided with a horse earlier in the day but now she was seemingly reluctant to extend that favour to Davina. She was not to know that Lady Thistledown saw any monopolisation of Davina's time by Lord Restharrow to be detrimental to the plan to marry her to Charlie. Lady Thistledown, unlike Great Aunt Sophia suffered no illusions. She had no expectations of Lord Restharrow wishing to marry Davina himself.

During the afternoon Lord Restharrow kept his promise to introduce Davina to Lord Thistledown. He escorted her to a separate wing of the house and opened the door to an enormous vaulted room full of books. There were stacks and stacks of tomes and pamphlets, many lying in drunken piles while others lined the walls in shelf upon shelf. Sitting amongst the mounds of paper was an elderly man in a bath chair. His hair was grey and wispy and a pince-nez sat across the bridge of his nose but his eyes were very alive with delighted interest.

'So you have brought me our guest,' he cried as Lord Restharrow ushered Davina across the room as though she was the only addition to the family household.

'Indeed I have, are you not impressed by her beauty and carriage?'

Lord Thistledown stretched out a gnarled hand clad in woollen fingerless gloves. 'Come my dear, come to me so that I can see you properly. Too many years of study have ruined my eyesight.'

Davina came forward and let him take her hand.

'Are you comfortable here, my dear, have they made you welcome?'

'Very welcome, thank you,' she replied formally.

'Tut, tut,' said the old man patting her hand. 'Now don't you pay any attention to the way my family carry on, young lady,' he said scouring her face with his eagle eyes, giving the lie to his earlier assertion of failing sight. 'If they give you any bother you come running to me, do you hear me?'

'Yes,' said Davina on a long outlet of breath, 'yes I do.'

5

*D*avina had spent a happy hour discussing Lord Thistledown's latest writings on the subject of botanical exploration untroubled by any thoughts of schemes and ruses to entrap her. The old man had swiftly dismissed Lord Restharrow and had encouraged her to show an interest in his studies. She had thoroughly enjoyed it and realised that she could, after all, get some pleasure out of her visit.

Once back in the main house, Davina saw the return of many of the day's adventurers. Ernestine returned desperately weary and was put to bed with a hot brick and a fire in her bedroom. Davina was rather concerned but Charlie was quick to reassure her that Ernestine often succumbed to weakness at the end of a long day in the saddle.

'Nothing ails her but fatigue,' he said cheerfully. 'It won't deter her though, she loves the chase and is a fine horsewoman. She will be in the saddle again on the morrow.'

Davina would have liked to demur, to suggest that perhaps Ernestine should have a day resting with her; however she could not do so in the face of Lady Thistledown's approbation so she spent the next day on tenterhooks fearing that Ernestine would return on a hurdle.

Instead it was Basil who remained at home due to his injuries. Whether it was good manners or genuine interest Davina could not tell but he applied himself to her entertainment. He escorted her to the music room and listened attentively to her piano playing. He ordered two stalwart footmen to go to the lumber room and retrieve the harp which had once been specially made for Amelia, then discarded when she lost interest. Davina was gratified to be allowed to use it although she would have preferred to be at leisure to visit Lord Thistledown again in his library.

Lord Restharrow did not appear and it was only at mid-morning when Lady Thistledown returned from the meet that Davina learned that he had ridden out that day. She thought she had been abandoned by him and did not know whether to be relieved or sorry.

After a light luncheon Davina escaped her escort and wended her way to Lord Thistledown's wing. She knocked on the door of the library and being requested to enter she opened the door. Lord Thistledown was sitting in his chair, a rug over his knees, scribbling rapidly on a long roll of paper. He looked up, irritated by the interruption. On seeing who it was however, he laid down his pen and rolled the chair forwards.

'Well, this is indeed a pleasure!' he exclaimed.

'I'm sorry, I can see I have discommoded you.'

'Oh, never mind that my dear. Have you come to continue our studies of yesterday?'

Davina smiled. 'No,' she said, 'for I can see you are busy. I just needed a haven for a few minutes and thought of you.'

He looked at her keenly. 'Who has been bothering you, my child?' he asked stretching out his hand, 'not that young whipper-snapper of mine?'

'No, oh no one,' she replied hastily to allay his suspicions. 'It's just when I am here with you my mind is clear. I can find repose. Amongst the others I feel naïve and foolish.'

Lord Thistledown patted her hand. 'You would never be foolish,' he said, 'I know that.'

'Do you?' She looked into his intelligent face and longed to be able to confide in him. For she knew soon she would have to confide in someone other than Nancy for Great Aunt Sophia's remarks at luncheon had become more and more pointed, expounding on the merits of marrying an older man rather than a younger one. This combined with Basil's unexpected interest had left her feeling besieged. The phrase 'bees around a honey pot' had leapt into her mind and she could not shift it.

'Come, you need some fresh air, a little light exercise; let me see if I can find you an escort.'

She would have preferred not to but as she knew he was much occupied with his writing, good manners overbore her reluctance.

The butler, a lean pinch-cheeked man answered the summons from the master of the house and was soon giving Lord Thistledown a list of the guests who had returned from the field.

'Ah! Lord Restharrow has returned early. Be so good as to ask him to visit me at his earliest convenience.' The butler withdrew and it was not many minutes before Lord Restharrow put in an appearance. He seemed surprised to find Davina with his host.

'I would be much beholden to you, my friend,' the older man said, 'if you would take this young lady for an airing.'

Lord Restharrow raised an eyebrow, then seeing that Davina was covered in confusion, gave her his arm and escorted her out of the room. Davina was bewildered, suddenly no longer feeling secure that Lord Thistledown was not furthering Lord Restharrow's pretensions to her hand. There was an embarrassed silence as they crossed a hallway to a side door. They waited for Nancy to appear once again with a warm outer garment. This time Nancy chose to follow them at a discreet distance. If Lady Thistledown was not around to act as chaperone, she felt her presence necessary.

Lord Restharrow appeared unperturbed by the maid's actions; he was more concerned by Davina's agitation.

He cleared his throat. 'We seemed to start so well yesterday, Miss Stanley but something or someone has put you against me, I fear. You seem no longer comfortable in my presence.'

Her eyes flew to his face. 'That is not the case, my lord,' she managed.

'Then why so much reserve? So much reluctance to converse with me?'

'There is none!'

'Oh but there is. Come, tell me. Is it Great Aunt Sophia's determination to wed you to every marriageable man on the premises. Or is it something more alarming?'

Davina sighed. 'Is it not so surprising that I am ruffled by her?' she asked plaintively. 'I am not used to her accusatory tone. She probes, she demands, she berates.' She stopped abruptly knowing it was unbecoming in her to pursue that line.

'You need not fear that anything you say to me will make its way back to her or Lady Thistledown, Miss Stanley,' Lord Restharrow said drawing her steps to a halt and looking earnestly down at her. 'I can be a good confidant.'

'I am grateful,' replied Davina, rather choked but only partly reassured. There was more reason to doubt his word than mere shortness of acquaintance. She sought to turn the conversation away from herself and learned that he had returned to the house early because his mount had thrown a shoe. He repeated his intention to teach her to ride and before she knew it the short afternoon was drawing to a close. Slightly chilled she returned with him to the house.

Dinner was early as befitted a home in the country and Davina found herself hungry. There was no sign of Ernestine so rather than join the throng in the with drawing room after the meal, Davina begged to be allowed to visit her friend in her room. She found her languishing in bed surrounded by pillows and cushions. As soon as the girl realised who her visitor was, she raised herself up to a sitting position and patted the bed to persuade Davina to sit down upon it. Her mood was far more buoyant than her friend might have expected.

'Oh I'm so glad you've come to relieve my boredom,' she cried ecstatically.

'Ernestine!' Davina was appalled. 'There is little amiss with you surely! I had understood you to be ill with fatigue. What game are you playing?'

'Oh is it not wicked of me,' giggled Ernestine. 'Charlie and I have enjoyed a day together, it is most diverting.'

'Diverting! Diverting, I am more likely to call it disastrous for you and for me both, if you are discovered.'

Ernestine's pretty face clouded. 'I did not expect you to be such a prude, Davina,' she grumbled sulkily. 'No one saw Charlie and I quit the field, they were all too occupied with the chase. We stayed safely in the grounds of the old gardener's cottage, beyond the park walls. No one goes there.'

'That is demonstrably untrue. If you went there for your clandestine meeting so might others.'

'They are unlikely to talk,' Ernestine pointed out reasonably. 'Have your wits gone wool gathering Davina, what has unsettled you so?'

Davina almost flung herself down on the bed.

'Oh Ernestine, I am in such a quandary; I have had no opportunity to talk to you since yesterday morning and I do not know what I should reveal to you.'

The deeply anxious look on her face forced Ernestine to lay out a hand and place it comfortingly on her arm.

'You must know that you can say anything to me, Davina,' she said carefully as though contemplating something of great import to impart to her friend. She gave a gusty sigh. 'You must know that I have no friends here above yourself and Charlie. None who see my interests as paramount.'

'Your aunt? Your uncle?'

Ernestine shook her head. 'Surely you see that my aunt interests herself in little above her own concerns except perhaps those of Lord Restharrow's and even they can be viewed as hers by association.'

Davina remained silent, conscious that Ernestine was confirming some of her worst fears.

'And my uncle, he is too frail now to give attention to anything but his studies.'

Davina stood up and walked to the window. It was very dark outside so she folded the shutters across the glass and then turned to lean her slender body against them. She gave an exclamation of decision; after all as Nancy had pointed out to her, neither Charlie nor Ernestine had yet failed her in their friendship.

Ernestine picked up a hairbrush from the solid chest of drawers beside the bed. She began to brush her hair in long rhythmic strokes while she waited for Davina to speak.

Davina found the motion of Ernestine's action vaguely soothing. She started to explain her predicament, haltingly at first but with more certainty as Ernestine carried on with her brushing. Methodically she unfolded the events of the last two days: the irregularities, the inconsistencies and the duplicities.

Ernestine remained surprisingly unmoved for someone of her mercurial temperament. Eventually though, when prompted by her agitated friend, she put down the brush amongst the covers and beckoned Davina to the bed.

'Come,' she said, 'let me take your hair down. I can explain away some of what you have seen and heard but not all.'

Davina did as she was bid and allowed Ernestine's clever fingers to undo the complicated twists and turns of her hair which Nancy had achieved that morning. Only when she was brushing out the tangled locks did she respond.

'Charlie told me of his conversation with our mutual aunt. We have been aware for some time that there have been stratagems to keep us apart. Hence the lengths we have been to to meet. If I had not retired to bed early tonight it would have elicited far more comment as I have always been exhausted by a day's riding. Perhaps if I had been one of fewer children I might have been prevented from participating in such energetic pursuits but we are a long-living family with few pretensions to frailty. My father sees it as a gift from God that he has so many healthy children; he can allow himself few concessions to my weakness.

Davina fidgeted, wanting to give her friend solace but it was rebuffed. Ernestine admonished her, demanding that she keep still while she braided the silky brown hair.

'Lord Restharrow,' she recommenced; 'has always been an object of pity amongst the family. Not a gamester himself he was prevented from marrying the lady of his choice because of the need to marry money.'

'But he has never married,' Davina struck in.

'No he has never married; it has always been surrounded by mystery. The stories hint of an elopement but they were never discovered to have attempted it, so it must have come to nothing.'

'What became of his lady love?'

'Little is known of her. My aunt was fascinated by his story for years and would speculate with my mother on how he could be so faithful to her memory when, as far as Aunt Thistledown could tell, there was no love-lorn damsel reciprocating his feelings. He withstood all efforts to marry a whole string of well-dowered young women willing to sacrifice themselves for a handsome husband. I believe there was one time when the family thought they had triumphed and were on the point of issuing an announcement in the papers when Lord Restharrow's father succumbed to his excesses and died. Of course once he succeeded to his father's dignitaries it was Lord Restharrow who called the tune. No more was said about marriage to anyone. I know he attempted to bring the estates back into order. He hoped the improved income would eventually enable him to pay off the family debts.' Ernestine broke off; she had finished Davina's hair. Putting her hands on the other girl's shoulders, she turned her around so she faced her.

'He reckoned without his younger brother,' she said with another sigh. 'Merlyn Winstanleigh, having married well in making a match with Lord Thistledown's sister, systematically drank and gambled her independence away. They were on the brink of ruin by the time Charlie was ten and lived hand-to-mouth until Mr Winstanleigh had an unlucky fall out steeplechasing. He lasted but a week after the accident. I believe the fall damaged his lungs.'

'What a chapter of accidents,' remarked Davina.

'Hardly. ' Ernestine gave a hollow laugh. 'Charlie's grandfather's death had been expected for some time. He had imbibed far too much wine on a regular basis for many years. Gout was only one of his afflictions. As for Merlyn, I believe his untimely death was viewed as a merciful release for the family.'

'Ernestine, I have never heard you speak with so little pity, so little restraint.'

'Have you not?' Ernestine's eyes clouded with misery. She leaned forward and took her friend's hands. 'That is because as yet you have not been thwarted in the one thing which matters more to you than life itself,' she said earnestly. 'It was not enough that Merlyn Winstanleigh should be a gambler but he has passed on his predilection to Charlie's brother, Lucien.' She caught up a sob. 'He will destroy our hopes as surely as anything that has gone before.'

Davina shook her head in speechless bewilderment.

'If you had loved, Davina, you would understand.'

'Oh do not misunderstand me, Tina,' Davina hastened to reassure her, 'it is the hypocritical nature of Lord Restharrow's stand I do not understand. Nor can I credit the well-ordered nature of this seat where clearly money has been spent and over spent, yet there is nothing to spare to support other members of the family.'

Ernestine was beginning to tire. She lay back against the pillows and drew the heavy coverlet up over her shoulders. She answered her friend in a thin thread of a voice.

'You mistake, Davina, Lord Restharrow makes no demands on us. He has assured Charlie that we have no duty to him. He has stated in the clearest terms that he will not ask Charlie to make the sort of sacrifice that had been demanded of him. It is Aunt Thistledown and Great Aunt Sophia who scheme, that must be obvious to you. You see the estate here is entailed, there is no land which is not governed by trustees. Since Uncle Thistledown's illness the trustees have handled all the affairs. While they will happily release money which will benefit the next heir as well as the present incumbent, they would not sanction throwing good money after wasted.'

'My aunt is conscious that had she had any form of dowry there might have been money unfettered by these restraints but she married above her station; my mother's family is hers. We are gentry not nobility. She feels it keenly.'

Davina could see that Ernestine's eyelids were drooping and that her face was pale. It was time to leave. She rose.

'We will talk more another time,' she said gently, 'but we have each other in this, Tina. We will not let them manoeuvre us into something regrettable.'

Ernestine smiled a weary smile.

'Good night Davina,' she said.

6

*T*he next day was inclement. The rain fell all day and there was no outdoor entertainment. The men took refuge in the billiard room whilst the ladies occupied themselves with chitter-chatter and needlework. Davina was pressed to play the piano to accompany their boredom which she did from time to time. The flatness of the day was something of a relief to her, giving her time to review what she had learnt from Ernestine.

Ernestine was cowed. The excitements of the previous day had left her debilitated and even she agreed that she should not ride out again that week. Amelia gathered up the younger ladies and cajoled them into accompanying her to the nearest village where spinning tops and juggling balls could be purchased for the tenants' children. It was customary on the Averbury estate to provide them all with gifts and to present them on Christmas Eve at a party in the servants' hall. Few failed to attend and Amelia, who generally appeared bored and disinterested, seemed to bloom under the responsibility.

'What makes her do it?' Davina whispered into Ernestine's ear as they watched her hand a gift to each expectant and delighted child.

'It is the one way she can be sure of her father's good opinion,' hissed Ernestine. 'He believes in all the observances but my aunt loathes their practice. Amelia is looking to be granted another season this coming year. I believe she hopes this might encourage him to persuade the trustees to allow it.'

Davina felt that Ernestine was being a touch uncharitable at a time of goodwill to all but she had to admit that at other times Amelia's behaviour had appeared calculating. Nonetheless she enjoyed the festivities and found Christmas-time in a large country house very different from the subdued affair to which she was accustomed. The only significant similarity was the morning service on Christmas Day but even this had its contrasts. At home, on the common, they would climb into their open gig braving the elements so that they could hail other would-be members of the congregation of the large church at Minchinhampnett. At Averbury it was a short walk to the estate chapel which, unlike Minchinhampnett, was filled with unfamiliar faces. Davina did not swerve from her devotions but she could have wished to be able to greet people by name and enquire after their friends and relatives.

The long service over, the guests returned to the house to prepare themselves for the Christmas banquet. The dining room was a blaze of candles from around three o'clock because the day was so short. Above half a dozen geese had been roasted for the occasion and there was a vast array of side dishes all served on gleaming silver plates. Once again Davina was conscious of the stark contrast between the opulence around her and the reported penury of other relatives.

Lady Thistledown's family presented a united front for the benefit of their guests. Lord Thistledown was wheeled out of his study and placed at the head of the table in advance of the procession from the drawing room to the dining room. On this occasion Davina was escorted by Basil, who seemed predisposed to entertain her with rather warm witticisms that she failed to appreciate. It did not however mar her enjoyment of the meal, not so much in the eating of it but its spectacle.

The day following being Boxing Day, Lady Thistledown made a show of distributing boxes to the tradesmen from the village who all presented themselves for the purpose. Davina could see why she preferred this form of giving to the more informal and rowdy tenants' party of Christmas Eve. Each recipient was suitably grateful and showed due homage to her position. Once the little pantomime had been accomplished Davina retired to the music room to pratice only to be interrupted by Lord Restharrow who was determined to arrange her first riding lesson. Somewhat reassured by Ernestine's championing of him, Davina agreed with a pretty show of gratitude and was pleased to awake the next morning to find a clear crisp day. Nothing now stood in the way of her first ride for six years.

Lord Restharrow had had a lovely bay mare, who was short of fifteen hands, saddled up. The mare blew warm air gently down her nostrils as Davina moved to pat her. Davina was well accustomed to handling horses from the ground or from a cart and was pleased to note that the mare was placid with an intelligent look in her soft brown eyes.

Lord Restharrow led the horse to the mounting block and helped Davina to climb the steps. Once she was in the saddle he guided her movements around the lady's pommel. Davina felt elated as she looked down into his kind worn face. It was a real thrill to be back on a horse. He led her to a small walled paddock which had clearly been used for schooling young horses and taking her on a long rein he let her walk around at its end.

The lovely mare responded easily to the instruction and walked buoyantly around the circle. Having settled with this for some minutes, Davina was tempted to show her mentor that she could remember most of what she had been taught as a child. The mare moved into a smooth trot and then on to a lolloping canter. Lord Restharrow, aware of what she was doing, laughed and drew the long rein in forcing the mare to reduce the size of her circle.

'I see that you need little tuition, Miss Stanley,' he laughed. 'Tomorrow we will go out on a more taxing ride. It will not be long before we can go further afield and explore the ancient stones I told you of.'

Davina's face was alight with pleasure. 'It is so marvellous to be in the saddle again. I am truly grateful to you, Sir, for overcoming my reservations. All my concerns have disappeared. I can recall much of what I was previously taught. Thank you with all my heart.'

Lord Restharrow looked up into her lovely face and felt an overwhelming surge of emotion he could not name. It was not attraction but more affection and an urge to protect this beautiful girl from all the vagaries of life. He could not prevent himself from putting up a hand to cover hers on the reins.

'You are most welcome, Miss Stanley, most welcome.' He withdrew his hand before its presence could become an embarrassment between them. 'Come, another canter, let me ensure that you have it correctly before I let you expose yourself to the exigencies of the highways and byways.'

The ride was such a success that Davina remained in a blissful dream of the wonders yet to come for the rest of the day. So deep was her reverie that she even managed to confound Aunt Sophia by not blinking in response to one of her barbed attacks on her lack of notable progenitors.

Lord Restharrow obligingly drew the old woman's fire and most nobly even agreed to take her as a partner in a round of whist. The younger members of the party, uninterested in this past time, conferred amongst themselves and begged leave of Lady Thistledown to be allowed to practise their dancing for an assembly the whole party planned to attend in Bath. Lady Thistledown nodded her consent while keeping a weather eye on the card table. She was no player but she knew the rules and she loved to watch a keen contest.

Gerard led his guests through to the saloon next to the music room. Having first opened wide the double doors between the two rooms, he rang the bell and on the arrival of a footman commanded that the grand piano be wheeled closer to the opening so that music could flood into the larger room. The rugs were rolled up and, giggling and chatting, some half a dozen couples took their places. It was only then that it was realised that a pianist was needed. All eyes were turned on Davina who was once again suffering Basil's attentions. Without listening to her protestations Basil led her to the piano and presented her with the dance music. Davina reluctantly capitulated and spent the next two hours drumming out an accompaniment to country dances and quadrilles. No one offered to take her place and no one, not even Ernestine, seemed to notice that she was being ill-used until Charlie strode in at about a quarter to ten. He had been supping with his maternal uncle in his rooms and had not been a party to the regular gathering.

He whispered a question into Ernestine's ear and on receipt of the negative he detached Amelia from her partner and took her to the piano.

'Come, come, Miss Stanley,' he said jovially, 'we cannot have you chained to your instrument all evening. My cousin Amelia will play us a tune while you give me the pleasure of this dance.'

'Oh no, surely you would prefer to dance with someone else. I am not a very accomplished dancer.'

'Then all the more reason for you to dance with me,' he responded gaily. 'We must have you footsure ready for the assembly next week.'

'You are very kind,' was all she could find to say. She did not like to be so conspicuous. She had not been unhappy playing the piano, she had just felt vaguely aggrieved that her hosts were so careless of her comfort. It warmed her heart that Charlie had put her interests above his own but misliked the interpretation others, including Ernestine, might put on his conduct. She went drearily to bed at the end of the evening, conscious that there was no comfort in entering this different world. There were pitfalls manifest everywhere and yet more that she could not see before they were upon her.

Nancy was a little preoccupied that night and Davina sensed it was due to her.

'You have heard something injurious to me, have you not?' she demanded after Nancy had vouchsafed nothing at all while undressing her.

'Certainly not,' her maid replied too quickly.

'I know you too well, Nancy,' Davina coaxed, 'come, tell me or I may think the very worst.'

'You are using mine own words on me,' smiled the maid, but the smile did not reach her eyes.

'Of course, see what an adept pupil I am; Lord Restharrow certainly thinks so.'

'Humph!'

'Ah, you do not approve of my riding expedition.'

'Oh no, it is not that,' Nancy said hastily, then fell silent. There was a strained pause as though she had meant to say more.

Davina cleared her throat. 'Please Nancy,' she implored in a small hollow voice, her eyes scrutinising Nancy's comely face. The maid could not withstand such an appeal.

'It's like this, Miss Davina,' she said as she turned to pick up the discarded dress from the bed, 'the servants see you fraternising with Lord Restharrow one minute, they hear that you are destined for Mr Charlie and they sees you being escorted by Mr Basil. They begins to think that you are an errant flirt. You do yourself no good accepting all this attention.'

Davina's face had gradually drained of colour; her astonishment and distress were very evident.

'How can this be, Nancy?' she cried, 'what is there about me which prompts this kind of speculation. There is nothing between me and any of these gentlemen. Lord Restharrow is too much my senior to be interested in me. Charlie clearly is attached irrevocably to Ernestine, and Basil,' she broke off, 'Basil may have shown me some attention but it waxes and wanes like the moon. He can have no real intentions. And what am I supposed to do: rebuff each and every one of them? That surely would earn me the stigma of being unforgivably rude.'

Nancy tutted despairingly at the warmth of her young mistress's response. She hung out the dress and then went to the dressing table to pick up the girl's mother-of-pearl hairbrushes. Davina moved from her position in the centre of the room and went to sit at the dressing table but she put her back to the mirror and would not turn around for Nancy to braid her hair until her questions had been answered. That they were unanswerable to any satisfaction was obvious to her but it did not mean that she was going to let Nancy off lightly.

'Now come Miss, let me ready your hair for bed.'

'No!' Davina put up a hand to ward her off. 'No, you are my only mentor here, my only adviser. You must tell me what I should do. How I should behave. I have no other guide.'

'Oh, Miss, I cannot. I know no more than you. I see Lord Restharrow as a kindly gentleman but you are a beautiful girl and there has been many an ageing man who has taken a beautiful young wife.' She took a quick breath. 'Mr Charlie, he is a charming young man with much sympathetic understanding of your position. He may well love Miss Ernestine but he must see an opportunity to make his future secure. And much the same can be said of Mr Basil. He too faces an uncertain future with the entail an' all. He will need a rich wife in time.'

'Yes, yes,' said Davina impatiently, 'but it was not their role which was being criticised here. You accuse me of flirtatiousness and then you excuse, one by one, those people to whom I have responded. Do you believe me at fault or do you not?'

'Oh hush, Miss Davina, pray do not go on so. There is no harm in what is being said at present. I only tell you to put you on your guard.'

Davina turned to the mirror and hunched a pettish shoulder. For once in her young life she questioned Nancy's wisdom in passing on the servants comments to her. She spent the subsequent night tossing and turning, reliving her meetings and interchanges with the three men, trying to see what she might have done to escape censure, but she could find nothing. She slept eventually but awoke hollow-eyed and found that tears were very near the surface.

She descended to the breakfast room late and was relieved to find no one but Ernestine there.

'This is an unusual circumstance,' she said as she placed herself beside her friend at the breakfast table, 'what brings you to breakfast here?'

Ernestine smiled a secretive smile. 'I cannot say,' she said mischievously.

Davina applied herself to her ham and eggs; she had no desire to know what contrivances Ernestine had prosecuted to meet up with Charlie.

'Well, are you not interested?' Ernestine queried.

'You have told me I cannot know, so I respect your wishes.' Davina knew this game of old. Today it irritated her in a way it had never done before.

Ernestine made a small growling noise in her throat like an angry kitten. 'You are no fun anymore, Davina,' she told her friend, 'you were never so careful with so much adult circumspection before.'

'I have never found the need before,' said Davina, turning her dark head to look into her friend's delicate face. 'Now my every move is being judged. Now I hear that I am being described as a flirt by the servants' hall. I feel very awkward.' Her voice broke. 'I just want to return home.' Individual tears began to roll down her cheek. She fumbled for a handkerchief from her reticule and dabbed furiously at her face.

Ernestine put down her knife with which she had been buttering her toast and put an awkward arm around her shoulders.

'You know,' she said conversationally, 'it must be some six years since I've seen you cry. I never thought to see your poise jeopardised in this way. You have always had the right word to say when we have been at odds with our respective parents.'

Davina sniffed and tried to sit up straight, dislodging Ernestine's arm. 'I have been brought to realise how little I know of life beyond my mother's house,' she said. 'Yet you seem familiar with a myriad of stratagems and deceits. You have no difficulty in avoiding chaperones and even censure, yet my every move is questioned.'

Ernestine thought for a moment. 'Perhaps it is the differential in our fortunes' she ventured.

Davina could not agree. 'I am beginning to believe it has to be more than that,' she said.

7

The visit to the ancient Avebury circle was arranged for two days hence. All who could ride would but Lady Thistledown and Great Aunt Sophia were to be conveyed there in a closed carriage piled high with rugs. The day started bright and clear but Davina, once she was settled in the saddle, felt a vague sense of unease. To her, attuned to the countryside, there was the unmistakable smell of snow.

Lord Restharrow noticed the furrow on her brow and was quick to question her concern.

'Are you unhappy, Miss Stanley, uncomfortable?'

She shook her head quickly. 'No, it is nothing like that Sir.' She paused while she searched for the right words. He brought his handsome chestnut gelding close to her so that he could catch her whispered utterances. Eventually she managed an enquiry of her own.

'How far is it to Avebury, my lord?'

'Oh not far, not above an hour and a half on horseback.'

'But in the carriage?'

'No more than two.' He tried to soothe her. 'You will be fine, Miss Stanley. A little stiff tomorrow perchance but otherwise fine.'

'You mistake, Sir, it is not for myself that I have a care but for the expedition as a whole. I feel the weather may close in upon us before we reach journey's end.'

Lord Restharrow laughed out loud at her anxiety. 'No, no,' he disclaimed, 'look at the sky, it is a beautiful blue, not a cloud to be seen, there is nothing to concern you.'

Unaccustomed to putting her opinion up in opposition against her elders, Davina subsided and allowed herself to be cajoled into cantering across an unploughed field with his lordship, Charlie, Ernestine, Basil and Amelia. Because Lord Restharrow was with them to temper high spirits, the little posse did not gallop hell for leather over the ground so Davina soon was able to relax and enjoy the mild speed. At the field's edge they traversed a small copse which was bleak and bare in the winter sunlight. Only the scattering of dark green yews and ivy columns acted as breaks to the fierce little wind which had arrived from nowhere to tug at the ladies' hats and the horses' manes.

They arrived at the stones some twenty minutes before the rest of the party who had ambled along accompanying Lady Thistledown's coach.

Davina was disappointed in the stones; they littered the ground over a great distance and near the central ring countless cottages had been built amongst them. One cottage even had a huge stone making up part of its wall to the eaves. Others lay drunken on their backs or had been broken to be used in barns and outhouses. It saddened Davina that something which had once been established by virtue of superhuman effort and commitment had fallen into such disrepair. She was thankful to reach the small inn where the party had bespoken lunch. Having dismounted and handed her horse over to an ostler she went in to warm her hands by the fire. Ernestine was looking chilled, so Davina drew her to the fire too.

'You must get warm before we set out on our return,' she told her friend.

Ernestine brushed aside her solicitude. 'Have not a care for me, Davina,' she said 'I have braved colder and more fearful conditions than this many a time.'

On her words Davina turned to look out of the low latticed

window of the inn's parlour. The sky had clouded over and there was a strange yellow hue. Davina's heart sank; she needed no further confirmation that it was going to snow and snow hard.

She did her best to encourage the rest not to tarry over their meal but the cold air and mulled wine had made them soporific so it was well past the hour of two o'clock before they all returned to their mounts.

It had not begun to snow yet but to Davina it was clearly imminent. She tried to persuade Ernestine to take up a place in the carriage but the girl would have none of it. They were almost at the mid-point between the village of Avebury and Avebury Place when the first flakes began to fall. Soon the occasional drifting softness turned to a flurry and then a frenzy whipped up by the fickle wind. The icy blasts blew fiercely into the ladies' unprotected faces and the horses bowed their heads against it. As the snow fell heavily it deadened the noise around them so those on horseback could no longer hear the coach coming on behind them.

'My lord, my lord,' Davina called out to the dark figure in front of her. Lord Restharrow reined back his horse and waited until he was alongside her.

'What is amiss, Miss Stanley?' he shouted.

'Miss Greenaway should await the carriage, my lord, she is very cold and susceptible to inflammation of the lung.'

Lord Restharrow quickly trotted back along the whitened lane where Charlie was manfully attempting to prevent the wind battering his lady.

'Put her up behind you, Charles,' commanded his lordship, 'I will lead the horse.'

'Should we not await the carriage?' Charlie repeated Davina's suggestion raising his voice above the now roaring wind. A blizzard had descended with mighty force.

'No, they may have halted on the route and taken shelter. We must not take that chance.'

Davina waited patiently, holding the head of Ernestine's mare while the gentlemen transferred their fair burden from one horse to another. Amelia, Basil and two others had ridden out ahead without them and were already lost to them in the swirling, blinding atmosphere, oblivious to the others' delay.

They moved off slowly keeping the horses close together for maximum protection. Ernestine was whimpering with cold; even the warmth of Charlie's body in front of her was insufficient to prevent her from becoming chilled to the marrow.

At last they reached the copse and were afforded some protection from the worst of the weather. The ground was less covered so they risked a faster pace, all deeply concerned about Ernestine's well-being.

From the copse the way was very exposed but thankfully short. There were a few uncertain moments while they tried to ascertain exactly where the lane ran. The ditches which ran beside them were filled with snow.

They battled on until they felt the firmness of the lane's surface beneath their horses' feet.

'A cottage! Should we not seek shelter there?' Davina hollered across what felt like a yawning space between Lord Restharrow and herself. For a moment he gave pause but then, out of the swirling, dancing snow, could be seen a number of cloak-clad figures making their way towards them. It was quickly revealed that Amelia, Basil and their companions had made it safely home and had sent out an army of rescuers. Soon Ernestine was wrapped in a huge blanket and Davina too was offered one. She declined, conscious that she was wearing many more layers beneath her riding habit than had Ernestine.

They reached the house eventually and Ernestine was hurried away by an alarmed Amelia. In the absence of her mother she knew herself to be responsible for her cousin and did not relish that responsibility.

'I owe you an apology, Miss Stanley,' Lord Restharrow said gravely as he escorted her to the bottom of the stair to deliver her into Nancy's waiting hands. 'Had I heeded your warning Miss Greenaway would not now be in such a grievous state.'

Davina could only shake her head in a wordless disclaimer. Her hands and face were tingling as they warmed and she could feel the snow melting through her clothes. She was eager to change her garments.

It was a depleted party which sat down to a late dinner that evening. Amelia had stayed above stairs to supervise the care of Ernestine. Lady Thistledown and Aunt Sophia had not reached home. All hopes were that they had found refuge along the route. Gerard, along with several others, had been escorting them, so he was absent too. Charlie was distracted with concern for Ernestine so he might as well have not been present. Davina ate a small and sombre meal, once again wishing she was back at Fromeview safely under her mother's gentle despotic rule.

Such was the irregularity of the circumstances that Lord Thistledown put in an appearance after the meal. He was unafraid for the safety of his wife as he knew there to be many inns and posting houses on the route she had taken but he was deeply anxious over Ernestine. He had sent his own doctor to see her and the elderly retainer had returned shaking his head.

'I would you could call out my esteemed colleague, Dr Cliffside, my lord,' he said to his employer. 'I have no expertise in the ailments of the lung. Dr Cliffside has treated Miss Ernestine on a number of occasions previous to this.'

'What is this?' cried Lord Restharrow, overhearing the best part of the doctor's speech. 'What is the good in having your own physician, Thistledown, if he is not capable of doctoring the sick.'

Dr Goodlaw looked pained and Lord Thistledown's elderly face was riven but he defended his own.

'Dr Goodlaw attends me on quite other matters. My illness has nothing to do with the lungs. My niece has always been a special case.'

Lord Restharrow gave an exclamation of annoyance and turned away from the ineffective pair to summon the butler, who answered the call with gratifying urgency.

'Dr Cliffside, Deepdene, where does he reside?'

The butler, who was inclined to be superior, had lost any inclination to superiority. Like many of the staff he had a soft spot for Ernestine and was aware of her delicacy.

'It is but five miles from here towards Swindon, Sir but I could not take it upon myself to send a man out in this. The snow is now two feet deep on the driveway. I have a notion that road, being more exposed, will have drifted badly.'

Lord Restharrow digested the words before accepting them as fact. He rounded on Dr Goodlaw. 'Well, it seems you are our only choice,' he said with an edge to his words. 'You must do what you can.'

At this point Davina, who had been sitting quietly in one of the straight-backed chairs stood up and came towards him.

'Do not be too alarmed, Sir,' she said quietly, 'I believe Ernestine's maid has a preparation with her which is used by Mrs Greenaway to alleviate Ernestine's breathing. I will go now and ascertain that Amelia is familiar with its use.'

Lord Restharrow caught up her hand and drew it to his lips saying, 'You are too kind,' which she did not understand.

Slightly embarrassed, she withdrew her hand and cast a sweeping glance around the room in search of Charlie. He was nowhere to be seen.

Davina hastened away and soon found herself at the door to Ernestine's room. She knocked gently and entered. The sound of her friend's laboured breathing was the first noise which assailed her. Amelia looked up from the bed, her rigid composure gone. Her hair was falling from its confines and her eyes were deep pools of anxiety in an over-pale face. Ernestine in contrast had a very flushed complexion and her chest was heaving in a most unnatural way. It struck Davina that each girl was feeding off the other's anxiety. She went to the bed and felt Ernestine's brow. It was cool.

The maid, a bright young woman Davina knew well, was hovering in an undecided way by the huge cupboard which lined the far wall of the room. She had in her hand the preparation Davina believed would be of benefit to her friend but was too diffident to put herself forward. Davina suspected that Amelia had not given her the opportunity.

'Sukey,' Davina said peremptorily, 'have you had the water boiled for the balsam?'

'No Miss.'

'Then jump to it, girl, we have need of it!'

The maid hurried away.

'Do you know what to do?' Amelia asked in hushed tones.

'Yes of course,' said Davina busily, determined that none of her own uncertainty would transmit itself to Ernestine.

She began to straighten the bed. Ernestine attempted to speak but Davina shushed her. When the maid returned with the bowl and a jug of steaming water Davina directed Amelia to help her sit Ernestine up and swing her legs over the edge of the bed. Once the invalid was in this position the bowl was placed on her knees and Davina dropped what she hoped was the right amount of balsam into it. Having stripped a cloth from an ornamental table she covered Ernestine's head with it and then poured the water over the aromatic liquid. Amelia watched in silence but the maid, Sukey, did what she could to steady the bowl and secure the cloth.

From a kneeling position by Ernestine's legs Davina looked up at Amelia.

'Why do you not go and get some sustenance,' she said, 'you must be both tired and hungry. We can manage until you are ready to return.'

Such was Amelia's relief that some measures were being taken which afforded Ernestine some benefit that she did not show any resentment at being so summarily dismissed.

For a few heart-stopping minutes the preparation appeared to be having no effect, but Davina took her lead from Sukey who must have carried out the procedure many a time before. The maid was looking calmer now that the right steps were being taken. Eventually the rasping noise from Ernestine's breathing began to subside and the girl was able to achieve a few halting words.

'Thank you, Davina,' she whispered, 'what would I do without you?'

Davina gave a little laugh, more from relief than humour. 'What you must do,' she said, looking Sukey in the eye directly, 'is engender your maid with the courage of her convictions. If she had but been able to administer to you earlier you might have been spared much distress.'

Ernestine released one hand from the bowl which was still being steadied by Sukey and she clasped the girl's free hand. 'You must not blame Sukey, she said, 'Amelia was very commanding until she realised she knew not what to do.'

'I am not blaming Sukey,' Davina assured them both, conscious that Ernestine was talking too much for her own good. There was still a catch of breath between the words. 'I merely wish to prevent a very unnerving event occurring again.' She patted Sukey's arm and then went around the other side of the bed to straighten it in preparation for Ernestine's return to it. It was some little while later that Amelia revisited her cousin, by which time Davina had managed a whispered conversation with Sukey and learned that Ernestine would continue to be assailed by the malady throughout the night. A watch would need to be kept, so that the process of inhalation could be revisited.

Braving Amelia's resentment, Davina explained the situation to her hostess.

'Would you be kind enough to set up a truckle bed in here so I might attend to Ernestine in the night if she needs me?' she asked.

Amelia for all her spoilt and selfish ways knew her duty.

'Would it not be a better scheme if we took turns to stay awake?' Davina nodded.

'Then if you would be so good as to explain the use of the balsam preparation, I will take the first watch until three o'clock for it is gone midnight already and I will wake you then. Sukey you may retire but please arrive promptly at six in the morning so that Miss Davina can seek her couch.'

8

*I*t was early afternoon before Davina awoke. Her throat was dry and she had a nagging headache across her brow. She had not expected to sleep so late, a circumstance she realised was the result of her inability to fall asleep while Amelia had been administering to her friend. It had not been that Davina did not trust Amelia, it was more the turmoil of her own thoughts which had kept her awake. On reaching her own room a little after midnight she had been taken to task by Nancy for exposing herself to illness and for agreeing to nurse Ernestine for half the night.

Wearily Davina explained that much of Ernestine's need was for firm and confident supervision so that she would not let her own anxiety exacerbate her condition. Nancy could not be convinced and eventually flounced out leaving Davina in high dudgeon.

Once between the sheets of the solid bed, Davina had tossed and turned, reassessing her own situation in the light of Ernestine's illness, and it had been with relief that she had greeted Amelia's gentle knock at three o'clock in the morning.

Amelia had had to use the balsam twice during her three hour stint while Davina had then had to use it once more. By the time Sukey had arrived at six, Davina had been fit to drop and had fallen asleep this time as soon as her head had touched the pillow.

Once awake, she had, without thinking, put out her hand to summon Nancy but the memory of their dispute the night before prevented her from tugging the bell rope. She got out of bed gingerly and found the pitcher and wash-bowl in readiness for her on the chest of drawers. The water inevitably was cold but the shock of it on her face cleared the fuzziness in her head.

Having towelled herself dry and put on her dress, a feat which took her some little time as the dress had a milliard of little buttons running down her back, she went to the window and looked out at the winter wonderland. Every tree was covered in snow, a great blue cedar had shed a branch under the weight and it was not possible to tell where the terrace ended and the lawns began. Davina sighed, and she very much hoped that Lady Thistledown and her party had found suitable shelter.

Davina wended a weary way down the stairs and came to the front hall. From the other side of the main door she could hear the scrape of shovels as the outdoor staff set about the Herculean task of clearing the drive.

Charlie found her still there some minutes later as she stood in some indecision not knowing which way to turn.

'How is Ernestine?' she asked him breathlessly, being sure he would have most recent news of her.

'I believe she is much improved. Sukey has had her sitting up in her chair this afternoon.' He paused and then clasped her hand. 'I cannot thank you enough for your care of her, Miss Davina, I am truly grateful.'

She was about to reply suitably when there was a flurry of skirts from behind them and Amelia appeared. Charlie dropped Davina's hand in haste. That Amelia had seen was clear but her face was inscrutable. Davina could not tell whether she viewed such intimacy with approval or disapprobation.

Charlie moved to greet her but noticeably did not thank her for the care she had given Ernestine. Davina wondered at it, then remembered that in the family's eyes the match was not sought. They would not accept Charlie's right to be grateful on Ernestine's behalf.

Conscious that the tension needed to be diffused, Davina

hurried forward too and asked if Amelia had had news of Lady Thistledown or her eldest brother. A shadow crossed Amelia's face.

'No, none,' she replied in a thread of a voice, 'and I cannot be as sanguine as my father and Lord Restharrow, I fear the worst.'

'Oh come now.' Davina's sweet face was at once riven with sympathy. 'I am sure they will be well situated, they were some way behind us and so could still command the services of cottages along the route. I am certain that the gentlemen have the right of it.'

Amelia gave a forced smile and grasped Davina's outstretched arm. 'You are most kind,' she said rather rigidly and turned on her heel before her feelings overcame her.

Charlie's eyes followed her in some alarm.

'I do not believe I have ever witnessed her so moved,' he said. Then he appeared to give himself a mental shake. 'Come,' he commanded, holding out his arm for Davina to loop hers through, 'let us away to find you some breakfast.'

They found the remains of some cold meats and fruit laid out in the dining room for those who had breakfasted at a reasonable hour. Many had already had luncheon leaving Davina little choice of menu. She was not however very hungry and so just picked at the food Charlie had laid on her plate.

Their companionable silence was interrupted by Basil who burst into the room.

'Where's Amelia?' he demanded without preamble, his pudgy face suffused with the heightened colour of exertion.

'She was with us in the vestibule a few moments ago but she was distressed. I suspect she has gone to her room.'

'Damn her, I need her in the stables.'

'It is most understandable,' Davina was quick to defend Amelia, 'she is very alarmed by your mother's absence.'

'Ha,' snorted the fond brother, 'she is only worried she will have to forego the next season if anything happens to Mother or Great Aunt Sophia and we have to go into blacks.'

'Basil, that is most unworthy of you.' Charlie, the good-looking antithesis of his cousin, could not conceal his disgust at the hasty and ill-judged words. Basil, with a look of loathing, turned on his heel and slammed the door.

Davina was left feeling shaky and alarmed. She pulled an embroidered handkerchief from her reticule and pressed it to her mouth.

'What can I say?' Charlie rushed to sit down beside her. 'How can I apologise? You should not have been exposed to such sentiments. It is the stuff of brothers and sisters and not for the ears of honoured guests. You should disregard it.'

Davina could only shake her head, unable to speak. Over again she longed for the tranquillity of her own home, its gentle sameness and inevitable cycle of events, but it could not now be. The roads were blocked and any escape was impossible.

In fact the situation did not improve for the next three days. It snowed on and off but not to the extent of the first night's blizzard. The drive could be brushed clean of the new falls rather than shovelled so the men had managed to clear a route to the gatehouse.

When she was not bearing Ernestine company, Davina would walk with Amelia to the end of the drive to view the road in the hope that it might become passable.

Each day brought fresh disappointment as there was no alleviation of the anxiety or the boredom. Time dragged and although Ernestine was showing signs of improvement Amelia's agitation had sopped up any excess energy Davina might have had. She soothed, she diverted, she pandered to all Amelia's fretting, conscious always of Basil's uncharitable view of the root cause of her concern.

When the thaw finally set in, Amelia was looking ashen and pinched. She had eaten very little and even the commands of her father demanding she take some sustenance had failed to have any impact.

Lord Restharrow had done his best to entertain the ladies but there had been little to do and cards and music had soon palled.

He did however win favour when he volunteered to go with Basil along the now slushy road.

If the wait while they were snowed in had seemed interminable, the time during which the men were absent was insupportable but the ragged patience they had managed to muster was rewarded. Just as the weak sun was setting, the clip-clop of many hooves and the crunch of cart wheels on the snow and gravel could be heard.

Amelia cast aside the embroidery with which she had been toying and ran, in a very unladylike fashion, to the door which she wrenched open before Deepdene could gather his wits. She hurtled down the steps to the carriage.

'Mama, Mama,' she cried, almost beside herself with emotion. Davina, following in her wake, could only be surprised by this unlooked for demonstration of affection, she could not believe it all to be orchestrated.

The carriage drew to a halt and once the steps had been put down, did in fact reveal that it was indeed Lady Thistledown. She was loud in her relief to be home and gave her daughter only a perfunctory acknowledgement. No one's ordeal could compare to what she had had to endure: the inn in which they had sheltered had been cramped, the sheets had been damp, the chimney had smoked and there had been insufficient food to feed them all according to their tastes.

Davina had to feel sympathy for the absent innkeeper and imagined the relief when these exacting guests had taken their leave. She wondered if their host had been paid enough to cover his costs and doubted it.

Lord Restharrow and Basil had met the party some six miles from home and had accompanied them on the last leg of their return. Great Aunt Sophia claimed to have suffered a slight cold as a result of the ill-fated expedition but the only real casualty had been Gerard who had been kicked by one of the restive horses during the blizzard and appeared to have broken an arm.

Lady Thistledown made little of his injuries but when Amelia was eventually allowed to tell her of Ernestine's indisposition, she was suitably alarmed. She had to be helped to a comfortable chair in the parlour and have burnt feathers and sal volatile waved under her equine nose.

Davina could only be relieved that Lady Thistledown had been from home when Ernestine was taken ill because she would clearly have been of little use in an emergency and might even have made matters worse. Undoubtedly some of the other guests who had been imprisoned with her had had a surfeit of her redoubtable character and were making moves to return to their own homes citing a possible further freeze as sufficient reason to make the bolt.

Lady Thistledown did not try to prevent them with any great conviction and not two days later the party was depleted to include only Great Aunt Sophia, Lord Restharrow, Charlie, Ernestine and Davina above the family members. Of these only Amelia and Lady Thistledown were much in evidence. Basil spent much of his time in the stables ensuring none of the horses had suffered any lasting hurt. Gerard had taken to his bed with the injured arm and Lord Thistledown had returned to his studies. Davina longed to be on her way home but ironically she was having to stall Lady Thistledown from arranging it. Lady Thistledown was very keen to return Ernestine to her mother in case of any recurrence of her illness, and this enthusiasm seemed to have driven any common sense from the lady's mind, if indeed it had ever been present. Ernestine would certainly suffer a relapse if she was forced to travel so soon after her indisposition so Davina had to sublimate her own wishes once again to ensure her friend's well-being.

Eventually however she could hold out no longer against Lady Thistledown's expressed wishes and had to finally agree to the travel arrangements which had been made without reference to her.

Lord Restharrow and Charlie had undertaken to accompany the coach until the point where the Bristol road crossed their path some four miles from their destination. They had business in that city and Davina knew she would be foolish to delay and therefore lose their escort.

They started out as soon as it was light, wanting to take full advantage of all the daylight available to them on the short winter's day. The ladies and their maids were packed tightly into the coach and pressed round with rugs and hot bricks. Ernestine still looked pale and unready for such a journey, which made Davina's words of thanks to her hostess stick in her throat. To her ears when they were eventually uttered they had an insincere and hollow ring. She was better able to thank Amelia, for putting aside any secondary motives, Davina preferred to thank her for what she perceived as genuine concern for Ernestine.

Davina's leave-taking of Lord Thistledown had been affectionate while that of Gerard and Basil had been formal and brief. Davina could barely bring herself to say a simple goodbye to Great Aunt Sophia so instead she had dropped a hint of a curtsy. The crowded coach seemed like a snug and friendly bolt-hole even though she had not quite reconciled her differences with Nancy.

The little party took the journey in easy stages, stopping regularly to allow the ladies to enjoy warming drinks at wayside inns and coaching houses. Lunch was a frugal affair just over two thirds of the way home as neither Davina nor Ernestine had much of an appetite. When it came to parting with their escort, Ernestine almost lost her grip on her composure. She dismounted the coach and clung to Charlie's outstretched hand as they stood apart from the vehicle on the other side of the road. She was fearful that she might not see him for some time. Davina too had alighted from the coach and was taking leave of Lord Restharrow.

Her face averted from witnessing the plight of her friend, Davina spoke. 'I wish that all could be resolved between them. They are so well suited and do not deserve to have their mutual affection blighted.'

Lord Restharrow's face quivered with suppressed emotion. He appeared to be going to make some retort then thought better of it. He merely nodded and led her back to the coach.

'May I call on you when you are once again at home?' he asked as he handed her tenderly into the coach. Surprised by such a request, she was glad to busy herself in settling into her seat and covering her legs with a rug. Finally she had schooled her face to hide her finer feelings.

'I'm sure Mama would be delighted to make your acquaintance, Sir,' she said.

'And you, Miss Stanley, would you wish to see me again?'

'But of course,' she said hurriedly, conscious that he was pressing her more than was seemly.

'Thank you.' He bowed and stepped back to allow Charlie to hand Ernestine back into the coach.

Eager not to keep his sweating horses standing in the cold air, no sooner was the door shut than the coachman had cracked his whip and chivvied the horses forward.

There was silence in the coach while its occupants digested the manner of their parting. A few moments passed before Davina realised that tears were trickling down her friend's face. She squeezed Ernestine's hand in a wordless gesture of sympathy but was unwilling to expose the girl's feelings to the curious maids.

All of a sudden and without any warning the coach lurched abruptly and Ernestine and Davina were thrown forward into the laps of their attendants. There was the scrape of the undercarriage on the ground and a shudder, and as the coachman pulled up his horses, the vehicle came to a halt.

'Good heavens,' cried Davina as she disentangled herself from Nancy's embrace. 'Whatever has occurred?' She looked about her and saw that Ernestine had a deep scratch on her face and her eyes were looking wild with fear. Finding her handkerchief she began to dab the drops of blood before they fell upon her friend's lacy bodice. The under-coachman's face appeared at the window.

'Are you all right, ladies?' he enquired anxiously, 'the rear axle has snapped, we can go no further.'

There was a squeak of dismay from Sukey.

'What of Miss Ernestine, Miss Davina?' she wailed. 'She cannot be made to wait out in the cold.'

Anger rose in Davina. This then was the outcome of Lady Thistledown's determination to rid herself of the vexatious problem of caring for Ernestine. No doubt they would now have her succumb to pneumonia all because the selfish woman would not put herself out.

'Quick,' she said to the stalwart attendant, 'go back and see if their lordships have set off towards Bristol yet.'

'Very well, Miss.'

To give him credit, the heavy man set off at a great rate but it was soon to be seen that he was blown. He stumbled back.

'I'm sorry Miss,' he gasped. By this time the coachman had disentangled the wheelers from their traces and was motioning to his assistant to give a leg-up on one of them.

'You'd be faster on horseback, Seth,' he suggested.

Away again went the under-coachman but to no avail for once around the bend he could see nothing of them. He returned to the wreck, crestfallen.

'So what to do now, Mr Ackroyd?' he asked of his superior.

The coachman looked to Davina, who so far had taken command of the situation. She was saved, however, from making any decisive moves by the sight of a coach and horses coming towards them from the direction from whence they had come. Mr Ackroyd flagged it down but it could be seen that the occupant was already aware that there had been an accident. The liveried coach, with an ornate crest upon its panel, drew up beside them and even before it had halted a young man sprang out.

'Well, this is a sorry sight,' the young man declared with laughter in his voice, 'what has occurred?'

Doffing his hat, Mr Ackroyd explained the nature of the breakdown and while he did so Davina made her perilous descent from the drunken coach.

Obviously taken aback by the sight of a beautiful young lady, the gentleman was momentarily lost for words. This allowed Davina to take covert stock of him. He was not handsome but striking. He had pale, pale skin, accentuated by the blackness of his hair and his eyebrows. His eyes were fringed by long dark lashes and carried a sparkle of laughter in their brown depths. He was tall with an upright bearing and fastidiously dressed in the latest fashion. Davina thought him the most elegant young man she had ever met, putting even Charlie's fair good looks in the shade.

'I would not trouble you, Sir,' she said hesitantly, 'if it were not for the gravest circumstance.'

'Madamoiselle, I am at your service,' he declared with a flourish, bowing and sweeping off his hat. 'What are these grave circumstances?'

'My friend, Miss Ernestine Greenaway, has of recent days been very ill and we are taking her home to the care of her mother. The accident has resulted in an injury to her and I am grievously afraid that if she remains in the cold air, she will become dangerously ill.'

'You paint a desperate picture, Madamoiselle, but all is not lost. I stand Lord Louis Twayblade at your service, command me as you will!'

'You are too good, my lord. Would it be too exacting a service to ask you to convey myself and my friend to the Rectory at Minchinhampnett, just short of three miles from here?'

'It would be a delight and a pleasure, Madamoiselle.'

'I think I should make myself known to you, my lord,' she said slightly haughtily as she was somewhat ruffled by his laughing use of the French.

'Please do, Madamoiselle.'

'I am Miss Davina Stanley of Fromeview Place, near Stroud.'

'A fine name, Madamoiselle and a fine sounding home. Am I to take you on to your home once we have delivered Madamoiselle Greenaway to the care of her parents?'

'That will not be necessary, thank you,' she replied tartly, 'I am sure the Rector will see me safely home.'

It seemed she had responded correctly because his lordship dropped his mocking tone and became business-like and efficient. He directed the attendants to transfer Ernestine from one coach to the other and it was clear that he was moved by her genuine plight. He saw no reason to leave any of the ladies behind but instead ordered his groom to help Mr Ackroyd and Seth, commanding him to rejoin him at a posting house in Stroud as soon as he was able. Then, having extracted directions from Davina, he swung himself up behind the horses to sit with his coachman.

The miles were covered quickly and easily, the horses being quite fresh and the coach well sprung. However it was with no little relief that Davina saw the scattering of cottages turn into the town of Minchinhampnett and then saw them draw into the Rectory's driveway and up outside the square front door.

Lord Louis jumped down from his seat and banged loudly on the door. Snow still lay in patches in the frost hollows amongst the trees of the garden and with the setting sun the temperature was plummeting.

His peremptory knock elicited a quick response and before Davina knew it, they were engulfed by what seemed to be the entire Greenaway family. Lord Louis took it all in his stride, brushing aside the Rector's grateful thanks as well as the man's offer to convey Davina and her maid home.

'No, it is a treat I have promised myself,' Lord Louis assured him, reverting to his jocular and slightly comical manner, 'it is nought but a step and on my way besides.'

'You don't know that.' Davina rounded on him when they were once more seated in the coach.

'Know what, Madamoiselle?'

'That my home is but a step away and on your route besides.'

He gave a shout of laughter. 'A guess based on sound foundation. You have clearly been acquainted for years, since childhood I'll be bound. That means you must have easy access to each other's company.' He looked out into the darkness as the coach slowed and turned off the road and onto the Place's gravelled court. 'See, am I not right?'

'Fie on you my lord, are you forever funning?'

Lord Louis's dark brows snapped together. 'Does it appear so to you Madamoiselle?'

'Yes indeed my lord,' she said, giving him back stare for stare. 'I fear you find my friends and I objects of ridicule.' She was astounded at herself for she had never spoken so boldly to any man, not even when the unwanted attentions of Basil or Gerard had raised her ire and made her long to call them to order.

'Ridicule is not the same as fun, Madamoiselle. Ridicule demands a perpetrator and a victim. Fun can be had together.'

Davina felt the warm rush of blood to her face. She was thankful that he could not see her heightened complexion in the darkness of the carriage.

Their arrival had drawn attendants out from the house and the stables. Suddenly there were lamps and flaming torches to light their way and they were encouraged to disgorge from the coach.

'Mama, oh Mama.' Suddenly Davina spotted her mother peeping anxiously at the throng. Throwing caution and decorum to the wind, Davina cast herself into her mother's arms, a gusty sobbing breath escaping her. Lord Louis alighted from the coach in a more leisurely fashion and was pleased to be ushered into the house by the elderly butler on the invitation of Mrs Stanley who had surfaced from her daughter's embrace and was gently leading her in too.

In the full light of the hallway, Lord Louis cast his gaze around the well-proportioned space. He was seen to approve as he once more accepted an invitation to enter the withdrawing room.

'What a splendid house you have, Mrs Stanley. I see now why

your daughter describes herself as Miss Stanley of Fromeview Place. It is certainly a domicile worthy of the handle.'

Davina threw him a darkling look, angry with herself for this exposure to more of his ridicule. He raised an eyebrow in response and sat down in the indicated seat, following the example of his hostess.

'I am truly grateful to you for conveying the girls home, my lord. I do not know what would have happened to them if you had not been on hand to effect a rescue.'

'Oh, you unman me, Madame with your graciousness but I am assured that your daughter, who appears to me to be very resourceful, would have found some method of rescuing her friend!'

'They are indeed inseparable, the closest of friends,' murmured Mrs Stanley 'I am sure Davina would have done everything in her power but I am most relieved that she was not called upon to do so.'

Lord Louis gave a slight smile. He accepted a drink of brandy from the butler and then surprised Davina even further by accepting her mother's invitation to partake of dinner with them.

Dinner sorely tried the cook who had been expecting to provide a light supper of boiled chicken and root vegetables for an unaccompanied lady. Instead she had to create a meal which would meet the approval of a member of the nobility, who was well known to the servants' hall, if not to their mistress.

The chicken stock was cast aside and the meat was buttered and sautéd into a more appetising dish. Lunchtime's game pie was recovered with pastry and baked hot and fast and the breakfast ham was heated and decorated with cloves. The apple store was raided and laced with damson jam and sweetmeats were liberated from the chef's secret store.

Mrs Stanley, who had given the kitchens as much time as she dared, looked at the spread with some relief. Cook had done her proud and would merit a visit later on from her grateful mistress.

Lord Louis ate well while chaffing Davina with his witticisms. Mrs Stanley, seeing her daughter's weariness, took pity on her and drew him off.

'So tell me Lord Louis, do you know this area well?' she asked, indicating to the footman to refill her guest's glass with red wine.

'Not so very well Madame, I have friends here but my home is in Scotland; my parents inhabit a vast and draughty castle on the banks of a deep loch.'

'Indeed,' smiled Mrs Stanley, humouring him, 'then you are a long way from home.'

'Yes, I fear so, but there is little point in repining. My travels bring me south every winter and I return in August after the Season. It is a vagabond lifestyle but it boasts variety.'

'Do you have any other family, my lord?'

He laughed. 'What is this Madame, a catechism? Do you wonder if I am heir to the granite pile?'

Mrs Stanley took a moment to answer; laying her cutlery down she looked directly into the young man's mobile face.

'You presume too much, my lord,' She paused but he did not retaliate. 'You presume that because my daughter is unmarried that we seek opportunities to associate her with any unmarried man with whom we become acquainted. You assume that because we are country folk we do not know the niceties of succession. You assume that you can laugh at our parochialism without us understanding the implied offence. I detract nothing from the service you have rendered my daughter and her friend but I ask you to observe the modicum of good manners in my house.'

Lord Louis listened to the gentle tirade with the merriment draining from his face. He stood up from the table and rammed the chair under it.

'It does not behove me to listen to this,' he said and, turning on his heel, he quitted the room and then the house, slamming the door behind him.

Lord Louis ... as well while chatting. Davina with her worldly wise
Mrs. Stanley ... acting as chaperone ... it appears ... to her
character and ...

9

*D*avina stalked to the bedroom window and drew the cord
from her dressing gown tightly around her waist. She
had spent a troubled night trying to fathom why her mother had
launched such an unprovoked attack upon their guest. To
Davina, in the cold light of day, it appeared a deliberate act of
sabotage. Any possible acquaintanceship between herself and
Lord Louis had been ruthlessly nipped in the bud. Davina's heart
contracted. She had met so many men in the last few weeks and
none of them had made her feel as alive and confident as her
rescuer. Even when he was teasing her with his affected French,
she had been able to articulate her irritation.

This had been a revelation to someone who had spent a
secluded and demure childhood.

One of Davina's chief reasons for wanting to return home had
been so that she could unburden herself on her mother the feelings of ill usage the Greenaways and their Thistledown connections had visited on her. However her mother's behaviour the
previous night now prevented any confidences. Although this
was at first a bitter blow, more rational thought drew Davina to
acknowledge the fact that she could not repeat to her mother all
the snide and abusive remarks she had endured from Great Aunt
Sophia as their main theme could only wound the beloved lady.
Davina considered creeping into her mother's dressing room
and gaining access to the box in which she housed her marriage
certificate. If Davina could see the name of her father written

large upon its surface and the date of their union, she could be satisfied and withstand the jibes and innuendoes.

She sighed and turned from the window to summon Nancy. It was useless to imagine she had the temerity to do such a thing. She would not even now wish to excite her mother's displeasure if she was caught rifling through her possessions. So Davina submitted to being dressed by Nancy in a thick overdress to keep out the cold.

'It is bitter again today, Miss,' said Nancy, attempting conversation with the rigid girl before her. 'Your mother will prefer you not to go out walking.'

Like a red rag to a bull, Davina saw her way clear. She could not rail and storm at her mother but she could retaliate with some subversive disobedience. No sooner had she breakfasted than she donned her leather boots and warmest pelisse to walk to Minchinhampnett to ascertain how Ernestine had suffered the journey.

The common was bare and drab. The sustained cold of early February had deadened the ground and the heavy snow had flattened the grass leaving it grey and rank. It was a dreary scene but it suited her mood. She saw no release from the trials of her situation, no comfortable future with an adoring husband. While there seemed to be many pretenders to her hand, none would be her choice. None would put her interests before theirs; of that she was in no doubt. Her footsteps dragged and she let the wind blow full in her face; she was not so eager to reach her destination.

Davina was welcomed at the Rectory with graciousness. Mrs Greenaway expressed herself very properly and thanked Davina again and again for her efforts on Ernestine's behalf.

'I would we could have stayed a few more days.' Davina ventured to say. 'I believe Ernestine had need of being a little more robust before we undertook a journey.'

Mrs Greenaway waved away the thought. 'If my sister thought her well enough to travel, you may be sure that was the case.'

A loyal statement this which gave Davina a poor opinion of Mrs Greenaway's understanding. To Ernestine's bedroom she was quick to make her escape and was delighted to see her friend in much improved spirits.

'Oh I miss him dreadfully,' Davina was told, 'but I feel so much better today. I cannot be downhearted.' She was still in her bed surrounded by frilly cushions and wearing a soft pink bedjacket. She looked even younger than her years. Davina felt a rush of affection for her.

'I am sorry that your time together was spoilt,' she said.

'What is this?' cried Ernestine, 'you are not usually so sympathetic to our plight.' She cast her friend a mischievous look. 'Is it that you have formed an attachment for someone and now understand my feelings?'

'No, of course not, do not be silly.' It was Davina's misfortune to have responded too quickly and to have a friend who saw too much.

'Ha, Davina, you blush. Am I not right? For whom do you have this unexpected partiality, not Basil?'

'No, no of course not.' Davina was too honest to deny that there was someone. 'You would not know him.'

Ernestine sat forward in the bed and scrutinised her friend's face. 'It's Lord Louis, that's who it is,' she cried delightedly, throwing herself back against the cushions.

Davina stood up from the chair she had taken by the bed, and clasped her hands together to steady herself.

'I was not aware that you had taken account of him yesterday, you were too distressed,' she said carefully.

Ernestine put an involuntary hand up to her damaged cheek. 'Perhaps I would not have done if he had been a stranger but I have made his acquaintance previously.

'You are already acquainted?' Davina could not mask her surprise. 'How is this?'

Ernestine considered for a moment. 'Let me see, yes, I believe his younger brother Etienne was at school with Charlie. His parents have numerous vast estates, he is very well heeled and the heir to a marquis.'

'That cannot be,' Davina jumped in, intrigued but suspicious of her friend's narrative. 'I understood that he has an elder brother.'

'A half-brother, a good many years his senior. Lord Campion resides the year out in Scotland; he is addicted to sporting pursuits to the exclusion of even a wife. He says the most generous favour his father has ever done for him was to remarry after the death of his mother and produce a bevy of sons, so that there is no need for him to marry. Lord Louis is therefore his heir presumptive.'

Davina's eyes were wide in wonderment. 'Surely you jest, Ernestine?,' she cried. 'What man would prefer his brother to inherit than his son?'

'A man who has no time but for his horses and his dogs and the sport they can provide.'

'So you have said, but I find it hard to credit.'

Ernestine was getting bored of this line of conversation. 'If you do not believe me, ask him yourself,' she said pettishly. 'Even in my sorry state I could see he was as taken with you as you are with him.'

There was no response from Davina but a gusty sigh.

'Oh, no love lorn display now please, two of us lovesick would never do.'

'Ah, but you have a better chance of securing your love than I,' said Davina rather bitterly.

'Oh come now Davina, this diffidence does not become you. You have face and fortune; even a family as prosperous as his would not sneer at £100,000.'

'Maybe not,' agreed Davina, taking her seat again, 'but for reasons I cannot divine, my mother drove him away yesterday evening. I believe that she offended him deeply. He will not seek me out again. In fact I think it highly likely that he will cut me should our paths ever cross again.'

Ernestine gave a little titter. 'We are a pair without a hope between us,' she said sadly.

It was these words which followed Davina home as she trudged back across the barren common. Beset as she was by so many people determined to engineer her future, she could not foresee a satisfactory conclusion to either her or Ernestine's affairs of the heart.

The next few days found her vetting every sentence she uttered in answer to her mother's persistent questions about her stay at Avebury. There were so many opportunities for it to go awry. Great Aunt Sophia had featured so heavily in the diminution of her enjoyment that even when she was describing an evening event or some jolly entertainment her name would creep in to slant it away from pleasure towards dissatisfaction.

'So name me the guests,' her mother demanded one night as they sat eating their dinner from opposite ends of a narrow dining table.

'Have I not done so?' asked Davina in surprise.

'Not as a list,' her mother assured her. So Davina dutifully enumerated the guests and the family giving thumbnail descriptions she hoped were witty. 'And Lord Restharrow plans to visit us next time he is in the area,' she said as she reached her conclusion.

Mrs Stanley dabbed her mouth carefully, then folded her white linen napkin and placed it carefully to one side of her plate.

'Did he say when he planned to call?' she asked after clearing her throat.

'No, but he was most insistent, so I feel sure it will be soon,' replied Davina more brightly than she felt. She was not ready to meet Lord Restharrow so soon after the rout of Lord Louis. Too perceptive, he would see more in her countenance than she cared to betray to him.

'Let it be weeks away,' she whispered as she took herself off to bed that night.

Weeks it was not but almost a week had past before he put in an appearance.

The Stanleys had early notice of it as two days before the appointed day, Mrs Greenaway imparted the information to Mrs Stanley when the latter was making her a morning visit.

'He has requested us to put him up for three nights,' she told a disapproving Mrs Stanley, 'and he brings both his groom and his valet. I know not where to put them. We do not have enough servants quarters to accommodate these men, so I am having to use one of the children's rooms; Henry and Cecil will have to share.'

'I can see that it is most inconvenient for you. Can you not hint him away?' Mrs Stanley suggested as she straightened her skirts about her. The beautiful dark silk rustled expressively.

Mrs Greenaway eyed her with a hint of loathing. 'It would be too base, too rude, he has had such an unhappy life. If he is wishful of staying here, then I will do my utmost to make it possible.'

Mrs Stanley raised her eyebrows and then herself from the chair. 'As you say, it is necessary to do whatever is possible to make it up to him,' she annunciated with a hint of sarcasm. She pulled on her gloves. 'I bid you good day,' she said, then she made her escape before the gentle irony of her words could seep into Mrs Greenaway's brain.

There had been no mention that Lord Restharrow would no sooner arrive than set out on a visit of ceremony to the Stanleys but Davina was convinced that he might. She had hoped that her mother would meet him and advise her on how to receive his advances but her mother had succumbed to a head cold which threatened to turn into influenza. She had retired to bed early the night before, heavy eyed and dabbing her nose regularly. Thus it was Davina alone who, on the watch for him, saw him arrive at Fromeview Place not two hours after he had put down at the Rectory.

The Rector's youngest boy, Cecil, a young lad of fifteen, had accompanied Lord Restharrow to show him the way. They came also with a groom on horseback leading a second mount.

Davina, for all her fears of this meeting, could not suppress a small thrill as she looked out at the scene. Lord Restharrow had promised he would find her a horse and if she was not very much mistaken, the spare horse looked like a lady's mount. Was this then a present for her?

She contained herself just long enough for Masterson, the ancient butler, to open the door, then she rushed out into the bracing air to greet the new arrivals.

'Miss Stanley, how do you do?' Lord Restharrow extended a hand down to shake hers. 'In good health I am glad to see.'

She released his hand and moved a little away from the horse so that he could swing his leg over its back and dismount.

'Come,' he commanded, drawing her over to the groom, 'see, I have kept my promise, I have found you a horse.'

'Oh , she is beautiful, my lord.' Davina put up a hand to stroke the beautiful bay mare. 'How did you come by her. She is lovely?'

The gentle horse snickered a welcome.

'She is one I bred. I have had her in my stables, unable to part with her, but whenever I look at her now, I think only of you.'

Davina was overwhelmed. 'How can I thank you? What can I say?'

'Merely enjoy her, Miss Stanley, that is all I ask.'

Overcome by his generosity, Davina took hold of the mare's halter and led her around to the stables. She had a vague sense that her mother would not approve of this most valuable present but she could not resist the mare nor inflict the unhappiness she knew its rejection would cause.

The visitors did not stay long nor did they enter the house. Lord Restharrow stayed only until he was sure that the mare was in competent hands and that there was tack sufficient for Miss Stanley to ride out with him the next day.

Because Mrs Stanley had retired to her bed with strict instructions not to allow Davina near her in case she was contagious, Davina found it unnecessary to pass on the information about her new mount. She suppressed her qualms with the certainty that the groom would convey the news to the servants' dining room and that Mrs Tulley or Nancy would carry it to her mother. It would then be reasonable to expect to hear via Mrs Tulley that she must return the gift to his lordship. Meanwhile she would enjoy the promised ride and experience some unexpected freedom.

Either the unidentifiable system which was the means by which servants knew all the dealings of their masters had broken down or her mother was indeed too ill to take in the information passed to her. For Davina heard nothing to prevent her from riding out the next day. She was happy to accept the groom's escort as well as Lord Restharrow's as she had no wish to offend the proprieties.

The sun had shone its weak might upon them and warmed the air as best it could. Davina delighted in showing Lord Restharrow the common and, on the following day, the winding steep lanes which gave him the best views of the river-filled valleys. She showed him the mills which were springing up along their length and tried to describe to him the area's beauty in spring and autumn.

'You astound me with your knowledge and understanding of your landscape,' he remarked as they came away from an area covered in snowdrops and aconites. 'I realise now that I should have heeded your warnings about the coming of the snow at Avebury. Can you tell me, Miss Stanley, what weather you antici-pate for tomorrow?'

'Why, more of the same, my Lord,' she laughed, 'there will be another day of winter sun.'

'Then grant me another ride with you tomorrow, my last before I leave for my estates in Berkshire.'.

Davina acquiesced but she had no expectation of being allowed to go. She felt her mother really should be improving in health by the morrow and would no doubt curtail her adventures.

Her mother, however, made no appearance at breakfast and information elicited from a grumpy Nancy was that she was still feverish. The ride was safe.

Davina parted from Lord Restharrow with some regret. He would never supplant Lord Louis in her interest and fledgling affections but with him she felt secure and protected, sensations which she had rarely been granted recently.

She watched his horse canter away until it had disappeared amongst the cottages on the outskirts of Minchinhampnett, then she resolutely turned into the house to suffer her mother's wrath.

10

*M*rs Stanley had recovered enough from her indisposition the next day to allow her daughter to visit her in her dressing room. As expensively and elegantly presented en déshabillé as in day wear, the only evidence of illness was the pallor of her face and the dullness of her usually lustrous hair. She was reclining on a day bed surrounded by cushions.

'Mama.' Davina gave a chaste salute upon her cheek and braced herself to hear words of reproach about her conduct while her mother had been absent.

Mrs Stanley was due to surprise her. 'How charmingly you look, my dear,' she said courteously. 'I do not recognise that dress. How did you come by it? Did you procure it while at Avebury?'

'Thank you Mama,' said Davina, taken aback. 'It is not new, I have just spent time embroidering the bodice and attaching ribbon to the hem. I am glad you approve.'

'Indeed I do.' Her mother fell silent but it was a portentous silence. Davina hurried to fill the gap.

'I have taken account of how the ladies of my new acquaintance dress and I see that I dressed too plainly. I do not have your chic, Mama, nor your bearing, so I must elevate my appearance by other means.'

'I would not have you put yourself unbecomingly forward, my dear,' her mother admonished her lightly, 'it would be most unladylike to be too conspicuous and might result in some unlooked for and indeed unwanted attention from gentlemen of the wrong character.'

Davina took this as censure for the attentions she had received at Avebury; she blushed rosily.

'I do crave your pardon, Mama,' she replied haltingly, 'but I had no one to whom I could turn who might advise me on my conduct.'

'What do you mean, child? What are you saying? Have you behaved unbecomingly at Avebury?'

Davina realised her mistake. Nancy had as yet not repeated to her mother the concerns she had expressed to the daughter.

'Oh no, indeed not, at least I trust not,' Davina returned with suitable circumspection, 'but you must know, you must have heard that Lord Restharrow has brought me a beautiful mare. He has given me her as a present.' Davina slipped to her knees by the bed in unconscious supplication. 'Please do not constrain me to return her to him,' she implored.

Mrs Stanley looked down into her lovely daughter's anxious face and seemed undecided. Instead of replying immediately, she began to attempt the rearrangement of her cushions. Davina rushed to her feet to aid her. Once the cushions had been placed to Mrs Stanley's satisfaction, which took no little time, Mrs Stanley seemed ready to approach the subject again.

'What manner of man is Lord Restharrow? How does he conduct himself with you?' she enquired.

'Oh Mama, he is most gentlemanly, most assiduous in his attentions towards me.'

Mrs Stanley seemed to receive this information with disquiet. 'Has he given any indication that he might wish you to become his wife?'

'Oh no, there is nothing love like in his manner, Mama. He treats me with affection rather than attraction,' her daughter hastily assured her. 'After all, Mama, he is quite elderly and has not succumbed to a wife for many years. I do not believe I am in any way singular enough to make him alter that situation.'

'Very well,' said Mrs Stanley. 'If that is the truth of it,' she looked straight into Davina's eyes, who nodded vigorously, 'then I will let you keep the horse for the time being.'

Davina was delighted and showed her gratitude as best she could by trying to put aside her grief at her mother's behaviour to Lord Louis. She ran errands for her, carried out her parish duties while her mother was still confined to the house and maintained the daily contact with the Rectory.

'Your mother has succumbed to a very severe catching of the influenza,' Mrs Greenaway was moved to comment when Davina arrived alone again four days after Lord Restharrow's departure.

'I am sure she will be able to attend church next Sunday,' was all Davina could think to say, 'but the weather has been so inclement for the last two days we fear the sharp east wind would do her a disservice.'

'You may be right,' agreed Mrs Greenaway magnanimously. For all that she was the Rector's wife she had little patience for the sick beyond her own family circle. She could even be said to view illness as a deliberate act on the part of the sufferer to inconvenience herself or her husband or the timid curate who had the unfortunate lot of having to live in the garden cottage at the Rectory. Unfortunate because he was always accessible and if Mrs Greenaway foresaw a duty as irksome she would shift it neatly on to the narrow shoulders of that curate. The only alleviation of this drudgery the curate found was to be in the company of Ernestine's sister, Annabelle, who was but a year younger than Ernestine and had a distinct predilection for his company. It was perhaps fortunate that the Greenaways had married their two eldest daughters well because it looked as though the next two had no plans to follow their example.

The possession of the mare allowed Davina to join Ernestine out riding as soon as the latter was fully restored to health. Through February and early March, while they did not go hunting, they had many delightful excursions into the surrounding countryside. The days were lengthening gradually and with the improvement of the weather Davina's enjoyment and peace of mind increased. She could look back at the time at Avebury as a brief interruption in her normal life. She could even sometimes think of it fondly as it had resulted in such a material improvement to her daily life now that she could ride.

There had been no further contact from Lord Restharrow either by letter or visit although Ernestine was still receiving secret and almost daily correspondence from Charlie. Davina had to admire his constancy and found it a living proof of the stories about Lord Restharrow that he should hold the memory of some lost love so dear that he could never look at another woman.

It came, then, as some considerable surprise when her mother received a letter inviting both herself and Davina to a spring ball at Lord Restharrow's sister's house. More surprising to Davina was that her mother should inform her of the invitation at all, especially if she planned to prevent her from attending.

'Shall we go, Mama?' she asked tentatively after her mother had read the letter out over breakfast.

Mrs Stanley, who had blanched as she read the contents of the missive, did not answer immediately. When she did, Davina had to struggle to catch the words. 'It will depend upon the circumstance of Ernestine having received an invitation,' she said quietly; then more firmly, 'you know well that I cannot attend.'

Davina nodded, unwilling to revisit old ground.

'We will await a visit from the Greenaways,' said Mrs Stanley, putting aside the matter.

They did not have long to wait. Shortly after they were privileged to be visited by Mrs Greenaway and her two eldest unmarried daughters, Ernestine and Annabelle.

'Both girls have been invited,' Mrs Greenaway announced even before she had been requested to sit down. 'I had no plans to bring Annabelle out this year, she is after all just sixteen, but Ernestine will be eighteen soon and I must give these girls opportunities where I can find them. I shall be taking both girls.'

'Then I fear you will not wish to be plagued with Davina as well.'

Mrs Greenaway eyed Mrs Stanley with her fierce determined grey eyes but Mrs Stanley did not flinch. 'You do not plan to accept for yourself then?' she said, capitulating before even battle was joined.

Mrs Stanley merely grimaced in acquiescence.

'It will of course be a great deal of work, chaperoning three girls and one of those only just entering society, but if it must be done, it will be done.'

'Thank you.'

Mrs Greenaway then remained only long enough to consume the refreshment which had attended her arrival before sweeping up her children and departing.

The party was to be in the first week of April, to ensure that most families had not yet left to start the London season.

Mrs Milfoil, Lord Restharrow's sister, had none of the alarming attributes of either Lady Thistledown or Mrs Greenaway, Davina was to find. She was most truly a gentlewoman, ageing gracefully, who made her guests feel welcomed and cared for. The low and rambling Elizabethan Manor which was her home had none of the impersonal grandeur of Avebury. It was well maintained though not lavishly. There was more likely to be an embroidered patch where a curtain had frayed or a pretty rug where the carpet had thinned but there was no dust and the wooden furniture shone from quantities of elbow grease. Davina loved it there. Mrs Milfoil had one married son and a married daughter so neither were in pursuit of a partner. The party was for pleasure, nothing more, and it was Mrs Milfoil's sole intent to ensure that all her guests enjoyed themselves.

In many ways it was possible that Davina enjoyed it more because of its contrast to the style of living at Avebury. At Mallowdown Manor she never had to fear boredom or the importunities of an unattached male, her hostess was always on hand to entertain her and include her.

To Ernestine's delight Charlie too had been invited and though their rendezvous were severely hampered by the presence of Mrs Greenaway, it was still possible for them to catch a stolen walk or ride together. Davina was made forcefully aware that their attachment was as strong as ever.

The evening of the ball arrived and Davina retired to her bedroom to dress. She was no longer reluctant to summon Nancy and their relationship had significantly improved in the uncritical atmosphere of Mallowdown Manor. Nancy's only moans were practical ones. Due to Mrs Milfoil's more restricted financial situation, there were not as many candles burning in the corridors or in the rooms and the fireplaces in the bedrooms were too small for the fire to throw out much light. Nancy kept the heavy drapes clear of the windows to allow in the last vestiges of daylight to lighten the room.

'Your mother asked me to present you with this new dress, Miss Davina,' she said once she had turned her attention to the serious matter of dressing a young lady for a ball. Davina was drawn to the bed on which lay a large flat box. She lifted the lid carefully and drew out the most beautiful pale pink dress of satin. The bodice was decorated with coral and pearls and there was a matching corsage holder and hair piece.

'Oh, it's beautiful, Nancy,' breathed Davina, delighted.

'It most certainly is,' said the maid, taking the dress off her charge, 'your mother has the most exquisite taste, nothing would have become you better.'

'Thank you,' murmured Davina, then a wicked glint appeared in her eye. 'What I have need of now is a beau to present me with some matching flowers.'

'Miss Davina!'

'There was a knock on the door and a maid was revealed holding a delicate posy of pink roses.

Davina had to smother a laugh but Nancy's lips pursed with disapproval as she read the note of hand.

'Tis from my Lord Restharrow, Miss,' she said.

'Oh how kind of him, he must know I have no admirer to do me the honour. See he has provided me with enough for each of my holders.'

'It is not seemly to be receiving flowers from him,' said Nancy, more in anger than in truth.

Davina looked perplexed. 'Why have you taken against him, Nancy? I can assure you that he means me no harm.'

Nancy allowed her shoulders to sag. 'I know Miss,' she said, 'but I still feel it improper that he pays you all this attention while having no serious intentions towards you.'

'What can it signify, Nancy?' Davina moaned. 'I know he has no intentions and the company here present know that he has no serious intentions. If we are all dancing the same steps, there can be no harm in it.'

Nancy gave the dress a vigorous shake before preparing to cast it over Davina's head. 'As you say, Miss Davina, we will not think of it again.'

Davina thought this would be impossible but such was the excitement of preparing for the ball, she could soon think of nothing else but her toilette and the effect it would have on the other guests.

Ernestine came to fetch her so they could descend the stairs and enter the saloon together. Annabelle was waiting nervously in the corridor. She was wearing the palest of yellow and had miniature daffodils in her hair. Davina thought she looked exquisite.

'Oh no,' demurred the younger girl rather breathlessly, 'no, you must look at Ernestine, does she not look lovely?'

'Ernestine is always turned out to perfection.' Davina linked an arm through each of the Greenaway girls. 'Come,' she said, 'let us go and make our entrance!'

11

*T*o Davina, the evening was a revelation. Mrs Milfoil had ensured that all her young guests had partners for the first two dances and after that she worked assiduously to keep the company circulating. Even before supper was announced Davina had danced with Mr Milfoil the younger, Charlie and an enthusiastic young man who was the son of the squire of the next village. He was much the type she was used to in her own circles at home so she could dance and converse with him with ease. It was only as he was taking her to procure a glass of lemonade that her equanimity was disturbed. Glancing towards the door to the hallway, she saw the tall figure of Lord Louis Twayblade making his entrance. Such was her surprise that she missed her step and had to be steadied by her partner. He was too young to know how best to deal with an apparently distressed young lady but he had the aplomb to lead her to her chaperone.

'Come now, Davina, what is the matter with you?' demanded Mrs Greenaway, seeing Davina pale-faced and trembling.

'Forgive me,' whispered Davina, 'make nothing of it. I have merely turned my ankle slightly. A moment, a moment is all I need to recover.'

'Foolish girl,' admonished her chaperone without much sympathy. 'Sit there then and wait awhile.'

Mrs Greenaway then dismissed Davina's escort and turned back to her animated conversation with a lifelong friend which was very much to the disservice of a mutual acquaintance.

Davina was grateful for the lack of sympathy. It allowed her to shrink out of sight behind the bulk of the lady and marshal her thoughts to handle this new turn of events. However she had reckoned without her hostess whose sharp eyes had seen the cause and effect of the little play between parties. Now Mrs Milfoil was not a mischief maker but she had a strong belief that one should confront one's fears and not allow them to reach mammoth proportions. She therefore gravitated to Lord Louis and drew him towards the seated Davina.

'Come, young man, let me introduce you to a young lady of my new acquaintance. I am sure you will be delighted with her.' Having reached her quarry she turned to Davina.

'Let me make known to you Miss Davina, Lord Louis Twayblade. Lord Louis, Miss Davina Stanley.'

Davina rose hurriedly to her feet and dropped a hesitant curtsy, afraid to look into his eyes.

'I believe we have met before, Madame Milfoil,' said Lord Louis, watching Davina slightly maliciously, 'there can be no need for introductions.'

'Then perhaps you would be good enough to lead her down to supper,' said Mrs Milfoil, moving away before he could refuse.

The young couple stood for a moment in awkward silence, an oasis of quiet in amongst the hubbub of voices and music. Davina was the first to find her voice.

'There can be no need for you to escort me, my lord, ' she said more evenly than she dared to hope. 'Mrs Greenaway is here to accompany me.'

Hearing her name, Mrs Greenaway turned and seeing that Davina had a potential escort misread the situation and said: 'Yes, yes that's very well Davina, you may go on to the dining room, do not await my coming.'

Lord Louis's love of the ridiculous came to his rescue. He put out his arm for Davina to take.

'It seems we must comply,' he said, 'so many are determined that we should Madamoiselle, we should not disappoint them.'

'There really is no need,' responded Davina rather haughtily.

'You think not,' he laughed. 'Then you do not know Madame Milfoil. She is all sweetness and light but woe betide any who puts their opinion against her.'

'You wrong her surely,' cried Davina, still not able to look in his face, so missing the teasing glint in his eye.

'I lay you odds, Madamoiselle, if I leave your side now she will be upon us to find out why.'

Davina shook her head; this conversation was going nowhere. She braved a look into his face and reaffirmed in her heart the attraction she had felt for him on their first meeting. It silenced her for a moment.

By now they had reached the dining room which was a long, low room ablaze with candles. The tables were laden with food all exotically decorated with spring flowers.

'Oh,' Davina gasped, 'how splendid.'

'It is indeed,' agreed her escort. 'I warrant you saw nothing like this at Avebury. Madame Milfoil keeps an excellent table. She may practise economy on her household costs but not her kitchen. You would be hard pressed to find a better spread throughout the land.'

Before Davina could respond Ernestine put up a hand from a table further down the room to attract their attention. They wove their way through the diners until they reached her.

'Quick, quick be seated beside me,' Ernestine bubbled. 'My mother does not know we have escaped down here. She would not have allowed me to be escorted by Charlie.' She tinkled a little laugh. 'Lord Louis, would you be so good as to be seated opposite me so that it looks as though I have come down with you?'

'But,' Davina was moved to protest, for she knew Mrs Greenaway had seen her make her way to the dining room with Lord Louis.

'I think Madamoiselle,' murmured Lord Louis, 'we will play this little game.' He pulled out a seat for Davina and once he was sure she was settled he went off to procure her some food.

'Is it not the best party?' demanded Ernestine once the two girls were alone, 'Mrs Milfoil is the very best of hostesses.'

'She is a lovely lady,' Davina agreed cautiously. A young man came up and made to sit beside Ernestine but she was quick to indicate that the place was taken.

Davina could not help but think that there were so many instances that Ernestine handled much better than she was able. She looked across the table at her pretty friend and wished she had half her assurances.

Charlie and Lord Louis returned together carrying plates laden with food.

'Oh my,' giggled Ernestine, 'I shall not be able to dance another step if I eat all this!'

Davina was just beginning to feel more comfortable. Lord Louis had not alluded to that disastrous evening at Fromeview Place and she hoped that he was inclined to forget about it. She had, however, reckoned without Charlie.

'I fear I have not had a proper opportunity to thank you for rescuing the girls from their plight on the open road,' he said suddenly before lifting a chicken drumstick to his mouth.

Davina gave a little choke, which made Lord Louis turn his head towards her.

'Ah you need have no concern for that, young Charlie. I'm sure the mothers of the mesdemoiselles thanked me well enough.'

'Fie on you, Lord Louis,' cried Ernestine, seeing her friend's distress, 'where is the gentleman in you that you should constantly taunt my sweet Davina?'

'Taunt! Taunt! Me!' he laughingly disclaimed, 'I do nothing.'

Davina felt this was too much and turned her beautiful brown eyes to look at him with a hint of reproach.

He read it there and threw up his hands in capitulation, knocking a wine glass over as he did so. There was a flurry of activity as they all rushed to mop up the heavy red liquid seeping into the tablecloth.

'Forgive me Miss Stanley,' he said as soon as calm had been

restored to the table, demonstrating his earnestness by dropping away any trace of the French accent. 'I allowed myself to be too much mortified by your mother's strictures and have wished since that day to apologise for my conduct. But when it came to it this evening I could not find the way of it. Forgive me.'

Davina's face broke into a lovely smile. 'And you too must forgive us for not being suitably grateful for your aid to us. You could not have expected such treatment after putting yourself out so significantly on our behalf.'

He smiled and would have stretched out his hand to clasp hers on the table if he had not looked up and seen Mrs Greenaway bearing down upon them.

'Come,' he said, hastily getting to his feet, 'let us return to the dance floor.'

They went as a foursome back to the saloon and the ladies were led out to form a set by their respective partners. Conscious, all of them, that they should not make a spectacle of themselves, they swapped partners for the following dance and sat out for the third.

Davina had never enjoyed herself so much and when she allowed herself the final dance with Lord Louis she knew that she was in love. What the gentleman thought, she could not tell, he still masked his feelings with teasing but it had a softer tone to it and she thought she could hope that there was a softening of his feelings too.

As a pair of couples it was much easier the next day for the young ladies to escape their duenna. Mr Milfoil kept an ample stable and was able to offer his young guests a mount apiece, so they set out to explore the countryside.

Once out in the expansive park which surrounded the manor, the little party dismounted and walked down towards a lake, leading their horses. Ernestine and Charlie were soon lost to the others.

After exchanging views of the previous night's entertainment and passing comment on the weather, Davina felt able to ask her escort some questions closer to home.

'Why, my lord, do you affect a French accent?' she asked.

'Affect a French accent?' he cried in mock affront.

'Most certainly. For I have seen that when you are much moved it deserts you. You cannot deny it.'

'But I must deny it, my sole defence is on being thought by you as a figure of romance and mystery. If you perceive my accent to be false, what of the rest, "Madamoiselle".'

'Ah, you need have no fear of that. What can be more romantic than a dashing rescue on the King's highway. No, pray tell me, why the accent?'

'Very well,' he said as he drew her to a fallen tree trunk and took the horse's reins from her hand. He secured both horses to a sapling and came and seated himself beside her. The tree might have been placed there, so perfect were the vistas down to the lake and across the rolling hills of the park. 'My mother has presented my father with a dark-haired son every two or three years since my birth. There is little to choose between us; I sought to make a distinction as my mother has a penchant for French as you can tell by my name, that is all.'

'But you are the eldest, what more distinction did you need than that?!'

'The eldest but not the heir. Not until I left school did I realise that I might have that honour.'

'You understand it to be the case then, that you are heir to your half-brother.'

'I am constantly told it but I do not believe it. My half-brother is fifteen years my senior, I grant you that, but that does not quite make him forty. There is many a man who sees old age before him and rushes into wedlock with a younger woman.'

Davina bowed her head and contemplated the blade of grass she had picked. She liked his frankness, his diffidence in assuming a great position. Many a man in his situation would have made much of being such an heir, but not he, he wanted her to know his true prospects.

'And what of you, Miss Stanley, how are you circumstanced?'

'I know little of my family, my lord,' she told him with more openness that she might have been reluctant to use had he not been so free with his own confidences. 'My mother too comes from the north, but south of the border in Cumbria, near the little town of Longtown. I believe we still have relatives there but my mother does not speak of them often. She moved south, I have been given to understand, because of her marriage but I have no knowledge of my father's family nor of him. He died of fever during his return from the Americas. My mother then went into genteel service, she became companion to two elderly ladies.' She paused and sighed. 'She felt either that or becoming a governess was all that was open to a gentlewoman in straightened circumstances and with a small child.' She brightened suddenly. 'But we were lucky and all that we have now we owe to our kind employers.'

12

That evening Davina retired to bed in considerable perturbation. Lord Louis seemed to have withdrawn from her and she feared that it was the disclosures about her family circumstances she had been lulled into making which had set him at a distance from her. She hoped to catch him at breakfast to reassure herself that this was not the case, so was disappointed to find that he had set out earlier with the Mr Milfoils on a ride around the estate. Ernestine had appeared bright and cheery that morning, so it came as a considerable surprise when a little while later a young housemaid, in some distress, came in search of Davina.

'Oh, Mr Charlie asks that you come quickly to Miss Ernestine, Miss, they are in the back parlour.'

Davina hurried to locate them. Knocking on the low door she did not wait for an answer and went straight in. The scene before her brought her to an immediate halt. Silhouetted against the light from the casement window was Charlie, letter in hand. Ernestine was seated at a small wooden table, her head bowed. There were tears streaming down her face and her whole body was convulsed with gusty sobs.

'Good God, what has occurred?' Davina cried.

'Please shut the door.' Charlie's voice was a thin reed betraying his shock and emotion. Davina looked more closely at him; his face was ashen and his blond locks were dishevelled and falling across his brow. She shut the door and came forward.

'Tell me, tell me what has occurred to distress you both so.'

Charlie made to hand her the letter, then thought better of it.

'My brother,' he said, 'my brother has been shot in a duel, not three days ago.'

There was a wail from Ernestine and her sobs intensified as though Charlie's articulation of the circumstance brought on a fresh wave of pain.

Davina did not know what to say. She had no notion that this brother, of whom she had heard nothing but ill, had so strong a hold on Ernestine's affections. She moved to put an arm around her friend to comfort her.

'How did this happen?' she enquired quietly.

Charlie came away from the window and flung the letter on the bare table.

'The information is scant but from the letter I have received from his adversary's second, it seems that my brother owed a debt of honour which he would not own.' He waved his arm in an expression of hopelessness. 'Lucien rarely owned to his debts! However it seems he was at his club when the matter was pressed. An argument flared up and a duel was demanded.'

'I'm sorry,' said Davina nonplussed, 'but a duel, Charlie? I did not know such things still occurred.'

'Tis true they have long been out of fashion but perhaps the man felt it was the only way to get his money. I know not. This is all the information that I have.' He grabbed the letter again and waved it at her then sighed heavily. 'Be that as it may, the duel was fought, pistols at dawn. My brother down, his challenger to flee the country.'

The bitterness in his voice left Davina with nothing she could say. She intensified her efforts to comfort Ernestine with words of sympathy when Ernestine suddenly let out a flood of anguished sentiments.

'I do not want sympathy for the loss of him,' she cried. 'What did he ever do but disservice to his friends and family?'

'Oh pray hush Ernestine, you cannot know what you are saying.' Davina was quick to try and stem the flow, fearing that Charlie might be offended.

'I will not be silenced, it was because of his debts that Charlie was no longer an eligible party for my hand. Had Lucien tried to repay his father's debts rather than compound them, we would have been wed by now. But no, he needs must run his own course. Game and gamble away what little money was left. We will never be able to marry now.' She collapsed forward on to the table and sobbed into her arms.

'How so, I do not understand?' Davina gave Charlie a look of enquiry, hoping for some enlightenment.

Charlie sat down heavily at the table opposite the two young women.

'I see you are not aware of the rules which govern debt,' he said. He took a deep breath. 'While Lucien was alive it was always within his power to win one of his gambles or marry wealth or sponge from a relative. His debtors lived in hope of repayment.'

'Now that he is dead, every trade account, every debt of honour, every bet will come to light and will have to be repaid either by me or my uncle. I, we, are staring ruin in the face, Miss Davina.' Davina tried to protest. 'But truly I am ruined,' he said emphatically, 'even if I and my uncle escaped debtors' prison I could never now marry Ernestine. I could not support her.'

It came to Davina as she sat there that she was not witnessing grief for the loss of a dear loved one but for the blighted love of two young people, so desperate for each other that all other considerations paled into insignificance.

'I wish I could bestow my fortune upon you.' The words escaped her almost involuntarily.

Charlie gave her a brief bleak smile in acknowledgement of the kind thought but Ernestine raised her head abruptly and the reddened eyes, framed by damp curls around her tear-washed face, had a sudden steely glint in them.

'Perhaps you might,' she said breathlessly, 'at least you might loan us an interest in it for a time.'

'Ernestine.' Charlie put up a hand to prevent her saying more but she would not be gainsaid.

'No, no listen to me, Charlie,' she hurried on, 'if you were to become engaged to Davina now, the creditors would be given pause.'

'They might,' agreed Charlie dubiously.

'But to what end?' asked Davina who found the fantastic nature of the proposal left her curiously detached.

'Don't you see,' said Ernestine, irritated by their lack of enthusiasm for her idea, 'if it were known that you intended to wed the creditors might be better convinced to wait until the marriage took place than to press their demands now when there is no money to meet them.'

'Forgive me,' said Davina, shaking her head slightly as if to detach the wool that appeared to be gathering within it. 'But how will that serve you when the engagement comes to an end as it surely must?'

'It will have bought Uncle Restharrow and Charlie time to find other means of payment,' said Ernestine triumphantly.

Davina looked at Charlie to try and gauge his feelings about this outlandish proposal. To her surprise he seemed to be considering it. She felt a surge of panic within her; they could not really expect her to pursue this course. Yet had she not already ascertained that they were single-minded in the pursuit of their own future.

'My mother would never permit it.' Davina realised she and she alone would have to call a halt to this little pantomime.

'But your mother is not one of your trustees,' Ernestine informed her promptly. 'I'm sure my father would give his permission. Indeed I know my mother would ensure it so. After all was not that one of the principal purposes of sending you to Avebury with me?'

'There is another trustee,' said Davina, rocked by this announcement.

Ernestine dismissed him with an airy wave of the hand. 'Old Romford does as father tells him.'

'But is not the danger that having agreed to the engagement my trustees might force the issue and insist on the match?'

'They will certainly not do so while we are all in deepest mourning,' said Ernestine, considering the question carefully. 'Seeing that year out will bring you to nearly nineteen, you need delay only a further two years and then they can no longer enforce their will on you. You will be in sole possession of your fortune.'

Davina was appalled that her friend knew so much more about her circumstances than she did herself. It made her wonder what else others knew which she did not. A hazy idea niggled at the back of her mind that Ernestine had confused trustees with guardianship. While the Reverend Greenaway and Mr Romford could withhold her fortune they had no say over her personal well-being. That still remained firmly under her mother's jurisdiction; however Davina did not raise the point, she was too busy trying to find expression of her deeper feeling of unease.

'There can be no thought of it,' she said with as much certainty as she could muster, 'people would not credit it, they know you and Charlie are as good as promised to each other.'

Ernestine looked crest fallen for a moment before rallying.

'Because it is known within the family it is assumed that others are aware of it too. But recall the circumstances at Avebury; Charlie manifested in company as much care for you as he did for me. And,' she said after a long out-take of breath, 'here you could have as well been partnered by Charlie as Lord Louis, so circumspect were we at the ball.'

'No, no this is madness.' Davina got hastily to her feet. 'You cannot persuade me that this is a reasonable course of action.' She rounded on Charlie. 'Come tell me, you think this is one of Ernestine's wild fantasies.'

Charlie had been lounging in the hard-backed chair, his long legs stretched out under the table and his hand twiddling a small twist of paper which had found itself within his orbit.

'We cannot force you down this road Davina,' he said quietly. 'You are our dear friend and nothing can change that but in making this gesture you would, indeed, be rendering us a service of great magnitude for which we will ever be grateful.'

The alarm bells were sounding in Davina's head. Her heart was racing and she felt nausea overcome her. She sat back down with a thump and with both hands smoothed her hair away from her face. An image of Lord Louis rose before her; she wished she could use this as fit punishment to him for his sudden coolness but she did not want some petty revenge, only reconciliation. The crux for her was whether that reconciliation could be bought at the expense of her friends' happiness.

'Are you sure that this is what you want?' she asked. 'Do you not want to take stock? Reconsider?'

Charlie shook his head. 'I need to tell my uncle Restharrow what has befallen us. This would soften the blow.'

Davina pursed her lips, unable to trust herself to speak.

'You will do it then?' asked Ernestine eagerly, covering Davina's hands with both of hers. 'You will do it for us?'

A great cavern of woe and uncertainties yawned in front of Davina's mind's eye but she nodded.

'If you have courage enough to bear it, then so have I,' she said.

Both young people embraced her. 'You will not regret it, Davina, I swear. We will not let anything or anyone harm you through this,' Charlie promised her before quitting the room in haste to find his uncle.

The two young women were left staring at each other.

'Have you considered what a trial this will be for you Tina?' Davina asked gently.

Ernestine's face was still blotched from crying and her eyes were still red but she held her head high and her back straight.

'I have no other choice,' she said with a catch in her voice, 'without your help I shall lose him for ever, with it he can be mine in three years' time.'

'It is a long time to wait.'

'A very long time but better than eternity. Forgive me.'

Ernestine turned and went to the door. 'I must go to my room and try and repair the ravages of this morning.' She blew Davina a kiss from the top of her fingertips and was gone. Davina found herself feeling totally bereft. She had the sensation that they had absorbed all the emotion from her, she felt sucked dry. She wondered at herself, how she could have been persuaded to agree. Reluctantly she acknowledged that had she believed there had been any chance of re-igniting Lord Louis's interest in her, she would have been better armed to ward them off.

13

*T*he news both of Lucien's demise and the unofficial engage-ment between Charlie and Davina ran rampant through the household. Davina was subjected to much curious question-ing and a small amount of restrained congratulations to which she found it very hard to respond. Lord Restharrow had merely pressed her hand before leaving for London to assist Charlie in the matter of his brother's estate. Soon after, the whole house party broke up and those guests who had expected to stay made their excuses and left for home.

Ernestine and Davina for a while believed themselves stranded as Mrs Greenaway would not leave without a male escort. However Mr Milfoil, the younger, was soon volunteered to perform the task. While his mother's affectionate heart was deeply saddened by the loss of her nephew, Mr Milfoil seemed relatively unmoved, appearing to expound the theory that Lucien had brought it upon himself.

It was a tired and sorry pair of girls who completed the uneventful journey back to Minchinhampnett. Davina did not alight from the carriage when the Greenaways were deliv-ered to their door first. Already there was a little constraint between them, Davina noted sadly, it had been an uncomfortable journey.

At home Davina waited for word from Charlie and could not prevent herself from going over and over what had happened just before Charlie had left for London.

Davina had seen the utter astonishment, swiftly followed by anger in the face of Lord Louis when the information of their betrothal had been imparted to him. He had wheeled out of the room to she knew not where but it did not stop her trying to follow him, afraid to explain but determined to do so.

She had eventually located him by the sound of his angry voice ringing down the passage from the morning room.

'My God, Charlie, what can you be thinking of? You cannot marry the Stanley girl.'

'I beg your pardon, I can marry whomsoever I please, and I would be grateful if you could speak of my affianced wife with more respect.'

'Respect, respect,' cried Lord Louis hotly, 'for what am I supposed to have respect, ha?' He was almost incoherent with rage. 'Certainly not her birth, nor her connections.'

'Her connections are my connections!'

'Nonsense there is no blood between her and them any more than there is between you and me, only friendship.'

'I see that as a secure enough foundation.'

'Then you delude yourself.'

Davina found herself rigid with shock; she stood in the doorway unable to make her presence known to them. Lord Louis's back was to her, his body obscuring Charlie's view of the door.

'Delude myself, in what way pray?'

'Why you fool, that her fortune will secure you a better future. You may no longer have debts but there will not be a lady amongst the upper echelons of the *ton* who would admit her to their ranks.'

'You seem so sure!'

'Of course I'm sure. Dammit Charlie, I have visited their house. There is no evidence of a father and the story her mother puts about of his loss is typical of a fallen woman attempting to pass herself off as a widowed one.'

'How dare you.' Suddenly Davina had found her voice and her legs, she had moved swiftly into the room and gone to stand by

Charlie's chair. 'I think you have said all you need say to us,' she said bitterly, 'please leave.'

Lord Louis's face drained of all colour and with deep mortification evident there, he had opened his mouth to speak, then making a gesture indicative of futility, he had turned with a snap of his heels and left the room. Davina had not seen him again.

No letter arrived from Charlie the next day nor the next but on the following day he arrived in person. He seemed tired and harassed but he made his formal bow to Mrs Stanley and very promptly requested to be allowed to pay his addresses to her daughter.

Mrs Stanley had not been taken completely by surprise as Nancy had been able to give her some indication of what had happened at Mallowdown Manor.

She listened attentively to Charlie's professions of regard and then summoned her daughter to attend the interview. When both were seated before her, she eyed them measuringly.

'So this attachment,' she began, 'is not of long duration. Some six weeks is all you have spent in each other's company.'

'True ma'am but...'

She held up her hand to halt his interruption. 'You, young man may have seen much of the world but my daughter is but going on eighteen. What basis is this six weeks for a lasting future for her?'

'I can assure you Mama, it will endure,' said Davina, attempting to deflect her from Charlie.

'And I say you know not enough of each other to have formed a lasting attachment, I cannot approve the match yet.'

'But you will not forbid it, Mama, please say you will not.' Davina's face was ravaged with anxiety.

Mrs Stanley looked at her briefly and then away as if unwilling to witness her daughter's distress.

'And your prospects, Sir, I have heard no mention of those. They will of course be significantly improved by marrying my daughter.'

'I acknowledge it, ma'am,' replied Charlie carefully, 'but my prospects are good. You may know that I recently became heir to Lord Restharrow's estate.'

'Fine sounding indeed, young man, but if my memory serves me aright, Lord Restharrow's estates are notoriously encumbered.'

Charlie coloured and stammered, and Davina rushed into the breach.

'That is all at an end Mama, Charlie and Lord Restharrow plan to restore the estates so that accounts can be settled.'

'All made much more easy my child, with the aid of your fortune.'

Charlie and Davina were silenced. They sat miserably forlorn in the ruin of Charlie and Ernestine's hopes. Mrs Stanley looked from one to the other and seemed to relent a little.

'And in what relationship do you stand to Lord Restharrow, Mr Winstanleigh?'

'I am his nephew, ma'am,' Charlie answered quietly.

'I see.' The lady appeared to consider for awhile; there was an extended silence that tried both young people's nerves. The clock on the mantelpiece ticked determinedly on towards five o'clock. Suddenly Mrs Stanley reached her decision.

'I will not forbid it,' she said, 'but I will not have it announced until I have determined that this attachment is lasting.'

'Thank you Mama, oh thank you.' Davina was up from her chair and at her mother's feet. 'You do not know what this means to us.'

Mrs Stanley patted the hand that was clutching her dress and stood up. 'Come,' she said as though nothing untoward or momentous had happened. 'Let us dine.'

It was an uncomfortable meal. Davina felt the full force of the moralist's arguments that deceit compounded itself. The deception weighed heavily on her shoulders, more so even she felt than on Charlie's. He was clearly distressed but with more cause on other fronts. Before he left he snatched a private moment with Davina.

'It is as we feared,' he told her. 'The vultures are gathering. My uncle has paid a few and parried more. The knowledge that we are betrothed is filtering through, there is less urgency from those who had heard it but still they want their money.'

Davina could do nothing but squeeze his hand; she had, after all, already done everything within her power.

Charlie did not stay long in Gloucestershire. Whether he visited the Greenaways, Davina could not tell. The social intercourse between the families had significantly reduced since the announcement within their circle that Charlie and Davina were to wed. While the parents had congratulated her appropriately, they seemed to want to keep meetings between their daughter and Davina to a minimum. Davina wondered at it for she did not believe it was a sudden surge of parental concern. After all it had been they who had most earnestly promoted the match.

The days drifted by with company becoming thin on the ground. All the occupants of the great houses locally had migrated to London for the Season. Davina felt abandoned. Charlie wrote regularly to keep up the pretence but briefly and, as what he did write was usually to do with his feelings for Ernestine, this was of little solace. In fact Davina had begun to merely scan the text rather than read it carefully so she nearly missed his request to meet her on the common in secret, three days hence.

Davina made her way there in some trepidation. The antics Ernestine clearly enjoyed were anathema to her, who would never disobey a convention unless it was unavoidable.

She found the spot Charlie had alluded to in his letter and waited obediently. The animals were out grazing, enjoying the stronger sun. Davina closed her eyes and raised her face to its warmth; she cared nothing for its effect on her complexion.

'Davina!' There was the sound of hasty footsteps, and Charlie was before her. He took her hand and raised it to his lips.

'I am a cad to request this meeting. I know how much you must dislike it.'

She shook her head, not able to express her feelings. Charlie seemed to have aged in the few weeks since she had seen him. His carefree, happy-go-lucky demeanour had completely deserted him and his brow under the golden locks was furrowed.

'Come, let us find a sheltered spot, I have much I have to tell you.'

She let him guide her to a spinney which teetered on the edge of the escarpment and brushing aside some of the undergrowth, he took off his coat and laid it on the ground for her to sit on.

'Tell me,' she urged him, 'tell me what has occurred.'

'It is not so much what has occurred as what has not,' he told her unhelpfully.

She gave an exclamation of annoyance and her brown eyes hardened slightly. 'No games, Charlie, I beg you,' she said.

He sighed. 'I do not know how best to say this,' he said dryly.

'Any way is better than not at all!'

'It seems so cruel after all your kindness.'

For a moment she thought he was going to ask her to declare their engagement at an end. She felt a flutter of relief before it was captured and penned by his next words.

'The traders and the debtors of a lesser order do not accept that there is an engagement. They see nothing of you and have no proof of your existence. If we are to benefit from this charade then I must beg you to come to London.'

'London! I cannot go to London,' she cried aghast. 'Where would I stay? Who would escort me about?'

'Oh I have thought of all that,' he assured her, 'I have prevailed on Amelia to invite you.'

'Prevailed!' After the one exclamation she was lost for words. Matters seemed to be going from bad to worse. She had no wish to be the unwelcome guest of an unwilling hostess.

Charlie apologised hastily and attempted a more acceptable rephrasing. 'I meant that I put it to her as a suggestion. I do not mean that she disliked the scheme, only that she had not previously thought of it.'

'And who can blame her?' cried Davina hotly. 'She goes on the expectation of pleasure and you demand a duty of her.' A thought occurred to Davina. 'How so can she go? Your family must surely be in full mourning for your brother.'

'It is so, of course. None of the Gloucestershire Greenaways go to London this season. Mr Greenaway feels that they should embrace mourning to its detailed observance because of his cloth even though their connection to us is a touch tenuous.. Lady Thistledown however, despite Lucien being her husband's sister's son, takes a more relaxed view. She and her husband have gone into full mourning but Amelia is allowed her season provided she eschews balls and any other form of dancing.' He sighed wearily. 'I can only assume Mrs Greenaway pursues this course for fear of a reconciliation between Ernestine and myself should we meet.' Another sigh and he dashed his hand across his face. 'Indeed I doubt I could hold out if I were to see her in company. She is much changed I fear. Her letters speak of her suffering. Her merry spirit has deserted her.'

Davina had to turn her face away as a small grim smile settled on her lips. It seemed Ernestine still had her methods of communicating with her amour despite the restrictions put about her by her family. Charlie appeared not to notice that Davina had been affected by what he had said.

'Amelia will be staying with Mrs Greenaway's eldest daughter, Lady Purslane, who rightly feels that Lucien's demise has nothing whatsoever to do with her. She will chaperone Amelia to dinner parties and musical soirées but not any grander affairs.'

'And has this lady been prevailed upon to include me?' Davina asked slightly acidly.

'Davina forgive me.' Charlie raised her hand to his lips again, 'we ask too much of you, I know we do.'

'No, no, it is I who should beg your forgiveness,' she assured him as a surge of guilt at her own churlishness assailed her. 'I know you are doing the very best in your power to help your uncle. It is wrong of me to hinder you.'

Her words and the implied tribute left him momentarily overcome. It took him a little while to make a recovery. Eventually he raised himself up from the ground and stood looking down at her.

'Lady Purslane cordially invites you to stay with her for the remainder of the Season,' he said. 'Your mother should be receiving a letter from her any day now.'

14

*L*ady Purslane's London house was charmingly decorated, with light and airy rooms and situated in a quiet, genteel area which was a pleasant relief from the noisome and noisy bustle of many thoroughfares of the city.

Davina had been more than a little concerned that Lady Purslane would resemble her formidable mother and aunt too closely and was greatly relieved to find that there was a leaven in her character that made her blunt utterances much more accept-able. Facially she had the look of her mother but she was still young enough to have escaped the hard lines of dogma in her face and a healthy self-discipline had prevented her from allow-ing her girth to increase after the birth of her two children. Davina warmed to her and was grateful for the welcome which made her feel immediately at home.

Amelia surprisingly appeared well satisfied with Davina's company.

'We shall enjoy more freedom as there are two of us,' she purred on the first afternoon of Davina's stay as they sauntered together, parasols aloft in Hyde Park. Amelia was keen to attract the attention of any of her acquaintances and was therefore a slow companion but Davina did not mind, it allowed her to go through the bare acknowledgements of civil responses without having to concentrate too hard. Not content with having the altercation with Lord Louis take up almost permanent residence in her mind, she also found a subsequent conversation with her mother jostling for position in her head. Mrs Stanley had been ill-disposed to the idea of Davina enjoying a sojourn in London but reluctant to prevent her daughter from going. These ambiguities had left Davina floundering and in a move braver than was her wont, she had challenged her mother on its reasons.

'Mama, do Mr Greenaway and Mr Romford have some power over you of which I am not aware, that you should be forever allowing me liberties which go against your inclination?'

Mrs Stanley had given her daughter a swift penetrating look. 'What can you mean?' she had asked sharply.

'This constant divide between what you want me to do and what you allow me to. It must have its roots in something.'

Mrs Stanley had stopped preparing the flowers she had been arranging and taking her daughter's hand had led her to a settle by the window. Outside there was glorious sunshine and the edges of the lawn under the trees were a mass of bluebells. Davina had glanced briefly at the familiar scene before turning her full attention to her mother.

'I have tarried too long,' the lady had said. 'I had hoped to keep you in ignorance of my youthful follies for some little while yet but the pressures exerted by the Greenaways and their connections make it impossible.'

By now Davina's heart had been thumping heavily. She had realised that she did not in fact want to hear any revelations to her mother's disservice. She had wanted to halt the utterances but knew she could not. She had sat, dark head slightly bowed, waiting for the blow which would wreck her future hopes.

'You are aware I know, my dear, that I hold your father's memory very dear,' Mrs Stanley had paused then for what had seemed to Davina like an eternity. 'I was a slave to my feelings for him long before we married. I knew he was an unsuitable party, that I must choose between him and my family.' She had clutched at Davina's hand and something suspiciously like a sob had escaped her. 'I am guilty of having put my youthful desires ahead of any other consideration. I married him secretly but the secrecy could not be maintained. I left my family and moved south hoping to make an independent life for myself and,' halting abruptly as though choosing her words very carefully, she had carried on hesitantly, 'as you know I lost your father. If it had not been for my godmother finding me employment with the Miss Leonards, I would have been lost too.'

Davina had returned the pressure of her mother's hand. 'But what has all that to do with me, Mama?' she asked plaintively.

'I do not want you to make the mistakes I made, my sweet.' Her mother's eyes had been so sorrowful, Davina had found tears welling up in her own in response. 'If the Miss Leonards had not taken me on trust, I could have been penniless, destitute. I fear putting too many obstacles in your way, in case you make the same mistakes as I did.'

Davina had not been blind to the flaws in Mrs Stanley's explanation nor the obvious differences between her mother and herself. She, after all, was independently wealthy. She had felt some relief that there had been no ghastly disclosure about her own birth but she could not be entirely satisfied.

'Have you never been reconciled with your family?' she had asked, hoping for some information about them.

'Never,' Mrs Stanley had sighed, 'but I do send them money.'

Davina had blinked with surprise. 'Indeed!'

'Oh yes, some years ago my godmother wrote to inform me that my father had suffered reverses on 'change'. My mother had to take up private tutoring but my father's health collapsed and my sister, whose mind is weak, is not capable of employment. I send them what I can from the housekeeping.'

'Have you ever suggested a reconciliation?'

Mrs Stanley had shaken her head.

It had been on the tip of Davina's tongue to ask why not but it seemed impertinent. She had waited for more information but it had not been forthcoming. Now walking with Amelia, Davina wished she had asked more questions, probed harder. The knowledge that she had a grandmother, grandfather and aunt had lightened the burden she was carrying and she resolved that, regardless of any protestations from her mother, she would visit them once she was of age. Mrs Stanley had spoken diffidently of the money she sent them but knowing her mother's goodness of heart, Davina felt sure that since the acquisition of her fortune, Mrs Stanley would have been contributing materially to their comfort.

If nothing else Davina felt she now had some answers, though possibly only partial ones, to some of the more barbed questions which came her way. She was no nearer knowing who her father was but nothing her mother had said gave credence to some of the darker inferences directed at her. She decided her best course was simply to ignore them.

Amelia was determined that they should take up every opportunity offered them within the restrictive cordon of mourning her mother had dictated. When the sun shone they either walked or rode but when it rained they strolled though the shops and bazarres or visited the library. Davina was amazed at how much pleasure Amelia derived from these simple pursuits.

'Do you miss the country?' she asked her one morning on their way to the library.

'Oh no,' laughed Amelia. 'I am a fickle creature, Davina. When at Avebury I love the grounds, the riding, the animals but transport me to the town and I am as happy,' she broke off to acknowledge the passing bow of a smart gentleman in a coat of rich burgundy, 'if not happier to enjoy its entertainments.'

'Is there anyone in whom you have a special interest?' Davina asked, emboldened by this openness.

'There have been two young men who have approached Papa,' she admitted, a saucy look on her face, 'but neither were suitable, they had nothing to offer me which I do not have already!'

Davina's mouth dropped open. This was an alternative view on marriage to that of Charlies and Ernestine's.

'So,' she hesitated, 'so what are you looking for in your marriage?'

Amelia shrugged her aristocratic shoulders. 'I do not believe that I have refined my thoughts on what I want. I know immediately when someone is not suitable.'

Davina was amazed. 'But is there no one with whom you think you could be happy?'

'Oh any number of well-heeled gentlemen but there are few eligible in both rank and fortune. I would hazard that the most eligible would be Lord Louis.'

Irrationally Davina found herself blushing at the mention of his name and had to turn her head away ostensibly to look at the stalls through which they were strolling. Amelia carried on in unconcern twirling the handle of the parasol so that its canopy spun in a drunken manner inflicting on any unwary passer-by a stab or a poke. 'If I hadn't known you were destined for Charlie, I would have advised you to fix your interest with him,' she went on airily. 'He is clearly very taken with you.'

Davina, while longing to listen to more prattle of this flavour, knew for her own comfort that she should not. Lord Louis no longer admired her, let alone respected her, even if he ever had. And to encourage such thoughts would be idle and foolish. She made efforts to turn the conversation and had thought that she had succeeded when who should be walking down the other side of the road but Lord Louis himself. Davina did not know where to put herself, how to act, whether to attempt to acknowledge him or to shrink behind Amelia and leave it to her. There was one thing of which Davina was sure, Lord Louis, whatever his feelings for Miss Davina Stanley, would not cut the Honourable Amelia. Just as their approach became imminent, Lord Louis turned swiftly down one of the side streets in the direction of St James and all the gentlemen's clubs. Davina did not know whether to be glad or sorry. This fleeting glimpse of him gave her no indication of how he intended to pursue his conduct towards her. She was however thankful that Amelia had not noticed him amongst the throng and therefore did not mention his name again.

Back within the secure confines of Lady Purslane's elegant town house, whose high-ceilinged rooms continued to be a pleasure to occupy in the sometime stifling heat, Davina wished she could just shut out the world and remain there occupied by her music. It was however her music which drew her once more from its portals.

While very few of the events to which Amelia had automatic entrance had opened their doors to include Davina, there was a musical soirée to which Lady Purslane had elicited an invitation for her.

In conspiratorial fashion she told Davina that she had promised her hostess a rare degree of musical talent from her young guest. The impression she gave Davina was that the evening would be quite formal and that Davina had been marked on the programme as one of the performers. This information had robbed Davina of any pleasurable anticipation she might have felt for the event and instead had her set out with clammy hands and palpitating heart.

Once there, in the opulent surroundings of a Mrs Bloxham's ballroom, it was seen to be quite the opposite. There were groups of guests clustered around the room, some listening to poetry, others to an instrument, either the piano or a harp. Down the centre of the room all that could be heard was a cacophony of sounds, all working in opposition to each other. Lady Purslane swept imperiously down the aisle, pausing to listen to each offering, casting a remark here or there until she reached the grand piano which was taking pride of place at the far end of the room. Once there she gave Davina a wry smile.

'I am held to be quite accomplished myself,' she said, 'quite an authority, but it is all nonsense. I just enjoy a thoroughly rousing time.'

Davina had to like her, for there was no side or guile to her. She might sometimes seem arrogant or self-important but she always lightened it with a hint of self-mockery. By now she had supplanted a rather insipid maiden who had been playing a whimsical tune heavy on the piano pedal so that it did not even reach much of an audience. Lady Purslane, with great aplomb, burst forth with a Bach fugue which reached every corner of the acoustically perfect room. Abandoning their less worthy pursuits, the occupants of the room gravitated to become her audience. As the recital came to a crescendo and ended with a flourish, there was a chorus of appreciative calls. Lady Purslane executed a brief encore, then made way for a rangy young redhead who played with gusto but with less accuracy than her ladyship. Davina watched their hostess's roving eye travel across the faces of her guests looking for likely performers. Davina kept her head bowed and hoped she would not be called upon to perform in front of such a large audience. There had been enough guests at Avebury but here the throng exceeded a hundred and fifty people.

It was not her hostess who betrayed her but her betrothed. She could only deduce when analysing his behaviour later that he had seen this as an excellent opportunity to parade her in front of his uncle's creditors. Charlie pushed forward through the crowd and led her to the piano, ignoring her whispered pleading that he should not. He pressed her to perform so ardently that Davina could not withstand him. She knew she risked being thought coy or missish. So swallowing a great gulp of breath she launched into her repertoire of favourite pieces. She did not have Lady Purslane's energy or power but her rendition was faithful to every note of the composer and it could be seen and heard that she and the instrument were one. There was a burst of applause when she had finished and cat calls for an encore which she resisted. Quickly she withdrew to make way for another performer.

Davina found herself shaking and was glad of Lady Purslane's escort to the dining room where refreshments were being provided. Lady Purslane was most generous in her praise of Davina's performance and keen to provide her opportunities to repeat it.

'No, please no,' Davina beseeched her, blanching under the

127

flush of her cheeks. 'See,' she held out her shaking hands, 'I am incapable of controlling my nerves, I suffer from them so. My music is much better kept quietly at home.'

'I challenge that view, Miss Stanley,' Lady Purslane cried, 'very soon you would become accustomed to an audience, I assure you. Do you sing?'

'No, not well, my voice has no power,' she replied quickly if not very accurately.

'Pity, I know someone with whom you could sing an excellent duet.'

Davina could only shake her head and sip her lemonade. The evening had outdone her fearful anticipation and she felt weak and ready for home.

Charlie found her not long after and made a move to congratulate her but such was the shocking state of her emotions that she could only look at him bleakly and demur at his praise.

Lord Restharrow had been present briefly at the beginning of the event but had soon retreated as a number of his erstwhile friends had been tempted beyond good manners to harass him. He had withstood it for a while but had quitted the building a little before the Purslane party so Davina had not even had a glimpse of him. She wished she could have a few moments of comfort from him. Just to look into his cavernous face would have strengthened her resolve to continue participating in this masquerade. As it was she longed, once again, to return to her mother and forget this strange double life.

She was not able to stay by the refreshments for long. Soon after there had been a break in the performances and everyone had moved into the dining room to help themselves to vittles. Davina retired to the back of the room. She thought she saw Lord Louis's dark head visible above the throng, his height making him conspicuous. She had not considered a musical soirée to be his penchant so she had had no expectation of seeing him. Now this set the seal on what was an abominable evening.

'There you are' cried Lady Purslane authoritatively making her way through the people to Davina's side. 'Come, there is going to be some more entertainment, let us make our way back to the ballroom so that we can get a prime view of it.'

'You will not suffer me to play again, will you?' begged Davina pathetically.

Lady Purslane subjected her to a penetrating gaze. Taking account of the genuine signs of fearful trepidation, she gave a brisk shake of the head and linked arms with her charge.

Amelia was nowhere to be seen but as a lady with at least four seasons behind her, Lady Purslane obviously felt she could take care of herself. Davina liked her hostess the better for taking such care of her in her noviciate.

As they passed through the doorway into the room Davina was conscious of a rich male voice warming up. To her surprise and embarrassment the beautifully pitched tenor was Lord Louis. Committed to a seat near the piano, Davina could do nothing but avert her face from him.

Lady Purslane beside her had started on a protracted eulogy in her ear on the qualities of Lord Louis's voice and the pleasure it gave his audience. Davina could only try to shrink deeper into her chair.

Lord Louis had cast one disdainful look in her direction and then had appeared to expunge her from his mind. The guests were returning from the dining room and taking up seats around them. Charlie came and stood behind Davina's chair. Once he squeezed her shoulder, much to her annoyance because she still hadn't quite forgiven him for the earlier part of the evening.

Lord Louis's performance began. He was accompanied on the piano by a flamboyant young man, who was currently studying music in the hope of being able to take up a place in Vienna. He could be seen to have indulged too freely in the heavy burgundy, which had been ample in its supply throughout the evening. Even before he had fumbled through the first piece, Davina could see the inevitable coming. The audience was restive and there was even an audible 'shame' as the accompanist fluffed a scale and made Lord Louis falter. Much as might have been expected, Davina was, suddenly, confronted by her hostess.

'Would you be so kind as to accompany Lord Louis, Miss Stanley? I am afraid young Mr Salter is not equal to the task.'

Davina turned to Lady Purslane and grasped her hand, imploring her with her eyes to step in and rescue her but a sinking feeling of inevitability assailed her as Lady Purslane rose from her seat and guided her to the piano stool. Lord Louis had moved to one side and was doing his best to persuade Salter to sober up. It was a fruitless task which he abandoned within moments. He turned to confront Davina who was continuing to stand stock still by the piano while Lady Purslane made a show of arranging the music sheets for her. Their eyes met, his defiant, hers apologetic.

'Come, come,' said Mrs Bloxham, their hostess, 'this won't do, we must have music!'

Davina, with one final look at Lord Louis's set face, capitulated and made her way to the stool. She allowed Lady Purslane to turn the pages for her as she knew if she lifted her hands to do it, those closest around her would see them shaking.

She struck up the first of Lord Louis's pieces and played as firmly as she could. There was nothing from him as she finished the introduction, no indication that he would sing. Inwardly furious that he was about to embarrass her in front of so many people, she smoothly doubled the number of bars into the song itself. She thought he would move away, such was the tension she could feel between them, then almost too late, he moved nearer to her and began to sing. Her faltering fingers steadied and her panic subsided. The beautiful song washed over her like a healing balm. Her spirits rose and she gave her all to forming a union between voice and instrument. Their performance was of such quality and depth that when the last strains of the piece died away, there was a silence before the audience gathered itself to give rapturous applause. After that there were calls for encore after encore until Davina's fingers were tired and Lord Louis's throat was dry. Finally their hostess took pity on them and reduced it to one final song. Lady Purslane, who had been juggling the scores all this time, produced a duet which was a gentle lullaby. Davina looked at her in horror, for it was for two voices, a man's and a woman's.

'If you cannot sing it, then I will,' hissed Lady Purslane, 'but I strongly recommend that you do.'

Davina cleared her throat. She had not pretended to any kind of voice at Avebury or here in London but she knew herself to be proficient and well trained. She nodded her agreement and started up the introduction. If the crowd, which had multiplied as they had played, had thought that they had enjoyed an unmatchable performance already they were now held spellbound by the purity and sweetness of the two performers' rendition.

The applause, which had been rapturous before, was now thunderous. Lord Louis found enough gallantry to take Davina's hand and draw her up from the piano for them to take their bow.

'Wonderful, wonderful.' Lady Purslane was loud in her appreciation but quickly shepherded the pair away from the piano and through the crowd. 'Let whoever dares follow that,' she said laughingly as she embraced Davina once they were clear of the throng.

'Now take her away and get yourselves some well-earned refreshments,' she advised and then melted away herself.

Davina and Lord Louis were left standing in some awkwardness trying to gather their wits and their respective dignities. After a pause, which yawned between them, Lord Louis cleared his throat.

'You have a very forgiving nature, Miss Stanley,' he said eventually, 'you need only have declined to play, I would have accepted it.'

She was stung. 'And expose our differences to public curiosity. I think not. Your credit may well be enough to stand it, but mine as you are so acutely aware is not!'

'I would say that after this day's performance your stock is in the ascent, Madamoiselle.'

She shot him a look, surprised at his reversion to playfulness. There was a twinkle in his eyes that she felt was misplaced. She saw nothing remotely humorous in their situation.

'Please return me to Lady Purslane,' she said haughtily, 'you need trouble yourself on my behalf no longer.'

His face clouded and he became at once serious again. 'Miss Stanley, you trouble me manifold,' he said. 'I fear you are being dragged out of your depth into a situation you cannot control. I beg you to return to your home where you can be quiet and safe. Here there are sharks and parasites who would bleed you if they could.'

She was rocked off her balance and could no longer look him in the face. She found herself staring at the large buttons on his beautiful deep blue coat. For a moment she remained mute while she thought of a way to put him off his guard without hinting what her real purpose in London was. She found she wanted to cry, his sympathetic understanding was such a surprise and so endearing. She wished she could furnish him with the truth and longed to cast all her troubles in his direction. However she counselled herself to resist any temptation to open up to him. He had already made it clear that her lack of connections was repugnant to him. He might well reject her further if he knew that she was trying to pass off a false engagement to society.

'Thank you for your concern, Lord Louis,' she said in a tight formal voice, 'but you need not fear for me, I have some good friends who are dedicated to my interests. They will protect me.'

'I see that you believe that, Miss Stanley, but let me be added to their number. If ever you need succour come to me for I shall surely help you.'

15

*H*aving sat for some time at Lady Purslane's escritoire trying to write a reply to her mother's letter, Davina sighed disconsolately. It had arrived the day before but it had taken Davina until now to decipher the heavily crossed and, in places, underscored letter. She regretted her efforts because the news it conveyed was very disquieting. Ernestine was reported to be in decline. Her appetite had faded, she was listless and much inclined to remain in her darkened room. Davina was not surprised but a leaden weight appeared to have settled on her shoulders. A small niggling part of her brain was bitterly resentful of the pressure under which Ernestine was putting her but such was her sympathy for her friend's situation that she speedily doused it and attempted to make a soothing and reassuring response to her mother. What she should say to Charlie she could not decide. However the matter was taken out of her hands late that afternoon when he strode into the room, ushered in by Lady Purslane's punctilious butler.

Charlie was looking tired and pale. His cravat was slightly askew and his coat a trifle crumpled. He had a sheaf of papers in his left hand which he waved at Davina before even he had spoken. She rose from the chair, thankful that he had found her alone, Lady Purslane and Amelia having gone out for a drive.

'Good heavens, Charlie, what has occurred?'

He grasped her hand briefly then swung away from her to the window. In a choked voice he explained that he had received a letter from Ernestine pleading with him to break off the engagement.

'She is in the Slough of Despond, Davina,' he said sighing gustily. 'She threatens to put a period to her existence. I fear for her reason.'

Davina's hand flew to her mouth, indicating her deep distress. 'Then we must.' She tried to say the words but they would not come out through her fingers.

Charlie ravaged his golden locks. 'But I cannot,' he said emphatically. 'My uncle is just beginning to see our efforts bear fruit. It is hard for our creditors to pretend you do not exist after that very public exhibition at Mrs Bloxham's soirée.' He turned back to Davina. 'What am I to do, Davina?' he cried. 'What am I to do?'

Words continued to fail her. She could only shake her head in mute sympathy.

Charlie, remembering the letters in his hand, made a move to scan them and indicate to Davina her friend's troubled words. Davina read them and was aghast at Ernestine's avowed desperation, but at last she found her voice. Laying a comforting hand on Charlie's shoulders she said: 'I think you should see her, perhaps it is her isolation that brings on these dark thoughts. If you were to visit her and explain what benefit you are deriving from this pretence, she may allow you to extend it.'

He was much struck by this idea. 'Yes, yes, I will go immediately, there is nothing but a few races on. I will make my excuses and ride to Gloucestershire to see her tonight.'

'Will they allow you to see her though, Charlie. Mr and Mrs Greenaway might think it inappropriate.'

For the first time since he had entered the room the gloom written on Charlie's face lifted. 'I shall not give them the opportunity. I will meet Ernestine clandestinely.'

Not wishing to put a damper on his improved demeanour Davina did not point out that if Ernestine was as ill as was reported, then she would not be able to rise from her bed and meet him. However Davina guessed that a secret missive from Charlie requesting a meeting would be all that was necessary to improve her friend's condition. This increasing suspicion that Ernestine was capable of manipulation did not endear her any less to Davina but it made her cautious.

Charlie did not remain long after he had reached his decision. Davina let him go without pressing him to refreshment, he was now very eager to get on with the job of making his excuses and packing his things. Davina began to suspect that he intended to make a much longer stay than one secret meeting required.

As a result of the musical evening, Lady Purslane had begun to receive invitation cards which included Davina. These were never the grand balls or big functions where the very cream of society might expect to be entertained, but usually the less formal dinners or musical evenings where Davina's prowess was expected to add to the evening. Amelia was delighted by the turn of events. She had not anticipated so many opportunities to visit other houses given her bereaved state.

'I am grateful to you, Davina,' she said unexpectedly one morning as she pulled on her gloves and tied her bonnet ready for a walk in the park.

'Grateful to me?' repeated Davina, rocked by this unexpected tribute.

'Why yes! Surely you must see that I have had a much improved season as a result of your presence. This invitation,' she picked up one which lay on the hall table, 'this one is from Lord Louis's cousin, Lady Evenlode. We would certainly not have been invited to that had it not been for your performance that night.' She picked up a second one, fumbling with it slightly through her soft gloves. 'And this one is from the wife of one of Lord Restharrow's closest friends, Mrs Etchwell, she has always considered her musical abilities well above ours and would not include us as a result.'

'Oh surely not, think of Lady Purslane's performance, she is an expert on delivering the more robust pieces.'

Amelia laughed and gave her friend a butterfly kiss on the cheek. 'Take the credit, my dear,' she said, 'you are too unassuming, take the credit and enjoy it.'

So Davina tried but it was rather overwhelming to be constantly pressured into performing.

'I am playing and singing for my supper each time,' she told Lady Purslane when she sank gratefully back into the squabs of the coach at the end of another musical evening.

Lady Purslane looked at her keenly through the gloom of the carriage. 'Is that how you perceive it?' she demanded forthrightly.

Davina coloured, not wanting to appear ungrateful, and mumbled an apology.

There was a silence as Lady Purslane gathered her thoughts. 'You are right, of course,' she decided. 'You were left to play far too long tonight. The *ton* are very selfish, they like to see and hear a beautiful young lady for their own enjoyment, and take no account of her comfort. We will ensure that it does not happen at Lady Evenlode's turtle supper tomorrow night.'

Davina was very nervous at the thought of visiting Lady Evenlode's establishment. She was sure that Lord Louis would be there and she had seen nothing of him since the night of their duet. She dressed with immense care irritating Nancy by requesting variation after variation to her hairstyle until she was quite satisfied with her appearance. She joined Amelia in the drawing room to await the carriage and was delighted to receive compliments on her appearance. Davina clasped the girl's hands warmly, acknowledging as she did so how easy it was to be mistaken by first appearances.

She had warmed to Amelia during their stay in London. Away from her family she seemed to leave behind a lot of her arrogance and pettishness. She was friendly and almost kind. It was a revelation to Davina who was suffering under the inconsistencies of Ernestine's behaviour.

Lady Purslane soon joined them and on this occasion, Major Sir Hugh Purslane, her hard-working husband whose absences were always explained by his commitments at the Horse Guards, also accompanied them. He was a tall jovial man, clean shaven unlike many of the officers, with auburn hair and green, humorous eyes. He teased the young ladies unmercifully but as it was always in good taste and he was more often conspicuous by his absence than his presence, the ladies forgave him and even encouraged him as it added a little spice to the event.

'We are all very smart tonight,' he said as he viewed the three ladies he was due to escort. 'I can see that I shall be mobbed because of my bevy of beauties!'

'For shame, Hugh,' laughed Lady Purslane as she rapped him playfully with her fan, 'you are there for our protection. You are not to encourage those young officers of your acquaintance. I am dependent on you to take care of our guests.

And great care he took of them, ensuring that none were allowed to walk unprotected from the carriage to the great portico on the front of Lady Evenlode's home in Russell Square. A summer deluge threatened to destroy their coiffure and elegant apparel, but Sir Hugh shielded them all with his huge, many-caped driving coat, careless himself of his own evening dress.

Once in the house the servants amassed aplenty to offer warm towels and rooms for the ladies to repair any damage to their appearance.

'Such a shame,' said Lady Evenlode, a spare woman who was much older than Davina had expected her to be until she reminded herself that Lord Louis had a much older brother too. 'I am sure a number of my guests will fail, unwilling to set out in the storm.' She shook hands with the Purslane party. 'I am so glad you would not be put off. Louis promised to come only if you were attending.' She made this remark general but it did not stop Amelia nudging Davina significantly. Davina waved her fan rapidly hoping to stave off any rush of colour to her cheeks.

They were ushered into a withdrawing room which did indeed seem light on company. Davina began to feel embarrassed for her hostess and disappointed for herself; she had hoped for an interesting evening and feared now it would be dull. Lord Louis was not in evidence.

Sir Hugh quickly assumed the life and soul of the party, his good manners making him appear well pleased with the arrangement. He allowed himself to be introduced to a dowager and several retired army types while keeping an eye out to ensure the ladies were not being neglected. Davina wondered how they had managed so well previously without him.

Much to Davina's consternation the next damp party to arrive included in its midst Aunt Sophia, late of Avebury.

'What's she doing here?' Davina hissed in Amelia's ear, 'I pray you protect me from her tongue.'

Amelia looked across the room and her face hardened.

'I will not speak to her,' she declared. 'She sent Mama a very strongly worded letter, determined to prevent my visit to London. It is you who must protect me.'

Sir Hugh made his leisurely way over to the ladies. 'What has happened to discompose you ladies?' he asked.

'Tis the presence of my elderly aunt,' Amelia was quick to point out. 'She has a poisonous tongue and neither Davina or I wish to speak to her.'

'Oh come now girls, you cannot cut a relative at a gathering like this. I will not let you make an exhibition of yourselves. Now, I will attend you, we will speak to her immediately and then maybe your paths need not cross again this evening.'

The girls looked sceptical but they did as they were bid and made their curtsy to Aunt Sophia. She had now affected a pair of pince-nez and she elevated these to her nose to view the girls.

'Well, Amelia,' she said, barely acknowledging their greeting, 'I did not expect to see you here. You are severely negligent of the state of mourning, I shall write to your mother first thing tomorrow. And you,' she swept on to look Davina up and down, 'you think you have done very well for yourself no doubt, but you have not secured your man yet. I see no sign of him tonight.

138

Where is Charlie Winstanleigh? Or is he at least honouring his brother's memory by absenting himself?'

Davina knew not how to reply so was grateful to Sir Hugh for replying succinctly that Charlie was out of town. He then made their excuses on the pretext of greeting a new arrival with whom he was well acquainted.

It was reported that the rain had eased off. The number of guests had risen as a result and soon dinner was served. Davina was surprised to find herself placed next to Lord Louis who had materialised late and had therefore not been in evidence in the withdrawing room. Her startled face made him laugh and he saluted her with unexpected good humour.

'Well met Madamoiselle Stanley,' he said as he waited for the liveried footman to place her chair under her before he took his seat. 'Are we to entertain the throng with more singing tonight?'

It was as safe a topic as any so Davina allowed herself to be led into a conversation about which pieces they might play if invited to do so. While he favoured Handel, particularly works such as *Silent Worship* and *Praise Ye the Lord*, she preferred newer scores like the songs of Haydn that were just finding their way over from the Continent.

'You are well informed Madamoiselle,' he said in wonder.

'I enjoy music, my lord, it is my recreation and my joy.'

'I can see that to be true when you play and sing. I am honoured that you are prepared to share it with me.'

Davina gave a mechanical smile, conscious that they had exhausted the subject. She pushed the food around on her plate as a diversion.

'Do you not like the turtle, Madamoiselle?' he asked solicitously.

'No, indeed I do not!'

'But it is a delicacy. It is that of which you have been invited to partake. My cousin would be most put out if you were not to eat it.'

'But I cannot, my lord; it is…' words failed her, 'it makes me nauseous.'

'Then,' he said lifting his napkin from his lap, 'you must slip it into this and I will eat it for you.'

Davina looked around a touch wildly, terrified that Aunt Sophia's eagle eyes might be upon them. Thankfully seeing the old harridan currently engaged in picking her teeth, with a quickness of hand that she did not know she possessed, Davina slipped the offending food into his napkin. From there he smuggled it in on to his plate, his eyes dancing with merriment.

'I feel very wicked,' Davina admitted as she watched him eat the turtle flesh.

'You need not feel so, Madamoiselle, no one need know.'

'Ah, but can I trust you with my secret?' she quizzed him, bewitched by his friendly attitude.

'Of course, with anything,' he said warmly, making her bite her lip in uncertainty on how to reply. Finally a gambit revealed itself to her.

'How did Aunt Sophia come to be invited?'

'Aunt Sophia?'

Davina indicated the old lady sitting at Lord Evenlode's left hand.

'Oh Sophia Bodwell, she is a connection of my cousin.'

'Good heavens, how closely everyone is associated with each other.'

'It is true of the *ton*, Madamoiselle, it is always necessary to practice caution when criticising someone, they could be connected to half your audience. I always make it my business to ensure I know someone's ancestry and affiliations before opening my mouth.' This was such an infelicitous thing to say that Davina stiffened. The day of their altercation at Mrs Milfoil's came back to her with a vengeance and she was struck dumb. Not so quick to realise that he had erred, Lord Louis continued: 'It is difficult not to invite Sophia Bidwell. No doubt she heard someone talking of the event and invited herself, or made it impossible for my cousin not to invite her.' He seemed to become aware that he had in some way offended Davina, and paused. She remained unhelpfully silent, then compounding the effect turned slightly to make desultory conversation with the retired military gentleman on her left. Lord Louis took the rebuff and had Davina been watching his vivid face she would have noticed when the look of deep chagrin indicated that he divined his mistake.

As soon as Davina had finished talking to the old colonel, Lord Louis claimed her again.

'Miss Stanley forgive me,' he said in a low throbbing under-voice, 'I meant to cause no offence.'

'Did you not, my lord?' Davina challenged him. 'I think in many ways you are like Aunt Sophia. You shoot barbs at people, the only difference being while her arrows come straight and true to the Achilles heel, yours dally and feint but when they reach their target they are seen to have a poisoned tip.'

'I swear you wrong me, Miss Stanley,' was all he managed to say.

Davina cast him a sidelong look and could see that he was much overcome. She was surprised at the depth of his feelings and a little flattered.

'Very well,' she said coolly, 'I will accept your apology, but,' she knew she must find a lighter note, they were too exposed sitting there at the dining table in full view of all the guests, 'only if you concede one of the Handel pieces for a Haydn.'

He recovered himself quickly and laughed at her triumph. 'You foil me at every turn Madamoiselle, I used to pride myself that I was quicker-witted than most of my contemporaries but you are ahead of me all the time.'

'I think not,' she disclaimed. 'For instance,' she said, looking up and down the table, 'I have no explanation for why you are seated next to me. Surely your rank demands a place nearer Lady Evenlode? I would say, Sir, that here you are almost below the salt!'

'Oh, my cousin is careless of rank, she would not let it weigh with her if there were others she wanted to honour.'

'I do not believe you,' said Davina, starting to giggle.

'What! Are you accusing me of altering the seating plan?'

'Oh no, you arrived too late for that. It was a genuine enquiry.' But both knew it was not, there was a clear indication of partiality in the move and while Davina considered him only to be entertaining himself, she knew she must be wary. Charlie's absence had been noted and she did not want to undo the limited but beneficial effects that her unofficial engagement was having on Lord Restharrow's circumstances.

16

In the following weeks there were a number of occasions when Lord Louis appeared at a function which would not normally have been graced by his presence just because he knew Davina would be attending. Amelia thought it a great joke and urged Davina to break off her engagement with Charlie in order to pursue a much more rewarding quarry. Nothing Davina could say would convince Amelia of her own view that Lord Louis was simply amusing himself. Whenever the girls were having these exchanges of views Lady Purslane would look on with a speculative look in her eye. Once she said: 'The lady doth protest too much, methinks!'

Davina coloured uncomfortably but was stalwart in maintaining her position. Only when Charlie returned from Gloucestershire did she take what was being said seriously.

Charlie arrived looking haggard and drawn and marched into Lady Purslane's first floor withdrawing room without waiting to be announced by the butler.

'Good Lord, Davina, what is this I hear about you making up to Lord Louis? You must know this does our cause no good!' were the first words he uttered, careless of Lady Purslane's presence.

It was Lady Purslane who responded for she could see that Davina was smitten with embarrassment.

'As an onlooker, Charles, I can say that Miss Stanley has done nothing of which to be ashamed. She has no control over Lord

Louis's movements and contrary to what you may have heard does not encourage his advances.'

Charlie was brought up short but such was the emotion suffusing him, he was unable to conceal it. He ground his teeth. 'You are bound in all honour to defend her Ma'am,' he said with an unaccustomed lack of chivalry. 'You are in the guise of chaperone and would have to own a fault if you acknowledged its truth, but my sources are reliable. I am aware that she has been seen everywhere with him.'

'That may be so but none of it was at her instigation nor choice. Others who could demand her obedience coupled her with him at soirées and musical evenings. You were at Mrs Bloxham's, you were a party to it then.'

'That's as may be…'

'Please, please,' Davina's voice finally made itself heard, 'I beg you do not brangle over me.' She stood up from her chair and walked towards Charlie. 'I know you must have had a very difficult time this last ten days, I am sorry if I have added to it.'

Lady Purslane snorted at what she saw as misplaced contrition although she had to observe that it was having a beneficial effect on Charlie. Rather reprehensibly she rose and left the room, leaving them alone together.

Charlie, defying convention, sat himself down on the edge of one of the chairs by the fireplace.

'I cannot tell you how gruelling this week has been,' he said at length having mastered his emotions. 'Ernestine suffers so. She will not allow the fact that the long-term gains will outweigh the short-term discomforts to compensate her. She rails against the force of circumstance but she cannot resolve our difficulties any other way than the course we have chosen.'

Davina came up and stood over him, clasping and unclasping her hands. 'Does she…' she hesitated, then pressed on. 'Does she acknowledge that it was she who set us on this course? I cannot bear that she has taken against me. We have always been such friends.'

Charlie put up a hand to grasp hers. 'She doesn't blame you, Davina,' he tried to reassure her. 'Please don't think that. She explained her actions to me. She finds it easier to fashion you the enemy in her mind. She knows it is not really so but it gives substance to her grievance in a way that self incrimination does not.'

'So she does blame me.' Davina pulled her hand away and walked to the window, fighting to keep her eyes from brimming over with tears. 'We should declare this engagement at an end. I cannot lose her friendship.'

'No!' Charlie almost shouted the word and leapt to his feet. 'No Davina, no. I have spent a week arguing with her, cajoling her into agreeing that we continue in this manner for a few more months. My uncle needs for us to do so and if I am his heir, it can only benefit Ernestine and I in the future. Don't concede defeat now, please I beg you.'

He was so sincere, so moved by his uncle's plight in the words he continued to utter thereafter, that Davina knew she could not turn her back on him whatever the voice of reason within her head was telling her. When he left she felt she had been wrung through a mangle. She sat by the window and looked out forlornly as he strode away up the street. Tears began to trickle and then run down her face unchecked. Once she put up a hand to wipe them away but it did not halt them so after that she just let them take their own path and fall to her lap, dampening her pale blue dress.

It was some minutes before Lady Purslane returned and when she did, she paused on the threshold for a moment, assessing the situation, then she turned in the doorway and required a servant to prevent them from being disturbed.

Having shut the door, Lady Purslane came into the room and made her way to sit across the window from Davina. 'There is more to this than I am being told, is there not?' she said quietly.

Davina managed a fleeting look at her hostess before averting her gaze. Her eyes fixed once again on the scene out in the street. The ensuing silence demanded a response from her but she could not find the words.

'I think you owe me the truth,' Lady Purslane said rather harshly. 'I have, after all, taken you as a guest into my home on trust. The least you can do is be honest with me.'

A sob escaped Davina and she put her hands to her face, the tears seeping through the gaps between her fingers.

'I'm sorry, I'm sorry,' she wailed in considerable distress.

Lady Purslane dropped her rigid pose and came and sat beside the slim girl. She put her arms around Davina's shoulders and pressed her head against hers.

'Don't cry, my dear,' she soothed, 'nothing is so bad that it cannot be mended, surely?'

'I don't know, I just don't know,' was the embattled but muffled cry.

For a while Lady Purslane just let the girl cry herself out. To the older woman it was a revelation. So much pent-up emotion was being allowed to escape, it would have been wrong to try and stem its flow. Lady Purslane had often seen Davina agitated but only prior to a performance or a public function; otherwise she had always seemed so serene and self-contained, while all the time she had clearly been keeping a heavy swell of emotion just below the surface.

The sobs had subsided and Davina had slipped sideways so that her head was in Lady Purslane's lap. In motherly response Lady Purslane began to stroke her damp head.

'Can you not trust me enough to tell me your troubles?' she asked.

Davina hiccuped and eventually sat up. 'A feature of my life since I left the closed confines of my own home is the number of people who recommend that I trust them.' She hesitated and cleared her throat. 'Before I visited Avebury, I don't believe I ever considered whether someone was trustworthy or not. I find it very hard to comprehend because since trust has been called into question, I have found that in fact I can trust very few.' She blew her nose defiantly.

Lady Purslane was horrified. 'What have I ever done to prevent you trusting me?' she demanded.

'Oh nothing, nothing at all,' Davina hastened to reassure her. 'I did not mean to include you, it is just that you saying that typifies my dilemma.'

Lady Purslane allowed herself to be mollified as Davina's tone suggested that she might be going to open up to her.

'Your dilemma?' she prompted.

Davina showed Lady Purslane a blotched and reddened face. 'I know I can rely on you to maintain the strictest secrecy if I tell you but I do not feel that I would be fair on you in doing so.'

'Why don't you let me be the judge of that?'

Davina sighed. 'Very well,' she said, 'but please do not think too badly of me.'

'I will do my best,' Lady Purslane assured her with the ghost of a smile. 'Come.' She stretched out a hand and guided Davina to a comfortable seat in the centre of the room. 'I will ring for some tea.'

They waited in companionable silence until the tea tray arrived and then Davina, haltingly at first and then with more confidence, related the cause and effect of her engagement.

Lady Purslane was horrified. Reading between the lines of the carefully worded explanation she saw the scheming hands of her mother and Lady Thistledown and she wondered at her father's part in this. She had always seen him as a stern moralist, viewing his calling as dictating a strict code of conduct. She had to assume that her mother had somehow manipulated him too. It was interesting though that the Greenaways now seemed to be supporting Ernestine in her role as supplanted lover. Lady Purslane saw more of the hand of her father in this and was tempted to believe that he had finally seen through his wife's machinations. She flirted with the idea that he might demand a halt to the scheme but had to admit that it would take a very committed moralist indeed to bring down a whole section of his wife's family. She suspected that unhappy he might be but reckless he was not.

Lady Purslane was in something of a quandary. She had no desire to become entangled in the deception but she could not stand by and see Davina made so miserable. Nor, if truth be told, did she want to acknowledge the weaknesses of her sister's character of which she had long been aware. She tempered this reluctance with a strict code of fairness which she had acquired from her father.

'I would venture to say,' she said looking away from Davina, 'that you should not refine too much upon my little sister's behaviour.' She attempted to justify her comment. 'It has always seemed to me that Ernestine would have been better as a petted and cosseted only child.'

'Like me you mean,' said Davina, slightly ruffled.

'No, no, of course not, you misunderstand me.' Lady Purslane grasped Davina's hand and shook it earnestly. 'Ernestine is the fifth of seven children; she would much rather be the centre of attention than have to give way to the precedence of elder siblings.' She saw Davina looking dubious. 'Oh come now, have you not seen it many a time?'

Davina shook her head. 'She is my friend,' she said quietly. 'I do not understand why she is doing this to me.'

In truth neither did Lady Purslane; she had to take Davina back to the explanation Charlie had given. 'She has such an imagination and very little handle on her own emotions. It may be make believe that she is the injured party but she has no difficulty in engendering it with some kind of reality.'

'I wish I could go home away from all this,' Davina wailed. 'I want to declare the engagement at an end and go home, but I cannot.' She gave a dry sob. 'I cannot.'

Lady Purslane stood up and went to the fireplace; there she absently flicked through the invitation cards which now mostly included Davina.

'I do believe that you cannot,' she agreed. 'It would excite too much comment and jeopardise the understanding Lord Restharrow is building with his creditors.'

'I wish I could see him,' Davina whispered.

'I'm sorry, what did you say?'

'I wish I could see him,' Davina spoke the words more boldly, 'I never see him.' She expanded her theme. 'He never comes to any events or has left before we arrive. I never see him.' She clasped and unclasped her fingers. 'I am doing this as much for him as for Charlie because he has been so kind to me but I have barely spoken to him since the death of Charlie's brother.'

Lady Purslane considered a moment and was about to speak when she was interrupted by a knock and the entrance of the butler wishing to know whether madam and her guests were dining in that evening.

Lady Purslane looked at Davina's weary and discoloured face and made a decision. 'Yes I think we will,' she said. 'We had not planned to but we will not be missed at the Riverdales. Please send a card round to inform them.'

'Yes, m'lady.' The butler withdrew, scarcely concealing his curiosity.

'Oh please,' cried Davina jumping up, 'do not curtail your pleasure to my convenience. I can remain here quietly, you and Amelia must go.'

'No, my mind is made up, we will have an evening in. And,' she said after a pause, 'I will find a time when Hugh is at home so that we can have Lord Restharrow here to dine. Would that please you?'

'Oh yes, it would indeed.'

'Then let us do that and see if we cannot see the Season out. You know that I will stand your friend and if ever you need my help you have it for the asking.'

'You are very kind,' murmured Davina, 'you and Lord Louis both, for he has said as much.'

'Don't tell me he knows of your masquerade? You have not told him, surely?' cried Lady Purslane, horrified.

Davina shook her head. 'No, but I think he suspects.'

17

*I*n thinking that Lord Louis suspected that the engagement was a fake, Davina was very far from the truth. Lord Louis was so taken up with the multiplicity of his own feelings that he had no time to divine the feelings of others beyond those they exhibited. His original feelings with regard to Davina had been gloriously simple. She was beautiful, he was taken with her but she was not suitable as a wife because of lack of connections and a dubious birthright. He still felt he had acted in honour to warn Charlie against marriage to her but his own heart was whispering opposition to the words he himself had expressed. As the glories of her talent and the generous nature of her forgiveness had unfurled themselves before him, less and less did he remember that she had no worthy name. He had considered his own status and wealth and had consoled himself that it was great enough to carry off a marriage to her. He had hoped as he and she had been more in each other's company that she would be worldly enough to see the greater benefits of being aligned to him rather than Charlie. He had hoped to see that engagement at an end before the conclusion of the Season. However, despite the malicious whisperings of the envious, coupling his name with hers, she had remained steadfast in her commitment to Charlie.

Disappointed, Lord Louis tried to find other outlets for his emotions in many of the pursuits which a year ago had seemed such fun but had now lost their allure. He had not taken up with any opera dancers this year much to the disappointment amongst their ranks. He was rarely seen at the races or in the cockpit. His friends chaffed him and teased him that he had lost his head to a pretty face but he could not shake off the malaise. As July turned to August and the *ton* began to disperse, Lord Louis was left in a quandary as to what to do. Even the knowledge that he would not have wanted her to trade Charlie for him simply because of their respective positions was little comfort, or that his own father, a great stickler from a bygone age, would almost certainly veto such a match. Lord Louis saw nothing for it but to return to Scotland and hope that distance would numb the senses and reduce the longing.

Davina felt a huge weight lift off her shoulders as she settled back into the squabs of the carriage which was to take her back to Fromeview. Basil had been dispatched by Lady Thistledown to fetch Amelia and her companion home. She had further magnanimously volunteered Basil to escort Davina home from Avebury. Davina had not welcomed this terribly, she would have been happier without a reluctant escort but Basil surprised her. He had been everything that was mannerly and helpful during the evening that they had spent in a posting house in Reading before moving on to Avebury, and once his sister had alighted and refreshments had been partaken he had been happy to speed on their way to Fromeview.

On this leg of the journey he had occupied the carriage rather than riding alongside as he had done previously. This was explained rather disingenuously: he was off to Bristol to visit a firm of solicitors who had written to inform him that an elderly godparent, after whom he had been named, had died and left him in significantly improved circumstances,

'Shan't need to hang out for a rich wife now,' he told her in some glee, rubbing his hands. 'Gerard's green with envy,' he chuckled, 'although I hardly know why. He's as good as spliced to the squire's daughter and she's bringing a tidy sum with her, not to mention the parcel of land my father used to have his eye on years ago before he became ill.'

Davina was finding these revelations fascinating but Nancy's homely face was a study of disapproval and as she was looking directly at Davina from her forward seat, Davina felt it behoved her to change the subject. The time was soon whiled away with talk of Gerard's impending nuptials. Basil saw himself as groomsman and talked as though Davina was certain to receive an invitation. Davina considered this unlikely. She had been no particular favourite at Avebury, merely a commodity to be bought and sold to the family's convenience. She played along though, listening to Basil's enthusiastic description of the rambling farmhouse which was being renovated for the bridal couples use. Davina remembered having passed it on a number of her rides and recalled the ample stables. She thought it unlikely that either the bride or the groom would take much account of the house when there were stables to be enjoyed.

The sun was lingering above the horizon when the coach pulled on to the gravel in front of Fromeview Place. Davina had tried to persuade Basil to sup with her and her mother but he was steadfast in his refusal. He had bespoken a room in an hotel in Bristol and thought that he could still achieve it that evening. Davina had to let him go with only her grateful thanks and that of her mother's to speed him on his way.

Mrs Stanley clasped her daughter to her in welcome as soon as the great door was shut behind them. Her embrace conveyed such an intensity of emotion that Davina was moved to hold her mother away from her and scrutinise her dear face. Davina was shocked at what she saw there. Mrs Stanley was pale and the lines had deepened on her face; the cheekbones and chin were more defined as though she had lost weight. Without quite acknowledging the reason for it, Davina felt a surge of protectiveness for her mother. It was an emotion which had never assailed her before but found its root in her own new-found worldliness. Davina was also taller now than her mother and an air of assurance clung to her, the vestiges of all those public performances.

'Mama,' she murmured, 'what is ailing you? Tell me you are not unwell.'

Mrs Stanley disengaged herself from her daughter and moved towards the saloon, forcing Davina to follow her.

'What can you mean?' she said evasively. 'There is nothing amiss with me. It is you who is much changed. I hardly recognised you in your modish clothes and dashing hairstyle.'

'Do you like it?' Davina asked, allowing her conversation to be diverted but not her eyes which continued to absorb every detail of her mother's countenance and bearing.

'Yes, very fetching,' Mrs Stanley smiled but with an effort, 'very fetching but you are no longer my little girl. You are a grown woman from the top of your shining hair to the tip of your spangled shoes.'

'It was inevitable, Mama,' her daughter ventured. Mrs Stanley nodded and turned away putting her handkerchief to her mouth. Davina would have gone to her and tried to give comfort for whatever was upsetting her but at that moment Mrs Tulley arrived with a tray of refreshments. Davina had to turn her attention to the good lady who was all amazement and exclamation about the changes in her young mistress.

By the time Mrs Tulley had been satisfied, Davina had concluded that after a long day on the road, she was not best able to cope with further emotional turmoil. She wondered whether after a night's repose she might feel equal to attending to her mother but went to bed in hope rather than expectation.

When she woke late the next morning, she had missed the opportunity for private speech with her mother over breakfast and, somehow, she never quite found an opening again. Mrs Stanley became even more adept at turning the conversation to Davina's pleasures and experiences in London, eager to hear about people that Davina had no idea she even knew. One consolation did materialise. Mrs Stanley, according to a vigilant Mrs Tulley, was eating better now that her daughter was home and her colour gradually returned over the following weeks. Davina was saddened to discover, though, that her mother rarely went out. The number of invitations she received to the cosy country house evenings that they used to enjoy had dwindled to only a trickle. When an invitation was forthcoming which her mother would accept the Greenaways were never present. Davina soon began to suspect that there was a conscious effort on the part of their friends and neighbours never to bring the two families together under the same roof. The Rector had no choice but to visit Fromeview Place because of his position as trustee but Mrs Greenaway never called and any information they had about Ernestine's condition was third hand.

Davina's only recourse was to write to Charlie and explain into what an intolerable situation this turn of events had put her mother. All her little pleasures had been withdrawn. All the small services she had been used to carry out for the parish had been stopped. Even going to church had become an ordeal with Mrs Greenaway never doing more than giving them a ghost of a nod. The two Stanley women began to go to Evensong in order to escape the titters and whispers which caused them so much pain. Davina had no need to demand explanations from her mother as to the state of her health, she could see what a drain facing these jibes must have been when Mrs Stanley had had to face them alone. Davina tried to forgive Ernestine but could not. Throughout her formative years Davina had never known her mother do anything unkind or cruel and she saw this ostracism as a deliberate act of cruelty.

The letters Davina received from Charlie were of little comfort. He beseeched her to stand firm. 'The situation,' he wrote, 'becomes graver by the day. Mine uncle receives fresh calls upon his resources as further debts of which we were unaware continue to surface. He is resolved to sell part of the estate but were he to do so there would be little for me to inherit and no chance of my winning Ernestine's hand.'

Davina brushed an angry tear from her cheek when she had finished re-reading this missive. She no more believed that

Charlie wanted his uncle dead than she did her mother but the manner of his writing showed how locked into his vision of the future he was. She could only feel for Lord Restharrow who, on the night he had visited Lady Purslane's for dinner, had almost moved her to tears. Had even a residue of the twinkle she had known in his eyes at Avebury remained she would have been comforted but there had not been even a glimmer. He had struggled to maintain his part in the jovial conversation instigated by Sir Hugh and when he was not being particularly applied to for an opinion or comment he had been silent, scarcely eating. He had taken affectionate leave of Davina knowing that she was to return to Gloucestershire in the near future but he had promised no visits and did not even ask about her mare. Davina knew she could not easily abandon him to his fate but it begged the question: why should he command more loyalty from her than her darling mother. If Mrs Stanley had not materially improved as summer turned to autumn and then faded into winter, Davina knew she would have called off this now hollow engagement. To the best of her knowledge Charlie still secretly visited Ernestine but he never called at Fromeview Place. Mrs Stanley had asked frequently at first and then at ever-extending intervals, whether Davina expected a visit from him. Each time she had merely observed that Charlie was much taken up with his uncle's affairs.

'You know, I feared that you would not return to me,' Mrs Stanley said one evening as Davina finished a chapter she had been reading out loud to her mother.

'What can you mean?' her daughter had demanded, startled.

'I thought you would be enticed away from me by the delights of London. Find some dashing young man to woo you.'

'I have a dashing young man,' she responded carefully.

'Do you, my dear?' asked her mother. 'Does he really care for you, he seems to keep his ardour well contained.'

Davina was appalled. 'Forgive me Mama but was it not your strictures that demanded that we wait. Are we not just abiding by your demands?'

'I wish I thought that you were, my dear, but I have seen no sight of him this last four months.'

'He has written,' Davina pointed out.

'Yes but you do not anticipate his letters with any great eagerness.'

Davina was silenced. This was an even more alarming twist. If her mother began to doubt the relationship then how must it appear to those for whom it was designed? She sent off another desperate letter to Charlie conveying her concern in tear-stained passages.

Charlie's response was swift and unexpected. He arrived at the village and bribed a farmhand to deliver a message to Davina. Wrapping herself in her thickest pelisse, Davina strode out on to the common to meet him. She found him standing on the escarpment looking out over her favourite view, which was barren and bleak on this cold December afternoon.

'Charlie,' she called as she neared his rigid figure. He turned and took her extended hands rubbing them between his.

'I am a selfish dog to have brought you out here on a day like this,' he acknowledged as his breath could be seen on the cold air.

'Nonsense, I am often here in much worse,' she replied, 'it may be cold and gloomy but it is not wet. Come, we have more important things to discuss than the weather. I did not expect such a swift response.'

'Response, response to what?'

'To my letter, have you not received it?'

Charlie shook his head. 'No, no I had to see you because Ernestine has been caught trying to leave her bed to visit me.'

Davina felt as though the air had been punched from her lungs. She gasped. 'By whom? When?'

'Her father.' Charlie turned back to the view as though not able to confront Davina's emotions as well as his own. 'Knowing nothing of the truth he believes her to be wearing the willow. He suspects her reason and has had her locked in her room and guarded. I fear she will be subjected to the most fearful doctoring.' A huge shudder coursed his body. 'I must save her, Davina. I cannot let them do the barbarous things they practise upon our King. We must declare the engagement at an end and make them see that she is sane.'

Davina was slow to recover from the shock, her mind in a whirl with the implications. She tried in that maelstrom of thoughts to see another route but could not. The consequences of such action, the ruin which could be delivered on them all left her colder inside than the piercing wind ever could.

'What of your uncle?' she managed.

'What of him?' growled Charlie. 'How can you ask that when you compare it with what Ernestine might be suffering?'

Even in the throes of such anguished emotions, Davina could not suppress the niggling thought that Ernestine had to some extent brought it upon herself. If she had been content to ride out the situation there need be none of the alarming results Charlie now foresaw.

'We cannot just abandon your uncle,' she said with firmness.

'We must.'

'We cannot, we must at least warn him.'

'No, I must rescue Ernestine now. Do you not understand the urgency?' He came up to her to try and impress his words upon her with his stance.

Davina lifted her fine eyes to his face. 'We must give your uncle due warning,' she said clearly and decisively.

'No, no, I must go to Ernestine,' he raged.

'You will come with me to warn Lord Restharrow first.'

'You cannot make me,' he shouted at her.

'Can I not?' Davina asked quietly. There was silence. 'This engagement was of your and Ernestine's making and on your terms. However,' she felt the wind dry and strong on her lips, and resisted the temptation to lick them, 'only I can terminate it. I have not done so because you asked, nay begged me not to. Now I am holding you to it until we have given your uncle due notice of what is about to befall him.

18

*H*uddled in the corner of the dark and chilly coach, Davina shivered. Though she had a rug across her knees it was inadequate and she could feel the cold creep up her legs. Tears pricked at the back of her eyes and she had to remove a hand from her muff to press her handkerchief to her mouth. She did not wish to give her distress away.

The last twenty four hours had felt like the longest in her existence thus far. Since she had delivered her ultimatum to Charlie the day before, her emotions had see-sawed from righteous wrath to utter despair. She had had to steel herself against the barrage of Charlie's arguments. She had walked away eventually, unable to repeat endlessly her insistence that Lord Restharrow had to be told that the false engagement was now at an end. She had returned to her mother's house and awaited Charlie's next move. The evening had yawned like a great void before her. She went to bed desperate for sleep but alienated from it by the misery of her own thoughts.

The next morning she had risen early and tramped into Minchinhampnett, determined to learn more about the situation at the Rectory. She visited the milliner's and the confectioner's but the little knots of people who were avidly discussing some morsel of gossip had fallen silent when they perceived her. Davina returned home stony hearted, her doggedly held opinion that Ernestine was her friend challenged at every turn.

At noon a billet was received from Charlie. Davina pounced on it with all the eager anticipation her mother had previously desired. The note was short and to the point. He had acceded to her wishes; he would be leaving that afternoon to meet with his uncle.

Such was the tattered nature of her trust, Davina could not be happy. No sooner had her mother risen from the luncheon table than Davina slipped up to her bedroom and dressed warmly in her outdoor clothes. After much soul searching she scratched a brief note to her mother.

'Dearest Mama, Fear not for me. I must away tonight but will return on the morrow. I have no choice. Davina.'

She sealed the paper with a wafer and left it on her bed. She could not afford to have it found too soon.

The early afternoon was a good time to make her escape from Fromeview. The old butler was in his rooms refreshing himself with a nap. The other servants were taking their time over the remains of their luncheon eaten after the dining room had been cleared and Mrs Stanley had withdrawn to the bookroom to check her monthly accounts.

Once away from the house, Davina picked up her skirts and ran to the coaching house from whence she hoped Charlie was hiring a vehicle to convey him to Hampshire. There was a coach and pair standing outside in the yard. Davina had felt a measure of relief; perhaps she need not have doubted his integrity so very much.

At that moment Charlie had come out of the hostelry wearing his many-caped driving coat and pulling on his gloves.

'Good God, Davina, what are you doing here?' he cried as she came towards him.

'I wish to accompany you. I must know what Lord Restharrow desires us to do,' she replied breathlessly.

'Now, look here,' Charlie exclaimed, righteously indignant, 'I have said I will attend to it. You have my word. There can be no need for your presence as well.'

'I will come, I must come,' she averred.

'Davina, you cannot,' he had said angrily. 'I will not reach there until long after dark. We cannot return tonight. You will be ruined unless you wed me and we have both agreed that that is not to be.'

There was silence as Davina digested this. 'Have we not thus agreed?' he barked at her imperatively.

'Yes, yes,' Davina had assured him hastily, 'but I will come with you Charlie; if I have to knock on some villager's door and sleep at their house rather than at the same inn as you, I will see your uncle.'

Charlie had shaken his head, baffled by her determination. He had moved to remonstrate further but the ostler came forward, concerned that his horses would be catching cold in the biting wind. Charlie had capitulated and helped Davina into the coach, handing her the only rug with a poor grace.

The coach set off and was discovered to be poorly sprung and the two horses unevenly matched. Davina very quickly began to feel queasy and knew more moments of doubt. Charlie had hunched a pettish shoulder and was seated as far from her as the post-chaise would allow.

It was a foolhardy errand, she knew. If it went awry no one would be more at fault than herself. Almost Davina felt that reason had forsaken her too. She longed for the certainty and the petty constraints of her earlier life when she had known the rules which governed her day-to-day living. By stepping outside that closed and comfortable world she felt she had lost all grasp on manners and morals. She perceived the wisdom of her mother's determination to keep out of society and wished the good lady had withstood the Rector's demands and had prevented her from ever entering the world of the Thistledowns and their like.

The cold was now nagging at her hands and arms; she tugged at the rug and hugged it to her. She longed to tell Charlie that it was not him she distrusted but the circles within which he moved. There was constant talk of honour and trust but she had seen very little of either and now needed the proof of her own eyes and ears to be sure. She wriggled her toes in her fur-lined boots trying to ward off the pervasive numbness of cold, but to little effect. The journey started so recently already felt interminable. She found, once again, that the tears were gathering in her eyes. She caught herself up on a convulsive sob but the noise had reached Charlie. Davina saw the pale shadow of his face turn towards her in the dark. He reached out his hand and groped for hers.

'Please Davina, don't upset yourself,' he begged. 'I do not think I can support your emotions as well as Ernestine's.' He paused. 'You were determined to make this journey, but it is not too late to turn back. Though it be very dark it is not much past the hour of five o'clock, I can return you to your home and set out on the morrow.'

'No,' said Davina in an emphatic whisper. 'I needs must see this through. I will be better directly. Perhaps if you could light the carriage lanterns I would be better able to support my spirits without your aid.' There was a bitter edge to her voice which was not lost on Charlie.

He grappled with his tinderbox in the dark and lit a match from whence he transferred the flame to the lantern on the side of the carriage. Mutely he indicated to Davina to pass her lantern over. This she did in some distress, conscious that Charlie had little sympathy with her stance or her feelings. She wondered at his patience with Ernestine yet his very blindness to the fact that she might have a valid grievance.

They sat back once again against the cushions isolated from each other in mind and body. The cold had begun to penetrate even Charlie's many-layered coat and he called out to the coachman to stop at the next inn. Some twenty minutes later he escorted Davina into a warm parlour and ordered her scalding coffee and a plate of vittles. While this was being arranged he demanded hot bricks and several more rugs for the carriage. Davina, while thankful for a break from the cold, found she was not hungry and could do no more than nibble an oatmeal biscuit.

They clambered back into the carriage and resumed their miserable journey, neither of them comfortable with their own thoughts or each other's company. Charlie, whilst his anger against Davina had raged, had not considered the long-term consequences of calling off the engagement above his desperate need to rescue Ernestine from her internment. Now, as the anger he could never maintain for long began to subside, he could begin to understand Davina's determination to give Lord Restharrow due warning. If bankruptcy was to befall them, there might yet be a few things which could be rescued before the bailiffs crossed the threshold.

As the evening dragged on he broke his silence.

'I must seem a monster of cold-heartedness to you,' he said at last.

Davina turned her eyes towards him in wonder.

'I believed all communication was at an end between us,' she said, her voice trembling with surprise, 'can it be that your friendship can be re-established or do I presume too much?'

'I would be the worst kind of cad or bounder if I forsook you now after all that you have done to try and help us,' he said.

'I cannot credit that I am hearing this,' she cried, 'what has brought about this sudden change in your sentiments?'

'My sentiments have undergone no change,' he assured her hurriedly, 'but I have come to appreciate your reasons for warning my uncle. If we cannot rescue some of the estate, there will be little point in me attempting to rescue Ernestine as her parents will not have me as a suitor for her.'

Davina gave a splurt of laughter, her initial surprise settling back to a reluctant respect that Charlie had not lost his way. His whole mind was still centred on Ernestine's well-being, he had merely extended its context slightly.

Of course Charlie wanted to know what had made her laugh but she could not tell him the truth. She turned the subject as adroitly as she could and asked him what latest news he had had of Ernestine's plight. He was at once serious and anxious. It was understood that a doctor from Bristol had been asked to attend her. There was little doubt that the family believed her case to be very worrying indeed.

'But will they listen to you, Charlie?' asked Davina.

'They must,' he ran his hands distractedly through his hair, 'and if they do not, I will fly with her to the border.'

Davina gave a little gasp of alarm but she held her own counsel, hoping it would not come to that, for she did not believe Ernestine's constitution could sustain such a journey in the prevailing weather conditions.

After a while the conversation became desultory and eventually Charlie appeared to fall asleep. Davina watched the dancing flame in the candle grow low and dull and longed for journey's end.

It wanted a little before eight o'clock when the final pair of horses turned through a tall pair of gates and headed up a long and unkempt driveway. Davina sat forward and peered out through the gloom but she could see very little except that the foliage flanking the carriageway was too close and would have been better cut back.

The jolt as they came to a halt awoke Charlie. He was instantly in possession of all his faculties and forcing open the door leapt to the ground without waiting for the steps to be put down. Davina alighted more sedately and became dimly aware of an imposing structure before her. Lord Restharrow's Hampshire seat was made from pale Bath stone and stood three storeys high. It had a vast frontage, which stretched either side of a modern portico under which the carriage had drawn. The freezing blast from an east wind did not encourage them to linger to admire the house. Charlie had already pounded on the front door rather immoderately. He was now demanding entry at the top of his voice. There was a noise from within and the great door was drawn open.

'Mr Charlie, this is indeed a surprise;' the smile lifted the wizened butler's features from dour to cheerful. 'Come, come in out of the cold. I know his lordship will be delighted to see you.'

Charlie and Davina needed no further encouragement to come into the vestibule. The butler, who could be seen to be dressed in rather worn and faded clothes had a suddenly arrested expression when he discovered that Charlie was accompanied by a young female.

'Let me make you known to Hudd, Davina,' said Charlie, trying to carry it off with a high hand. 'Hudd, this is a young friend of mine, Miss Stanley.' The butler gave a cautious bow in Davina's direction, then, having supervised the removal of their various coats and rugs, escorted them across the hallway and through a long, grand gallery.

Davina would have preferred to keep her pelisse on for the house was decidedly chilly but good manners had forestalled her.

The gallery through which they travelled was poorly lit but Davina did not need any light to tell her that decay and neglect surrounded her. After one cursory look around she kept her gaze level and fixed on the back of the butler's grizzled head.

Eventually they reached the door to a large saloon. Here at least there was a roaring fire in a wide grate.

'Who was it, Hudd?' came Lord Restharrow's weary voice.

Charlie strode forward. 'Uncle, it is I and I have Miss Stanley with me. It is imperative that we speak with you.'

Charlie drew Davina into the room and brought her up to the fire. He turned to his uncle.

'We have something of great import to impart to you. Will you hear us?'

Lord Restharrow dismissed the butler with a tiny flick of his head.

'Well, it looks as though I have little choice,' he said, echoing Davina's letter to her mother.

19

*H*ungry for reassurance, Davina scrutinised Lord Restharrow's face and knew defeat. He still carried himself erect although she sensed that he had straightened his stance for their presence. The furrows on his brow had deepened and the crows' feet around his eyes had multiplied but it was the depth of sadness in those eyes which smote her to the core.

'No, Charlie,' she choked, 'you cannot do this.'

'But I must, I must,' came Charlie's anguished response as he tore distractedly at his golden locks.

'Come! Enough!' said Lord Restharrow sternly. 'Let me be the judge. Speak, man.'

Charlie, unable to settle, paced the poorly lit room. Lord Restharrow's eyes followed his progress but the older man did not repeat his command.

Eventually, taking pity on them both, Davina began the tale.

'You will perhaps remember, my lord, the sad day of Charlie's brother Lucien's demise.'

'I do, of course.'

'Charlie and Ernestine were in such sorrow. Their future together had been destroyed in one fell swoop.'

'How so, I do not see it?'

'I hate to wound you, mine uncle, but it was so,' said Charlie, intervening at last. 'My brother's debts, even though then unknown, I foresaw as crippling. I knew neither you nor I could meet them, I believed we faced ruin.'

Lord Restharrow linked his hands behind his back, forcing his shoulders straight. 'You may have been right,' he conceded.

'Ernestine perceived it too and she divined a way through it. She believed that if I was betrothed to an heiress we might confound the creditors and buy you time to ameliorate the situation. She,' he caught himself, 'we prevailed upon Miss Stanley to enter into such an engagement.'

'Good God!'

Davina raised her head in surprise, she had presumed that Lord Restharrow, if not party to the information that the engagement was a fake, at least might have some suspicions of it. The shock she witnessed on the lined face disabused her immediately of such a notion.

Charlie too had been drawn up short. 'Did you not suspect? Had you not considered how providential the timing of our announcement?'

'No of course not.' Lord Restharrow walked to a cabinet against the wall and helped himself from a decanter there. He knocked back the brandy with a deft jerk of the head. 'I had no inkling. I could think of nothing but the sad boy's death and my failure to bring him to heel. I thought nothing of the debts until the leeches started knocking at our door.' He paused, trying in vain to grapple with this news. 'My God, Charlie, how could you be so calculating, so manipulative at such a time?'

There was silence now as the conspirators bowed their heads. The only noise was the spitting of the fire and the ticking of a huge wall clock in the corner.

As the silence lengthened, Lord Restharrow tossed back a second drink.

'I should have guessed,' he said suddenly as if the liquor had delivered him clarity of thought. 'That girl, I might have known, she has always been a schemer.' He put the cut glass down firmly and strode across the room to his nephew. He put his hands on the young man's sagging shoulders and forced them back so that their eyes met.

'I thought,' Lord Restharrow gave an exclamation of disbelief. 'Nay I wanted to think that you had finally broken from her coils when seeing them in relief against the purity and generosity of spirit of Miss Stanley.' He flung away again. 'No, it is more of the same, she has encased you in her schemes and now has dragged Miss Stanley into them too.' He came up now to confront the sitting Davina. 'What did she promise you, Miss Stanley. Eh? Eh? What did she promise you? Eternal gratitude and friendship? For what else did she have to offer? Eh!'

Davina placed her face in her hands and sobbed into them. Lord Restharrow gave a derisive snort. 'Foolish girl,' he said angrily, 'could you not see that you were being duped?'

'Uncle, I beg you, Uncle please.' Charlie was moved to intervene. 'We did it for you.'

'She may have done,' responded Lord Restharrow, pointing his finger at the sorry figure by the fire, 'but neither you nor Miss Greenaway will have given me more than a passing thought. Your determination was fuelled entirely by thoughts of yourselves.'

So true were his words that Davina could not help emitting a gusty sob. She thought of all her mother had endured as a result of the engagement and wished she had had the strength of character to deny them in the beginning.

'So,' said Lord Restharrow in a more moderate tone as the depth of Davina's suffering reached him, 'what have you come to tell me? What must I know which has resulted in this extravagant gesture of making this journey alone and unattended?'

'Ernestine has been taken ill, Uncle. She suffers from our separation and her parents suspect that she is losing her mind. We must declare the engagement at an end.'

'Ha, so the girl suffers does she? What of it Charlie? I thought her foolish beyond permission when I understood her to be wearing the willow for you. Now however you tell me she has known all along that it is a sham. The girl is a narcissus, Charlie, she needs must be the centre of attention. Can you not see that?'

Charlie was confounded. He had never heard his uncle speak so derisively of anyone let alone his lady love. He gawped and stammered and fell silent.

Now that the intensity of his anger had been vented, Lord Restharrow went to Davina and drew her to her feet.

'You have been shamefully used, Miss Stanley,' he said gently. 'I acquit you of any grosser misconduct than that of being naïve and persuadable.' He took out a great linen handkerchief and began to dab the tears from her face. Her own very damp and ineffectual lace hanky fell to the floor. 'Come! Come to the window embrasure and collect yourself, I will ring for some tea and bread and butter. You will feel more the thing when you have had sustenance.'

She went unresisting to the large window alcove and sat on the padded seat. She could feel the draught coming through the ill-fitting window but she endured it, knowing she could not present a swollen and reddened face to a servant.

Charlie came over to her and patted her ineffectually on the shoulder. She caught his hand in a silent gesture of sympathy. She knew Lord Restharrow's words had been harsh but they had also been true and she could imagine how they might affect soft-hearted Charlie.

Lord Restharrow had tugged on a bell-rope beside the mantel-piece and not long after the sound of footsteps could be heard hurrying up the long gallery.

The saloon door was flung open and a cloaked figure entered the room, followed closely by the butler who was much agitated.

'My lord, I'm sorry, I could not gainsay her, she would see you. I tried, I tried to say you had company but she would have none of it.'

'My lord.' The great hood of the cape was thrown back to reveal Mrs Stanley, her face suffused with trouble and anxiety. 'My lord, you must help me for they have gone, they have eloped. I beg you save them from our folly. Go after them.'

Lord Restharrow seemed to be turned to stone. He stood as frozen as a statue, his face drained of all colour. Mrs Stanley came forward and shook his arm. 'My lord, I beg you,' she cried.

Recovering from her own stupor on perceiving the new arrival, Davina rose out of the shadows of the alcove and came to her mother.

'Mama, Mama,' she cried, 'what is this? What brings you here?'

Mrs Stanley dropped Lord Restharrow's arm and wheeled round. 'Davina, Davina. Oh thank God!'

20

*F*ar too taken up with the implications of her mother's arrival, Davina failed to notice the extreme nature of Lord Restharrow's reaction to Mrs Stanley's appearance. Charlie, however, was not. He went to the decanter and poured two good measures of brandy into a pair of crystal glasses and handed one to his uncle. He recognised Mrs Stanley, of course, although he had had little contact with her during the near year of his engagement to Davina. His uncle, though, he believed had never been introduced to the lady.

'What is this woman to you, Uncle?' he demanded once he had taken a swig of the potent liquid.

'Davida!' Finally Lord Restharrow spoke but it was in a hoarse whisper that did not penetrate the exchange of explanations which were going on between Davina and her mother.

'Not Davina,' said Charlie, mishearing him. 'Uncle, Mrs Stanley, what is she to you?'

At the audible use of her name Mrs Stanley had drawn away from Davina and she now looked towards his lordship.

'She is my wife,' said the man on a shuddering sigh. 'My wife.'

The shock amongst his auditors was tangible. The words hung in the air, portentous, cathartic. Mrs Stanley sank into a chair and shaded her eyes with her hand. Charlie was thunderstruck but with a dawning look of understanding stealing over his face. For Davina it was the final straw, she simply fainted away and landed in a crumpled heap on the berugged floor. It broke the spell as nothing else could. Mrs Stanley rose quickly and began to loosen the girl's dress at the throat, Charlie started to wave an embroidered chair coverlet over her and the butler who had remained in the doorway unnoticed throughout the scene turned on his heel to procure some water. Lord Restharrow, at last in full command of his senses despite the brandies, rather roughly pushed apart the others. He bent down and gathered up Davina's inanimate form into his arms, and moved her to the settle. Mrs Stanley, recovering her balance after being so unceremoniously shoved aside, rummaged in her reticule and withdrew her smelling salts. Charlie once again took up fanning the invalid.

It was some little while before Davina began to come murmuringly to her senses. As her faculties returned she reached out her hand and grasped Lord Restharrow's.

'Pray tell me,' she whispered, 'pray tell me that it is true, that it makes you my father?'

Lord Restharrow made no move to give her any such assurance. In truth it was not his to give. All eyes turned on Mrs Stanley and after a significant pause when the room was once again held spellbound she capitulated and gave a small, decisive, nod.

'Good God.' Charlie wheeled away from the group by the settle and strode over to the fire. Leaning against the mantelpiece, he looked into the flames searchingly. 'I think I am owed some explanation,' he declared, 'how has this come about?'

'More simply and truly than you imagine,' said Mrs Stanley as she stood up from her place by Davina's recumbent form. Davina shifted her position so that she was more upright but her eyes never left her new father's face, for what had been a tired and wan expression now registered a profound joy. She felt it too, a deep warm glow, a sense of justification for all she had put herself through. She could almost convince herself that she had known there was an affinity between them. He was her father and she his child. For that moment that was all that mattered. The implications and complications could come later.

However, Charlie was agitating for an explanation. Mrs Stanley, still standing, clasped her hands together against her beautiful bronze dress. She did not look at Charlie but at Lord Restharrow, her eyes begging him to understand.

'We were very young,' she said, 'very much in love. My home, was not only close to the border with Scotland but was situated near one of Lord Restharrow's smaller estates which has since been sold.'

She saw him wince and looked away. It had not been meant to be a jibe at his financial predicaments but he took it so.

After an infinitesimal pause she continued. 'It seemed like a game. Neither set of parents would approve the match. Mine because we were country folk without town connections who feared the high-spending, free-living upper ten thousand. His because they had already spent too freely and needed a good match to save their estates. Being so close to Gretna Green was tantalising; we were too young to look ahead, we thought if we could prosecute a clandestine marriage our parents would accept it.'

She broke off as the butler appeared with a tray of tea and macaroons which he had left to attend to soon after pouring Davina a drink of water.

Lord Restharrow moved towards him. 'I will not insult you by requesting your discretion in this matter Hudd,' he said, 'but I believe we need the Parson here to advise us. Will you send out for him.'

'Now my lord?'

'Yes.'

'But it wants twenty to ten, my lord. Reverand Cowfold is likely to have retired to his couch.'

'That's as may be,' said his lordship testily, 'but we must have him here please.'

The butler withdrew to break the news to the youngest footman that he must don his greatcoat and go knocking on the Parsonage door. Hudd was not sure how he was to do this without initiating a great deal of gossip in the servants' hall.

Within the saloon, Mrs Stanley had resumed her tale.

'We found a way, as the young do, to be free of our family and friends. Your father even found a farmer willing to have his address used for the banns. Then we crossed the border together, and were married. Such was the joy of our union and the thrill of secret meetings that we did not hurry to tell our families. Indeed I believe we feared to in case they attempted an annulment. It was however already too late. Not two months on I began to feel queasy and unwell, and some fine intuition prevented me from consulting the family doctor. I went alone to the village wise woman who was renowned for her discretion. She told me what I had already begun to suspect: that I was with child.'

Lord Restharrow clearly knew nothing of this development; he was as avid as the rest for more information. Mrs Stanley bent down to the tray and took up a cup of tea but she did not sit down. After a couple of sips she put the cup and saucer down.

'I realised now was the time to have my husband tell our families but before I could, I received a billet from him. The family had been urgently recalled to London, his brother had lost a considerable sum at the gaming tables and capital had to be raised to settle the debt. I dashed off a note begging him to meet me first but they had already left, leaving no date for their return.'

'I did come back for you, Davida,' Lord Restharrow said in a husky voice, 'when I received no reply to my letters, I came back to see you but you were already gone.'

Mrs Stanley nodded. 'But can you not see, my lord, it was too late. By now I had been with child more than three months. The servants were becoming suspicious and I could not divulge our marriage until I had your permission to do so. I also saw at last the force of the many arguments that had been ranged against our union. Your family were falling deeper and deeper into debt and although my parents had a comfortable living at that time, they could not have secured your future with any dowry I could offer. I had to act. I went to my godmother and begged her indulgence.

'Your godmother, of course, I never thought of her.'

'She took me in without a word to my parents.' Mrs Stanley carried on as though she had not heard his interjection. 'She supported me while I had the baby and then found me employment with some elderly sisters with whom she had spent her school days. They lived in Gloucestershire and kept very close, never enjoying much company. My godmother would have me alter my name entirely but I could not. At that time before your father's demise, my lord, I was The Hon Mrs Winstanleigh, I would commute it to Stanley, no more.'

Charlie was bemused by these revelations and now made his voice heard.

'But this was nigh on twenty years ago. Why, why prolong the secrecy beyond my grandfather's death?'

Mrs Stanley looked at him fully for the first time. A candle guttered in its socket on the wall and Lord Restharrow went to replace it with a fresh one. Everyone waited in silence until he had concluded his task.

'You forget, Mr Winstanleigh,' his new aunt resumed, 'that I had set myself apart from him, so that he could remarry a fortune. I presumed him able to annul the marriage after my disappearance and indeed thought that he had done so when it appeared that he was on the point of taking another woman to wife.

'I never did so,' said Lord Restharrow quietly.

'Did you not? Yet you were preparing for another marriage.'

Lord Restharrow threw up his hands as if to ward off a blow. 'Enough, say no more of it. I was very conscious of the duplicity, the evil of what I was undertaking. Mine only mitigation was the torment my mother and sisters were suffering with every fresh charge on the estate from my father or brother. I was never more thankful than when my father's death allowed me to withdraw.'

Davina at last found a reed of a voice. 'When the Miss Leonards died, Mama, and left us well endowed, could you not have sought him out then?'

'Perhaps I should have done,' she conceded; 'had I known then what we were to endure this last year, I would have felt the scandal it risked a worthy price to pay. Instead I thought we could continue to live quietly with none the wiser. I was not to know that the Rector would pitchfork us right into the family and friends I most wished to avoid!'

'So now it is explained why you tried to prevent our engagement.'

Mrs Stanley nodded.

'And why you retired to your sickbed when Lord Restharrow, my father, visited.' Davina's voice was becoming stronger.

'Yes, my dear,' her mother acknowledged. 'While I had followed his progress through the court circulars and society pages of the journals, he had had no word of me in two decades but I knew he would recognise me as he did tonight.'

'So,' Charlie slapped his thigh and left his place by the fire, 'what now?' He looked from one to the other. 'It seems I no longer need to be betrothed to Davina because, as your daughter, she is much more valuable than as my fiancée.' There was an edge to his voice, a cold anger which drew Lord Restharrow to him.

'Some harsh words have been said this evening, Charlie, which I would gladly unsay. You find me as someone who has erred and who has small right to take you to task. Forgive me.' He held out his hand and stood watchful as his nephew grappled with his feelings. Finally Charlie took the outstretched hand.

'So what now?' he asked. 'There will be a deal of scandal when all this is revealed.'

'That depends on the wishes of my wife,' said Lord Restharrow turning back to Mrs Stanley. 'Well, Lady Restharrow, do you wish now to acknowledge the truth or do we return to our separate lives and pretend this revelation never happened?'

'Oh no,' the denial burst from Davina.

As the truth had filtered through the annals of her mind, she had felt a surge of elation; she was now a fit wife for Lord Louis should he ever seek her out again. Her love for him had been like a bruise, painful if touched; now she thought she could rejoice in it unfettered by either her false engagement to Charlie or the mystery of her birth.

'But consider Davina,' said her mother before anyone else could speak, 'if we announce to the world our folly, we will once again be shunned as we have been in Gloucestershire. The only way I can see for us to in part resolve the situation is if your father and I re-enact some form of marriage ceremony. You could then be acknowledged as his daughter in law if not in blood and your father could have access to my wealth if not yours.'

Davina bit her lip and shook her head sadly. It seemed the duplicity was not, after all, at an end as she had hoped. 'Perhaps the Parson will not undertake the service,' she mumbled hopefully.

Lord Restharrow shrugged. 'That will be for him to decide of course. Until he makes that decision we will not look for alternatives.

Charlie, though weary, was standing as though about to take his leave.

'You are going back to Miss Greenaway?' Lord Restharrow queried.

'Yes I must,' Charlie met his gaze squarely, 'she is my life's chosen partner, will you give me your blessing?'

'My blessing has little value, nephew, but you have it if you will, but I beg you for the time being, keep your own counsel over this matter.'

Charlie nodded and strode out leaving the remaining three to await the Parson's verdict.

21

*T*he Reverend St. John Cowfold smoothed his baldpate with a weary hand then rubbed his tired eyes. The quill with which he had been annotating ideas for his forthcoming Sunday sermon was blunt and needed sharpening but the Parson was disinclined to do it. His sister, Martha, had retired to bed some little time earlier and he had not made up the fire since then. The austere room was cold and did not encourage him to linger at his desk.

The Parsonage was a fair-sized house but due to the want of funds, Revd. Cowfold and his sister were reduced to living in the kitchen and one of the smaller parlours. Revd. Cowfold's living was dependent on the fortunes of the Restharrow estate and therefore it had remained unpaid for more than a decade. The Cowfolds subsisted on a small income inherited from their mother. While they could afford the purchase of logs for the fire, their purse did not stretch to the wages for a servant to chop the wood. Thus Revd. Cowfold limited his use of the fire to what he could chop or when he was feeling particularly extravagant the amount the farmer's stripling youth could chop in a morning for a few pence. Miss Martha Cowfold had some years before taken in mending which, while they both believed it was demeaning for a parson's sister, they tacitly agreed had to continue.

The sermon the Parson had been trying to write that evening had at its centre the passage from *St Mark*, chapter 10 verse 25, 'It is easier for a camel to go through the eye of a needle than for a rich man to enter the kingdom of God'. While he was not bitter that his benefactors had abandoned him to his fate, he did have stirrings of doubt when he reviewed a world where there were some unworthies given great wealth who squandered it without a thought to their responsibilities towards those lowly dependants entrusted to their care. He had seen much suffering over the years as the Restharrow family had wasted its inheritance on excess. He was not thinking of the lesser members of the family who had clearly suffered themselves but of the tenants and the servants who had gone without wages and proper repairs for their homes. Sometimes his conscience smote him at his questioning and required him to offer some penance such as to give up the Parsonage, as proof of his devotions, so that it could be sold or rented out but he had never made the gesture. Although his failure to do so had caused him many a sleepless night during which he consulted with his God and challenged his faith, in the cold light of morning he would see his sister valiantly cut him a thick slice of bread and take but a morsel herself. He had wrought with his conscience and remained where he was, deep in the knowledge that they could not afford any other lodgings.

'God, you must be the judge,' he found himself saying once again and wished that he could be spared the constant drain of this dilemma which had become more difficult as Lord Restharrow's financial crisis' deepened. For Revd. Cowfold knew that Lord Restharrow had never been guilty of overlooking his obligations, only unable to meet them.

The knock on the door did not at first alarm the cleric. It was part of his ministry to go out to the sick or dying at any time of day or night. He rose from his desk and moved stiffly to the hallway hoping the noise had not roused his sister. She was one who needed her sleep.

Opening the door revealed the bulk of young Arthur, the second footman from the house.

'His lordship requires you at the house, Reverend,' said the stalwart flinging his arms across his chest and stamping his feet to ward off the cold. Revd. Cowfold ushered him into the hallway and closed the door hastily. The hallway was not appreciably warmer than outside but at least there was no wind.

'But it wants a little before ten, my boy. Surely his lordship does not wish to see me at this hour.'

'That's what he said,' affirmed the footman, 'he's got visitors, Reverend, surprise visitors,' he said portentously.

The Parson's heart sank. He heard a slight noise from the stairs and turned to see the thin form of his sister silhouetted against the candles on the half-landing wall. She was wrapped in her woollen night jacket over her flannel nightgown and her head was covered in a bonnet but Revd. Cowfold knew she must be cold. He was about to remonstrate with her to return to the warmth of her bed but something in her stance prevented him.

'This is the end of it, then,' she said in a voice with an audible tremble.

'I fear so,' he replied.

Miss Cowfold began to walk down the stairs.

'I will await your return,' she said and went past him into the parlour.

The Parson put on his thickest coat and followed Arthur out into the perishing night.

At the house, they awaited the Reverend's pleasure in some trepidation.

Davina, now that the initial shock had been overcome had begun to advance the arguments for a total revelation of the truth but her parents would not be persuaded. Clearly the ostracism of the last few months had affected Mrs Stanley deeply and she was determined not to offer the gossipmongers anything further.

'If we can announce our marriage before Charlie's engagement to Miss Greenaway becomes generally known, we can ward off the most vociferous of our creditors,' Lord Restharrow told her. 'However if we admit to a long-standing union, the gossip alone will have everyone beating a trail to our door and demanding their money, fearing that we will take flight and go abroad out of their reach.'

'Money! Always money! Always the first consideration!' cried Davina. 'I would rather present you with my whole fortune so that you can settle all the debts and be allowed to acknowledge you are my true father, than submit to more subterfuge.'

'Hush, my dear.' Her mother had tried to comfort her but Davina brushed her off. 'Your fortune could not be used even if your father was acknowledged, it is in trust for some little time yet,' she continued, following her daughter's progress up the room with sad eyes. 'My fortune is but a third of yours and though it can make your father's life much more comfortable, it will not pay all that is owed. We must practise a degree of circumspection.'

Davina collapsed into a chair, unable to sustain any further emotion, she felt battered and bewildered. Even the people whom she had thought immune to duplicity and betrayal were embracing it now, indeed had lived a lie for more than twenty years. The whole foundation of her very existence was turning to sand around her.

She looked at her parents with eyes as bleak as a moorland hill in winter and when she spoke it was with a hollow voice.

'So,' she said, 'suddenly, after all these years of separation you will arrange a charade of a marriage service and live as husband and wife. I fear I do not understand why it can be so simple now when it has been so assiduously avoided for so many years.'

Mrs Stanley drew a chair closer to her daughter's and attempted to take Davina's hand. Once again she was rejected. The lady did not try again.

'My dear,' she said patiently as though speaking to a recalcitrant child, 'have I not explained it to you?'

'Not well enough for me to understand,' bit back the rejoinder.

Mrs Stanley sighed. 'Very well then, I will try again to make you accept my reasoning.' She paused to collect herself. 'Until the

Miss Leonards made us their beneficiaries, my reason for leaving your father remained the same: I had no fortune. I could not help him, our marriage had been an idyllic summer's youthful madness. There were no benefits to either of us in being reunited.' She smoothed the beautiful material of the dress, which had been crumpled by her sitting down and arranged it in neat folds.

Davina waited in silence exhibiting no obvious signs of impatience. Lord Restharrow fiddled with a nutcracker that had been placed with attendant assorted nuts next to the brandy decanter. He had not taken another drink but it was clear from his demeanour that he would like to.

Mrs Stanley resumed her narrative. 'When Lord Restharrow appeared to be on the point of remarrying, it led me to assume that he had arranged an annulment and that my appearance would therefore be most unwelcome. It was only as you, my dear, were drawn into his family that I began to indulge the suspicions that we might still be married. The general acceptance that Lord Restharrow would never marry implied to me that there was an impediment preventing him from doing so. I guessed I was that impediment.' She cast a shy look in the direction of his lordship. 'What I might have done had your seeming flight with young Mr Winstanleigh not driven me here now, I cannot say. I had certainly considered and rejected a number of possible modes of making myself known again to his lordship.'

'This is all very well, Mama, I am familiar with being locked into a form of conduct from which one later wishes to escape', her face expressed her bewilderment. 'But you both seem intent, within minutes of making each other's reacquaintance, in formalising your marriage and becoming husband and wife in more than just form. It is twenty years or thereabouts since you were known to each other; so much including yourselves must have changed.'

Again Mrs Stanley cast a shy glance towards her husband but what she saw in his expression seemed to reassure her.

'In law, my dear, we are married. Your father has rights over me and my fortune under that law. We may have much to learn about each other but that fact is inescapable: it would be most wrong in me to attempt to walk away now that the truth is known to me.'

Lord Restharrow put down the nutcracker and came back into the body of the room.

'What are you afraid of Davina?' he asked gently. 'Are you afraid I will squander your mother's fortune and have us both live in penury? I shall not, I swear it.'

Davina finally showed some sign of life. 'I know you will not mean to,' she said levelly, 'but the magnitude of your debts, my lord, how can you possibly protect my mother?'

He smiled a rare mischievous smile. 'The beauty of the isolated existence she has lived means few know the extent of her wealth. We can mete it out slowly living on the promise of your wealth, my darling daughter.'

Davina stood up, she could take no more. 'I think,' she said carefully as she swayed slightly, 'that I would like to retire. Is it possible to have a room readied for me? Perhaps it will all seem more reasonable and acceptable in the morning.'

22

*O*n being ushered into the saloon by Hudd, the Reverend Cowfold was surprised to find it occupied by more than just his lordship. He had assumed that the visitors had been some vicarious creditors who had finally pushed Lord Restharrow into realising some of his assets. It was a measure of the man, the Parson had argued with himself, that he had wished to put him in possession of the facts immediately.

Finding himself in the presence of a lady, however, he was completely thrown off his balance even before the manifestly entangled story was laid bare before him.

'Would you perform the ceremony we require, Cowfold?' asked Lord Restharrow at the end of his recital, 'we can see no other way through the maze.'

The Parson considered for a moment, steepling his fingers and drawing them to his face. This was not an everyday tale. To his mind, these people had both suffered for their youthful indiscretions. He would have wanted to help them even if his own future security had not depended on it.

'I would have to read the banns,' he said.

Lord Restharrow looked pained. 'I dare not risk the delay,' he said.

'I cannot do otherwise, my lord, unless you return to London and procure a special licence which I do not recommend.'

Lord Restharrow nodded. 'Very well,' he conceded wearily, 'I must ensure that my nephew does nothing before that.'

'It will of course have to be a very private ceremony, a reassertion of your vows,' continued the Parson, enjoying himself, 'with no signing of the register but it will serve,' he smiled seraphically at his two parishioners, 'I am sure it will serve.'

The lady dropped him a grateful curtsy then, turning aside and shielding what she was doing from their guest, she handed a small pouch to Lord Restharrow and whispered urgently into his ear.

Taking it from her, Lord Restharrow came up to the Parson. He seemed a trifle uncertain.

'Please take this,' he said, handing the bag to the clergyman, 'you will no doubt have some church expenses that must be met.'

The older man palmed the money and acknowledged to himself that it must have been a rare experience for Lord Restharrow to be able to pay his dues in advance.

On leaving Restharrow Hall, the Parson had stuffed the pouch in his pocket so it was only while he was waiting in the stable yard for Arthur to ready the gig to drive him home that he was able to look and see how much he had been given. The bag contained some twenty guineas. He gave a silent prayer of thanks and on reaching his home he slipped one of the golden guineas into Arthur's hand.

Surprised, the young man looked at the Parson.

'I cannot take this, Reverend,' he protested.

'Of course you can young man. I have never done it before and may never be able to again, but I have just received a small windfall and I wish to spread a little happiness with it.'

'Well that you have, Sir, that you have,' said the delighted servant and to both men the night did not seem so dark, cold and cheerless anymore.

Davina awoke betimes the next morning. Despite the previous day's exhaustion her sleep had been fitful and troubled by complicated dreams. When she woke finally not to return to sleep it was still dark but she knew she was at the end of the night by the clatter of a servant along the corridor.

She rang for a pitcher and bowl and when it had come, splashed cold water on her face. She hoped it would freshen her mind as well as her body so that she could keep pace with the latest turn of events.

She did not delay with her dressing, as the room was unheated. The floor was cold to her feet and the windows were covered with a million frost crystals all laid out in intricate patterns. She had slept in her petticoats as she had come unprepared and the bed had been made up for her hastily the night before. Taking a cover from it, Davina wrapped it around her and set out in the gradually lifting gloom to find her parents.

Eventually, after a couple of wrong turns, Davina found the grand stairwell and descended to the ground floor. She found the grimy, derelict state of the place depressed her spirits and she longed to escape. It was as though hope had not walked these corridors and passages for many years. Even the portraits and miniatures of the family members looked grieved and disapproving. Davina had no concept of what it would cost to restore this place to order but she feared her mother would be run off her legs should she make the attempt.

She finally returned to the saloon where she had spent the evening before and pulled the service bell. After some minutes Hudd, the butler appeared; he too had had little sleep and was looking tired but an air of elation clung to him. He had discovered from Arthur that the clergyman had come into some money. He had surmised that the money had come from the lady formerly known as Mrs Stanley. He was enveloped in an uncharacteristic optimism. He smiled encouragingly at Davina and led her to the breakfast parlour.

Davina was not to know that the spirits of the handful of remaining servants had all lifted mysteriously overnight. The breakfast parlour which the morning before she would have found dismal and uninviting had this morning a cheerful fire jumping in a clean grate. The silver dishes that contained a more plentiful breakfast than usual had been polished and now shone brightly in competition with the fire. The floor had been swept clean and the dust removed from the corners and along the skirting board.

Davina was much heartened by the appearance of the room, it contrasted so favourably with the others she had seen so far in the house. She took her seat at the table and allowed herself to be served without waiting for her father and mother. Once she had had her fill, she asked the footman to guide her to her mother's bedchamber. When he had provided her with this service she naturally tipped him. She was not to know she had given further proof that the fortunes of Restharrow Hall had finally improved. The servants' quarters became a place of chatter and excitement.

Davina knocked gently on her mother's door and entered on her instruction. The lady was already in her beautiful bronze dress but was grateful for her daughter's appearance to aid her with its fixings as she was without a lady's maid.

'What becomes of us now, mama?' Davina asked as she began to unbraid her mother's soft brown hair.

Lady Restharrow shifted slightly under her daughter's dextrous fingers and fleetingly met her eyes in the mirror.

'It is not for me to say, my dear,' she murmured 'The Parson desires the banns and we cannot deny him.' Her voice became stronger. 'It is vastly unfortunate as we cannot remain here for the next three weeks, it would excite the sort of comment we wish to avoid.'

'We cannot stay here whatever the circumstances, Mama,' replied Davina, rhythmically smoothing with her hands her mother's hair which was now loosed from its bonds, 'we have no clothes, no baggage, no hairbrush even, it will most certainly excite comment if we attempt to stay.'

'You speak as though you wish to return home.'

'Yes, I wish it,' said the girl, beginning to twist up her mother's tresses, 'if you will not let me be my father's child, I do not wish to remain here to live a lie.'

'You have become a high stickler overnight, Davina,' said her mother on a note of caution. 'Do not presume that you can set yourself above us for you cannot. Whatever its mitigation, your false engagement disqualifies you.'

'Do I not know it.' Davina gave a gusty sigh.

Lady Restharrow captured her daughter's restless hand. 'Come tell me, why must you pursue this to its very end? Can you not settle for a hazy picture?'

'No, no I cannot,' cried Davina, 'you cannot ask me to make that sacrifice.'

'What sacrifice, my dear?' asked her mother, caught up by the emotion in her daughter's face. 'What are you trying to conceal from me?'

Davina, who prior to her introduction to polite society had not been a lachrymose girl, burst into tears. While Lady Purslane had become used to a demonstration of emotion from her, Davina's mother was not. This meant that the tears had a profound effect on the older woman.

'My darling, what can be the matter? What has provoked this response from you?'

Davina shook her head, unwilling to admit to a love she had only latterly admitted to herself. Eventually though her mother's soft words of encouragement prized the information out of her.

Lady Restharrow was inclined to think that Davina had read too much into Lord Louis's behaviour and said as much.

'He is one of young Mr Winstanleigh's closest friends, Davina, he would be bound to gravitate to you and him.'

Davina did not attempt to disabuse her of that view. It seemed futile to tell of the many events where she had been present and Charlie had not. Nor did she repeat the whisperings and gossip, which had so upset Charlie; her mother would surely have taken it as a fault in Davina's behaviour.

'And my dear,' went on Lady Restharrow, 'you have to acknowledge that if he cavilled at your birth when he had no knowledge of your father, he will undoubtedly be turned away by the gossip. I am very sorry Davina but there is little chance of you making yourself acceptable to him, whichever course we choose.'

Davina saw the futility of her own arguments and the flaws in her mother's but she was beyond reasonable and coherent thought on the matter. If Lord Louis was lost to her then she saw no future for herself. As the step daughter of Lord Restharrow, she could take up a life in this derelict pile but she did not want that, she wanted a life of her own which she could order and arrange to her own satisfaction. She knew it would not be acceptable for her to reside alone at Fromeview while her mother removed to Restharrow Hall. She dried her eyes and tried to think of what alternatives might present themselves.

Eventually she was composed enough to accompany her mother to the breakfast parlour where she administered tea to her but did not partake of anything further herself. Not long after Lady Restharrow had seated herself, his lordship appeared. He was dressed in top boots and riding dress and had clearly been out for a morning constitutional.

'Had I had a suitable mount for you, my child, I would have encouraged you to come with me,' he told a silent and embarrassed Davina. She flickered a brief tight smile but said nothing.

Lady Restharrow hurried into speech. 'Davina and I must return home at your very earliest convenience,' she said slightly breathlessly. 'We have none of our chattels and it would be unsuitable for us to remain here.'

'Devil take the Parson for his delay,' said Lord Restharrow with a good deal of vehemence as he laid down his whip on the side table, only then conscious that he had brought it with him, such had been his haste to renew the acquaintance with his new family. He had also failed to put off his gloves, and he began to pull them off finger by finger.

'It is only natural that he should want to give it a correct appearance, my lord,' said his wife.

'Yes, yes, but what are we to do with the intervening time? I am impatient to claim you as my wife. God knows I have waited long enough.'

Davina lifted her head from contemplating her hands and directed a long look at him with her fine brown eyes.

'I want to claim you as my father but you will not allow it,' she said boldly.

Lord Restharrow's face altered subtly as he turned to look at her. 'I'm sorry, my child, truly sorry,' he said, 'but there is nothing I can do to alter it.'

'Then,' said Davina pressing on, 'can we not spend these next weeks reacquainting ourselves with my mother's parents and sister? If I cannot claim you as my father, I must surely be able to claim them as grandparents and aunt.'

23

*L*ady Restharrow was most reluctant to consider such a journey, while it was still winter. Her protests had a slightly hysterical air to them and both husband and daughter sensed that her stated objections masked a dark fear that her family would reject her. It took some time of patient argument and not a little pleading from her daughter to convince the lady that within a day of returning to Fromeview Place they should pack up and travel north to the little border village which had been the home of her youth. Lord Restharrow magnanimously agreed to accompany them, which set the seal on the decision.

'And while we are absent from here, the servants can make the house ready for us, I suppose,' said Lady Restharrow once she had conceded defeat.

Lord Restharrow looked pained and withdrew from the room circumspectly to order the horses. Davina ran to her mother and cast herself down at her feet.

'Mama, you cannot ask him to command the servants to carry out Herculean labours. There are barely enough of them left to carry out the daily chores and they have not been paid since Lucien died.'

Lady Restharrow considered a moment, then drew out a roll of notes from her reticule.

'I did not come unprepared, my love,' she said with a brief smile. 'I admit I had expected to use the money chasing you to the border, not accompanying you there, but this money can be used to pay the servants. I have more at Fromeview, which will cover our journey north.'

She then rang for a servant and sent for the housekeeper. Mrs Hudd was not the butler's wife but his sister-in-law. Mr Hudd's younger brother, Samson, was a seaman and saw little of his wife. It had seemed prudent when money was scarce for her to seek employment but without much experience of service she had struggled to find a post. When the Restharrow housekeeper had retired after many years' service, the butler had recommended his brother's wife for the position. Too entangled in the web of debt, Lord Restharrow had been happy to engage someone who came so cheaply.

Hudd had spent some time coaching his kinswoman in the ways of housewifery and she was now well versed in the running of a large house. She was however unable to work miracles and with only two maids and the old gardener's wife she struggled to keep standards to a bare minimum. When she received the summons from her future mistress she armed herself with excuses but when it came to it none were necessary.

On entering the room, she found Lady Restharrow seated with her back to the dressing table; she had had her daughter pull a small table in front of her. She looked very businesslike. Mrs Hudd found herself bobbing a curtsy almost before she had closed the door.

'Mrs Hudd?' Lady Restharrow enquired.

'Yes ma'am,' acknowledged the stocky woman.

'I am Mrs Stanley, you must know that I have become betrothed to Lord Restharrow.'

'Yes ma'am, and may I wish you happy?'

Lady Restharrow raised her fine brown eyes to the flushed face of the servant.

'Thank you,' she said, 'I hope that we will all be happy with the arrangement.' She paused and fingered her reticule, which lay on the table. 'I presume you have records of what is owing to the staff, Mrs Hudd?'

Mrs Hudd bobbed another curtsy and put a hand with fingers which felt suddenly wooden up to loose the strings of her cap. 'Yes ma'am,' she said again, this time with a hint of breathlessness.

'Then please bring your books to me. I wish to hire more servants to put the house aright but we must reward those who have been loyal enough to stay.'

Never had there been such music to Mrs Hudd's ears; with almost unseemly haste she bustled to her room to retrieve her records which had been laboriously kept, under the critical eye of the butler.

The score of wages owed was soon settled. The two women made provision for a further two maids and enough to clear the slate with the local suppliers. The butler and the housekeeper did their best to prevent younger members of staff from squandering their newfound wealth; only Arthur divided up his shillings and sent some home to his parents and long family before heading for the taproom of the local hostelry. Mr Hudd was very put out but Mrs Hudd, more familiar with sailors and their binges, was quietly philosophical.

'It's a lesson that has to be learned,' she said sagely before squirrelling away her portion.

Lord Restharrow and his recently acquired family were ready to set out for Gloucestershire before noon. His lordship rode beside the chaise and the ladies entertained themselves as best they could within the vehicle. Both were weary but Lady Restharrow's thoughts sat more comfortably then her daughter's and she fell into a doze. Davina, with nothing but her troubled musings to preoccupy her, sighed a little sigh and looked out of the window at the winter landscape. Of Lord Louis she had heard nothing for months; his movements were no longer reported in the papers so it had to be assumed that he was still in Scotland. This circumstance was at such variance with what she knew of him that Davina was bound to wonder what kept him there. Her thoughts divided themselves between hoping that he languished for the want of her and fear that he had found some other young lady who suited him better.

'There can be no one such,' she said almost audibly as she thought of the evenings when their combined voices had soared to the rafters and filled the great halls, enthralling the guests. 'There cannot!'

Lady Restharrow, disturbed by the murmurings had opened her eyes but Davina averted her gaze and pretended to be much absorbed in the countryside. Lady Restharrow settled back into her corner and Davina was careful not to utter her thoughts out loud again.

They arrived at Fromeview Place late that evening and were welcomed with much excitement and relief. Nancy was even moved to embrace Davina, so thankful was she to see her returned. The news of the forthcoming marriage was not advertised to the servants to explain Lord Restharrow's presence, he was merely their escort; the ladies fed him then sent him off to the Ragged Cot to seek his couch and his valet who they had deposited there earlier. He did not protest and went as soon as he might to recruit his forces for the following day's journey north. Nancy did her best to extract an explanation from Davina for her flight but Davina returned only evasive answers. Too much was still uncertain for her to feel information could be imparted freely.

The next day Nancy and the housekeeper, Mrs Tulley, made every effort to dissuade the ladies from undertaking another even more fatiguing journey. However Davina would not allow them much access to her mother and parried all the questions herself. She explained endlessly to them that they must travel now before the weather broke. A day's delay might see snow. They must go while the weather was bright and clear.

They left, this time with all attendant luggage and with more available light. They made good time to Wolverhampton where they spent the night, determined to start early the next morning. Davina was confident they had two more days before snow might fall but she counselled the use of roads nearer the coast just in case she had made an error of judgement. The end of the second day's journey found them in Lancaster and well pleased with their progress. The next day's journey although shorter in distance was hampered by the paucity of the roads. Recent rain and snow had left many a pothole and as they climbed towards Shap the snow could be seen to be lying on the ground. Davina shivered and harried her parents not to tarry over nuncheon. Lord Restharrow who had had previous experience of her weather wisdom was happy to do as she asked. Lady Restharrow was becoming increasingly agitated at the prospect of discovering herself to her parents.

The short day had been exhausted when they reached Carlisle and Lord Restharrow immediately bespoke rooms at the posting house. He had no plans to go further that day. Both ladies were looking strained and he felt they should be well rested before they tackled what could be a very emotional day on the morrow. He failed to take account of the effect of a long night's anticipation on his wife's constitution. The next morning saw her pale with great dark smudges below her eyes, a stark betrayal of how she had spent her sleepless night.

All three rode in the chaise this time, each trying to draw courage from the others. When the chaise eventually drew up outside the pillars of Mewing Grange as it had been instructed, there was a moment's silence amongst the travellers.

'I cannot go in, I cannot,' burst from Lady Restharrow, 'what must they think of me. I cannot see them.'

Lord Restharrow dismounted quietly from the chaise and walked up the short drive to the square, rather gloomy house which was fabricated from a dark grey stone. Peeping out of the carriage window, Davina watched her father lift the great brass knocker and without a moment's hesitation hammer it against the door. Davina slipped out of the carriage and before the door had been opened was beside him.

In answer to his summons there came a liveried manservant who looked rather imperiously upon the visitors on the doorstep.

Lord Restharrow held out his card. 'We have come to see Mr Burdock,' he said stiffly, misliking the servant's manner.

The man ignored the outstretched card and sniffed.

'Neither Mr Burdock nor the rest of his family have resided here for a decade or more. The gentleman who owns it is a Mr Redberry.'

'Then may I speak with Mr Redberry to ascertain what he knows of the whereabouts of Mr Burdock?'

'I can give you that information,' said the servant. 'He lives at Dale End Cottage out the far end of the village.'

'Thank you for that information,' said Lord Restharrow, 'but I prefer to speak with your master.'

The servant sniffed again. 'I will discover if he is at home to visitors,' he said after a pause, then went away leaving them on the doorstep.

After some little while there was a noise from within the house and a jolly young man appeared rubbing his hands.

His manners and dress spoke of his origins in trade but he was much friendlier and more jovial than his servant.

'Come in, come in do,' he cried enthusiastically. 'Forgive my man, I beg. He does his best to ward off visitors. It is his only entertainment in this quiet little backwater.' He executed a neat bow. 'I am sorry, I did not catch your name nor the business which brings you here.'

Lord Restharrow forbore to blame the servant and while giving his name handed out his card.

'My lord, this is indeed an honour,' cried Mr Redberry, reminding Davina of a bright robin after whom she felt he should have been more aptly named.

'And who is this charming young lady?' Mr Redberry demanded. There was a moment's hesitation before Lord Restharrow found the right term.

'May I introduce Miss Stanley, my ward.'

Davina bit her lip to stop her crying out in dispute and bobbed him a curtsy. 'She is Mr Burdock's granddaughter and is anxious to make his acquaintance. We believed this was his address.'

'No, no.' Mr Redberry discarded his merry tone and moved closer to Davina. 'I am sorry to have to pain you but he fell upon hard times and had to sell the property as far back as '87. I believe, yes, yes I think that was when I bought it.'

Davina cleared her throat. 'My mother was used to send them financial assistance. Would you know if they received it?'

'Oh most certainly they did for I have been in the habit of delivering it myself, not wanting it to fall into the wrong hands.'

'You are most kind,' murmured Davina.

'Then if you could furnish us with their direction we will not trespass on your good nature any further,' said Lord Restharrow.

This he did then the jolly man accompanied them to the door with every good wish for a happy reunion between the parties.

On reaching the chaise it was clear that Lady Restharrow had discovered that her parents were no longer in the family home.

'What has become of them?' she cried as Davina re-entered the carriage. 'Tell me, I beg you, tell me their fate.'

Gently Lord Restharrow explained the history of the change in the Burdocks' circumstances. Lady Restharrow sank back against the squabs emitting an anguished sigh. They rested there for some little while, while father and daughter tried to calm her.

'It is worse than I feared,' she moaned, 'it is even less likely that they will receive me with good grace now.'

'By no means,' said Lord Restharrow bracingly, 'I have every confidence that their delight will be outstripped only by their relief. Onwards,' he called to the coachman, and gave them the direction before swinging up into the chaise as it moved off.

The cottage was down the far end of a narrow lane that petered out into a farm track. It was a picturesque abode with white-washed walls and a thatched roof but it was small and had never been designed as a gentleman's residence. There was a clipped hedge, which protected it from the road, that also formed an archway over the wooden gateway and there were the bare branches of climbing roses up the cottage wall as though every effort had been made to enhance the ambience of the cramped conditions. Even the small front garden had been planted with winter pansies whose cheerful little faces welcomed the visitor. The valiant nature of the whole ensemble lifted Davina's spirits appreciably. She tugged at Lord Restharrow's coat.

'Pray, let me go in alone, my lord,' she begged. 'I would break it to them gently.'

Lord Restharrow covered her hand with his and cast his eyes across the chaise to rest upon his wife. Her demeanour was cowed and she was dabbing her eyes with her lace handkerchief; he must have concluded that she was in greater need of his sustaining presence than his daughter was for he nodded his head.

'Very well,' he said.

The chaise had drawn up outside the gate and as Davina stooped to get out of the door Lady Restharrow put up a hand to stop her but let it fall. There was no going back now.

Davina went resolutely through the gate and knocked on the black door. It was answered with a speed compatible with the size of the cottage. No one therein would have been far from the front door.

A young and comely maid in painstakingly tidy but simple uniform opened the door.

'My name is Miss Stanley and I have come to call on Mr and Mrs Burdock,' Davina stated as calmly as she could in answer to the girl's look of mute enquiry.

The maid ushered her into the cottage and Davina found herself immediately in the parlour.

A tall grey-haired lady arrayed in cheerful blues and mauves stood up from her chair. On spying Davina she gave an exclamation of surprise but before she could say anything, there was a joyous squeak from a woman with childlike features. She made a rush for Davina.

'Davida,' she cried, 'Davida, I knew you would come home one day.'

24

*M*rs Burdock made a move to constrain her simple-minded daughter but when she saw how sweetly the visitor handled her, she halted.

'Hello Aunt Grace,' said Davina, smiling into the strangely vacant eyes. 'Yes, I have brought Davida home for you, but I am not she. I am her daughter, Davina.'

Mrs Burdock let out an exhale of pure excitement. She clapped her hands together. 'If you only knew how long I have waited for this day,' she cried. 'Come quickly, tell me where my daughter is.'

'She is out in the chaise, fearful that you might not wish to receive her.'

'Not receive her, good heavens why should I not? She has been our saviour over the years. We have known we were ever in her thoughts as she was in ours.'

'Then let me fetch her in,' said Davina, turning to the front door.

'No, no.' Grace's anguished cry as much as the force with which she clung to Davina's arm, prevented the girl from moving. 'Don't leave me again, don't leave me,' she wailed.

'Betty, Betty,' Mrs Burdock called back the maid. 'Fetch Mr Burdock from the kitchen garden will you please?' she commanded, then she walked up to her agitated daughter and tried to comfort her but she was pushed away.

'Davida, Davida,' she repeated over and over again.

'Perhaps it would be better if you went out to the chaise ma'am,' said Davina, 'I will remain with her.'

The older woman nodded and slipped out round the front door.

Davina stood for a little while with her arms around her aunt trying to think of how to settle her. Then gently she attempted to guide her to a chair.

'Come sweet aunt,' she said, 'let us be seated and you can tell me what you recall of your sister Davida. I would like to know more about her childhood.'

'She was as beautiful as you,' said a deep voice from the doorway at the back of the room, 'with glowing hair and a capacity for love well beyond the norm. You have the very look of her.'

Davina would have liked to go to him, so drawn was she by her grandfather's kind face. He was a thickset man with grey sideburns that travelled far down the side of his ruddy cheeks. He was dressed in working clothes and his hands were callused. Davina did not need reminding that he had been recalled from the garden to know that he had been labouring there. However she could not go to him because she was pinioned by her aunt's attentions. The troubled lady was now patting and stroking Davina's arm.

'Have you travelled far?' asked the old man, trying to find his bearings.

'From Minchinhampnett in Gloucestershire, a four-day drive.'

'Well this is marvellous indeed,' he said drawing closer and reaching for a log from the basket by the fire. He began to stoke the embers. 'And what has prompted such a trek?'

'I'm afraid it was at mine insistence,' said Davina in a small voice, 'I could no longer support the absence of a wider family circle. I wanted to know my relations. I am conscious that I may have over-persuaded my mother to her detriment and,' she broke off and looked at the bowed head of her aunt, 'I did not realise it would affect my aunt so adversely.'

The old man had risen from his place on the hearth and now

stood over her. 'Do not let that give you a moment's disquiet. Although I would not wish your mother to know it, there has not been a day in nearly twenty years when your aunt has not asked for her. You must know that the weakness of her mind means that she is locked into her childhood forever. Davida was a daily part of that childhood which was suddenly and inexplicably wrenched away.'

Davina did not know what to say. She marvelled at the even way the man spoke and the manner in which she had been received. These people who had been dealt many a blow throughout their lifetime had found a cheerful form of acceptance and had filled their lives with simple pleasures like the abundance of the garden or the charm of the decor in their tiny parlour.

The front door was opened and suddenly the room seemed very full. Lord Restharrow, a tall man, appearing even taller under the low ceiling of the cottage, Lady Restharrow and Mrs Burdock all came in from the cold. Mrs Burdock appeared as reconciled to the situation as her husband. It calmed Davina's qualms but as yet had not quite soothed Lady Restharrow's misgivings.

'Come,' said Mrs Burdock, taking her prodigal daughter's arm and leading her to her sister's chair, 'make yourself known to Grace.'

'Hello Grace,' said Lady Restharrow in a voice that quivered slightly.

The childlike woman in the floral dress looked up at the use of her name but there was no recognition there.

'My sister Davida has come home,' she told the stranger looking down at her, 'she has come home. She is never going away again.'

'I will have to go in a sennight Grace,' said Lady Restharrow, not quite grasping that she was not her object but Davina. 'I have a marriage ceremony to attend in Hampshire. Let me introduce you to Lord Restharrow, my husband, do you not remember him?'

Grace moved her eyes to the man's face but they still held the blank look of incomprehension they had contained when they had rested on his wife.

'Davida is here,' she said, 'Davida has come home.'

There was silence as each member of her audience adjusted their thinking to take account of this new twist. The poor woman's ailing mind could only recognise Davida as she had been and could make no allowances for the passage of time. She had a brand new Davida restored to her; no older alternative no matter how chic and beautiful would do.

Mrs Burdock turned to her husband who in response to her look quitted the room and went to the kitchen. It was not many minutes before he returned with some wine. Betty, the maid, who brought in a tray of figs, walnuts and hazelnuts at which Davina could only exclaim, followed him.

Seeing her expression her grandfather smiled. 'Succession houses were always my hobby,' he said. 'When we moved here with no library or pool table to pass the time of day, encouraged by your grandmother, I built cloches and a small glasshouse. I have grown figs and a magnificent walnut tree in the centre of the garden. We also gather hazelnuts on walks with your aunt.' He cracked a walnut for her and handed it to her.

Grace watched doe-eyed as she ate it. Gradually the tension eased and Lady Restharrow was persuaded to take one of the two vacant chairs.

'You are too good,' she said to her mother, 'to receive me so.' She paused and let a shudder of escaping emotion wrack her body. 'You have suffered so much in my absence and I am guilty of having abandoned you.'

'How can you speak so,' demanded her mother. 'We were distraught when you disappeared, but as the days passed and there was no news of you, we came to think of you as not wishing to be discovered. Other troubles assailed us, your father's stocks became worthless and he tried to restore our fortunes by gambling on new ventures. I am afraid the upshot of these ventures resulted in the sale of the house. Those were dark times and I knew not where to turn for the money to keep your sister and your father, who was ailing at this time because of the collapse of his hopes. Then came the day when Mr Redberry arrived with a package from you. From that day on our fortunes improved. You gave us back our self-esteem. I could buy the little luxuries for Grace. Your father recovered his health and took up his gardening. I knew that one-day you would find your way back to us.' She smiled at her daughter warmly. 'What I did not expect was that you would return in the guise of this beautiful young woman;' she indicated Davina still sitting tranquilly attending to Grace. 'Now tell me what has become of you over this time.'

The rest of the day was taken up with the telling of Lady Restharrow's life history thus far. There was no attempt to disguise the truth. Lord Restharrow was drawn into the story of her youth and though Mr Burdock shook his head disapprovingly when he heard of the contrived border marriage, he did not castigate them. They asked for his forgiveness and were given it absolutely.

When talk turned to the forthcoming marriage ceremony, the Burdocks nodded sagely and agreed that it was necessary. Davina demurred again, citing her wish for recognition as her father's legitimate daughter. Her agitation conveyed itself to Grace and it unsettled her again. She clung closer to Davina.

'No Davida, no,' she whispered, 'stay with me. Let them go. You stay with me. We are safe here.'

It was a wearing day for Davina; it was not until Grace could be persuaded to bed that Davina was eventually released from her grasp. Davina sat holding her hand until she fell asleep as abruptly and as deeply as a child. When Davina tiptoed down the narrow wooden stairs there were gentle tears cascading down her cheeks. She had to pause in the dark little hallway behind the parlour door to compose herself.

When she returned to the parlour her grandmother and then her grandfather embraced her.

'You have been so kind to her,' said Mrs Burdock, 'I trust that a night's repose will steady her.'

Some little while later Lord and Lady Restharrow moved to leave. There were only two bedrooms and a boxroom in the cottage; nowhere for them to stay.

Mr and Mrs Burdock made no attempt to stop them but invited them back for the next day. Davina stood undecided; she wanted to stay, not only for herself but for the aunt who she feared would react adversely if she was not there the next morning.

'What troubles you, my dear?' asked her grandfather, watching the delicate face transparent in its dilemma.

'Would you permit me to stay here with you?' she asked tentatively. 'Would it inconvenience you too much if I remained here?'

Mrs Burdock flurried into action. 'No, no, indeed an excellent idea. Grace will want to see you as soon as she wakes. Come, I will put up a truckle bed for you in her room.'

The next few days were a blur of happy revelation to Davina. With her aunt, who accompanied her dog-like wherever she went, she marvelled at her grandfather's kitchen garden, she admired her grandmother's stitchery which outstripped even her mother's in excellence and she cosseted the chickens which nominally belonged to Grace. Grace's adoration did not diminish nor did she waver from her certainty that Davina was her sister. Lady Restharrow looked on more in sorrow than in envy. The clinging nature of her sister's attention smote her with remorse and left her deeply concerned for the future. Her only solution, which she discussed persistently with Lord Restharrow when they were alone, was that they should take her parents and sister south with them. Although she saw this as imprisoning Davina by her own good nature, the distress it would cause Grace to be parted from Davina was almost too much for Lady Restharrow to contemplate.

She put her suggestion first to her mother.

'Would you consider coming to Restharrow Hall with me,

Mama? Lord Restharrow assures me that you would all be most welcome.'

Mrs Burdock knew that her daughter was driven by feelings of guilt and considered this a very unhealthy basis on which to make such a momentous change in their circumstances. Thus her initial response was tentative and unenthusiastic.

'The upheaval, my dear, would be too much for your sister and I cannot ask your father to give up his garden.'

However, when he was asked, Mr Burdock merely laughed and with a merry twinkle in his eye assured his daughter that he would be quite willing to be given another chance to sport the character of a gentleman again.

'You could not leave all the work you have done here, surely?' his wife demanded, aghast at his response.

'But I could, you know,' he said, 'the labouring takes its toll and my body has begun to protest its age. And if in forsaking it, I miss it, no doubt you would provide me with a small patch on which to continue my craft.'

'Yes, of course,' agreed his daughter hastily. 'I am so glad,' she continued on a deep sigh, 'then we are agreed are we not?'

It was only when they were gently trying to explain the move to Grace that Davina became aware of the machinations,which were proposed and halfway to being executed.

'But this cannot be,' cried the girl in much distress, starting up from her chair. 'I am not living at Restharrow Hall. You cannot expect it of me.'

'Davina, Davina,' cried her mother, considerably alarmed by the witness of her daughter's reaction, 'what are you saying?'

Mindful of how heightened emotions upset her aunt, Davina drew a steadying breath. 'Mama, my lord, you know I have tried to be a dutiful daughter, the biddable child, but you must let me have my way in this, I beseech you.'

'What is your way, Davina?' asked her grandmother.

'That I might return to Fromeview Place and take up occupation there,' said Davina quietly.

'Good heavens, child, why should you want to?' demanded her mother.

'It is my home, Mama.'

'Your home yes but we are no longer welcome there!'

'Outside its gates possibly but within its walls it has served us well. I would go there with Grace and my grandparents if they would come.'

There was silence as her audience digested this alternative. Mr Burdock was the first to speak. 'It is a wise choice, Davida,' he said. 'You and your husband have been thrown together after twenty years of separation. You need to know each other again, to plan your future. You are still young enough to have more children.'

'Father, please,' protested Lady Restharrow blushing.

The old man gave a mock bow. 'We would be much in your way and you tell us the house is in bad repair. Sparing your feelings, my lord, such a place would not be safe for Grace. Davina is more right than she knows. We would be much better staying quietly and safely in Gloucestershire.'

The decision reached, it did not take long to pack up the few contents of the cottage and have them loaded on the carrier. Mr Burdock had taken a last look around his garden before handing the keys over to Betty, the maid. Providentially Betty was due to wed a young labourer from the neighbouring estate. The two of them were to make Dale End Cottage their home and had promised to keep up the gardens.

So the family was waved a tearful farewell by Betty not eight days after the surprise arrival of their elder daughter. Progress was good at first, while Grace was enthralled by everything like an excited child, but the second day boredom had set in and she could not be settled unless Davina played endless, foolish games to entertain her. Mrs Burdock became anxious that Davina would become too tired and begged a day's rest at a little place called Siddington just south of Manchester. The day was spent walking through the village to watch the blacksmith and playing with a bundle of kittens belonging to the guest house's cat.

The following day was not so fatiguing as Grace had one of her sleepy days so she dozed for hours as the chaises continued south. When they finally reached Gloucestershire some three days later, no one even for a moment thought it would be reasonable to convey Grace any further.

Time was marching on and the wedding day was looming large. Lord and Lady Restharrow could not afford many a day to settle the family into their new home but luckily Mrs Tulley took to Mrs Burdock and had sympathy for Grace, so there was no great need for them to tarry.

Davina, still revelling in the warmth of the regard of her grandparents witnessed her mother's departure without a pang. She knew that her mother had a real chance now of happiness. Lord Restharrow was clearly as smitten with the real Davida as he had been with the memory of her. Davina could only be glad because the relationship between herself and her mother had undergone such a material change. She no longer saw herself as the unquestioningly obedient daughter, she now knew she had a will of her own. This will as it stood was impotent. Opinions in the district had not changed in the time they were away. Whatever Charlie might have said to the Greenaways had not yet altered their behaviour towards Miss Stanley and the village took their lead from the church.

25

*R*everend Greenaway had made his decision. Initially after the revelations about the duplicity his child, her lover and friend had practised on the world, he ruled out of hand any engagement with such an unworthy recipient of his blessing. However as the days passed it percolated through his thoughts that he might find he had rejected the only man who could support Ernestine's histrionics and who was conscious of what she was capable. Some uninitiated fool might be gulled into any manner of scrapes. Charlie at least loved her and was well aware of her faults. It was even possible that given the rumours about her unsteadiness, no other man might come forward. Reverend Greenaway, toiling away in his study late at night, eventually came to the conclusion that he would have to sanction the betrothal between his third daughter and Charles Winstanleigh, however much he disliked it and notwithstanding his many reservations.

It took him some days to inform his wife of his decision. He still carried with him a certain grievance against her. As hard as he might try to rationalise her behaviour, he could not shake off the feeling that she had put her own considerations ahead of his daughter's. He also felt it had been wrong to expose Davina to the censure of polite society but she had done it in an attempt to keep her sister's family out of debt. Both Ernestine and Davina had been sacrificed without a qualm. This did not rest easily with his ministry of care for his flock. He had promised before the

Fromeview family had returned from the north that Mrs Greenaway and Ernestine should go and make their apologies to Miss Stanley. This had not been done, Mrs Greenaway clinging to the pretext that the arrival of the unknown Burdocks made it much better form if Revd. Greenaway made a visit of ceremony first.

So the weeks drifted by with the occupants of Fromeview remaining in isolation. It was only when Lady Purslane, accompanied by the Honourable Amelia, came to bring her children on a visit to their grandparents that the omission was discovered.

'I cannot presume to dictate to you Mama,' said Lady Purslane angrily, 'but I will take Ernestine to visit Miss Stanley. She owes her that much.'

As good as her word, Lady Purslane abandoned Amelia to the few entertainments of a rural community and took Ernestine to Fromeview Place.

The arrival of a smart carriage caused quite a stir, such an unusual occurrence as it was. On hearing its description Davina's heart fluttered with the hope that it was Lord Louis although she was not much disappointed when she discovered who it was in his stead.

She embraced Lady Purslane warmly but found she could only execute a chilly curtsy to Ernestine.

Ernestine was still pale from her ordeal. She was dressed much more simply than had been her habit. The frills and lace were gone along with the soft curls around her face. She had lost weight and Davina felt a stirring of pity for her.

There was an awkward silence after the greetings had taken place. Davina, still constantly shadowed by her aunt had been fortunate enough to escape her attentions for an hour as Mr Burdock had taken her off to see an early lamb which had been spotted on the common. Davina indicated to the ladies to sit down and then perched herself on the edge of a chair.

'Do you make a long stay, Lady Purslane?' she managed after an inner struggle.

'Some three weeks,' replied the lady. 'Sir Hugh has been posted abroad, so I took the opportunity to visit my mother. The children have not seen their grandparents this year out.' She cleared her throat slightly and straightened her back. 'Amelia has been good enough to take up residence with me while Sir Hugh is away. You know you would be most welcome to stay the Season with us.'

'You are very kind,' said Davina quickly, 'but I have my family staying and my aunt does not like to be much parted from me.'

'So I understand,' said Lady Purslane although Davina could not fathom where she might have come by her information. 'Is there no cure for the poor soul?'

Davina shook her head. 'No, it is an accident of birth, she has been like it all her life.'

'You are to be pitied.'

'How so? I think not, she is a delightful and easy companion,' countered Davina defensively.

'Oh I mean no disrespect, my dear, but if it curtails your activities you must surely find it a little tedious?'

'It curtails my activities less than the treatment we have received from our sometime friends and neighbours,' said Davina looking briefly but coldly at Ernestine.

'Oh Davina do not say so,' wailed Ernestine at last, her voice almost a whisper. 'If you knew how much I long for your forgiveness, you would not use me so harshly.'

'Long for my forgiveness,' said Davina in patent disbelief. 'I have no evidence of that, I have seen nothing of you since my return to Fromeview in the summer and I am sure you would not be here now if it were not for your sister's insistence.'

'Indeed I know it but it is not lack of inclination but lack of courage which has prevented me.'

Davina emitted only an exclamation of annoyance and turned her head aside. Ernestine got up unsteadily from her chair and sank to the ground at Davina's feet.

'Davina, I am so sorry,' she said grasping at Davina's inert hands. 'Please, please forgive me. I know I have behaved abominably. So many times I have wished I had not done it.'

Davina braved a look down into the mobile face below her. 'Why Ernestine?' she said quietly, 'why did you do it? Why did you feign so much illness, why did you put Charlie and I through the emotional mangle? If you knew how much we suffered. We were playing a dangerous and difficult game and you increasingly exposed us to more censure.'

'I know, I know.' Ernestine waved her head from side to side. 'I know I did, it was unforgivable.'

'I think Davina is entitled to an explanation,' said Lady Purslane from her point as witness to this scene. 'Indeed I feel the need for some explanation. You were the instigator of this plan, Ernestine. It was put in place ultimately for your benefit yet you sabotaged it at every turn. Instead of giving Charlie time to exhibit his new attachment, you kept summoning him back to Gloucestershire to attend your sickbed.

'But don't you see?' cried Ernestine in some anguish. 'Can't you see? Look at Davina. Is she not beautiful? Is she not talented? Does she not exhibit a natural charm of manner and obvious kindness? When I compared my charms to hers, I found myself profoundly wanting. I had conceived the plan in the height of our anxieties but when I had leisure to study it, I realised I had forced my love into the arms of someone so much more appealing than myself.'

'What nonsense,' said her sister heartily. 'Your charms may be different from Davina's but I am sure she would be the first to admit, they are as many.' She turned on Davina in mute interrogation.

Davina however was silent, her head now bowed over her lap. The others waited for her to break that silence. When she lifted her head it was to be seen that there was an angry light smouldering in her eyes.

'You were my friend, Ernestine,' she said in a voice which throbbed, 'my friend. Do you really believe that I would steal your fiancé? Do you really believe that I would? That is the unkindest cut you could make. I would never have failed you, never,' she fumed.

'I know that now Davina, but picture me, I beg. Far away from the man I loved, confined to home when you were enjoying freedoms of the Season. I had no other pastime than to fancy myself ill used.'

'That's as maybe,' said Davina unmollified, 'but you were living a better life than many. Could you not have gritted your teeth and waited it out?'

'I wish I had, I so very nearly paid the ultimate price for my folly.'

These words gave Davina pause. 'I know you did,' she said at last, her voice gentler now. Suddenly she pulled Ernestine to her feet and embraced her. 'I forgive you!' she said.

26

*T*here was no immediate improvement in relations between the censorious world and the occupants of Fromeview Place. The Rector, hard pressed by his Christmas commitments continued to put off his visit of ceremony. Mrs Greenaway assumed that the visit from her daughters would do the trick but the visit had gone unnoticed by the gossips and Ernestine, still cowed by her own culpability did not advertise it. The many services at Christmas should have allowed for a much more public reconciliation. Sadly Grace was unable to sit through a lengthy church service without becoming bored and noisy so Mr and Mrs Burdock had to leave her behind with Davina while they carried out their worship, and Davina had to content herself with attending the early morning communion before her aunt awoke. As her swift departure at the end of each service smacked of flight, this arrangement only fuelled the gossip. It was obvious, to those who enjoyed making the connection, that Miss Stanley preferred the early morning service because it was conducted by the meek curate and not the Rector. Nobody took much account of the fact that she sat in the same pew as Miss Annabelle Greenaway and that they exchanged conspiratorial smiles.

Davina had hoped that once the announcement of her mother's marriage to Lord Restharrow was made known and the betrothal of Charlie and Ernestine made public that her old friends would return to her, but they did not. There was much smug sniggering and a sense that justice had been done in the fact that Davina remained a spinster and nothing altered. Inside Fromeview there was the quiet dignity of carrying out the daily chores but their inclusion in the Minchinhampnett society was non-existent.

Lord Louis Twayblade had remained in Scotland so long that his mother was beginning to be seriously concerned for his well being.

The second marchioness, Lady Sainfoin, was a remarkable woman. Despite having been pressed by her father into marrying a man twice her age some six and twenty years before, she had maintained both her dark beauty from which her sons got their colouring and her lively spirit. She had always longed for excitement but had known as soon as she was committed to the Marquis that her place would be in his turreted Scottish castle, divorced from the society she longed to embrace. Lord Sainfoin, much like his heir, Viscount Campion, had never been addicted to assemblies or balls, he enjoyed the chase or the shoot. His lovely young wife was left to make the best of it. The first long winter, she thought she would die of boredom and then she was delivered of her first son and her world changed. She was a fond and doting parent, who was forever finding ways to entertain her ever-lengthening line of sons. She indulged her love of France and instructed them in French, naming each fresh son with a romantic French-sounding name. To date she had presented her husband with Louis, Etienne, Fabien, Patrice, Henri, Jean Luc, Pierre and most recently Guillaume.

It was while she was nursing her youngest son and marvelling at the contrast between the dark quiff of hair against the whiteness of her breast that her mind began to wander to her concerns about her first born. She had been so delighted when she had discovered in him a wanderlust that had never been sated in her. She had encouraged him to take up any invitation, to travel as far and as fast as the mood took him. Her only stipulation was that he should write her exciting descriptive letters, which were not sanitised for his mother's eyes. He had been faithful in this regard and she had travelled by proxy now to so many house parties and enjoyed such numerous seasons that she no longer felt hard done by. Lord Louis had, it seemed also encouraged others to take up their quill and she now had a whole host of penfriends with whom she corresponded regularly. It was their letters to which she turned to try and discover what lay at the bottom of Lord Louis's uncharacteristic behaviour. He had left Sainfoin Castle only once since the beginning of August and her intuition told her that that had only been because Lord Campion had been roasting him that he must be getting old to stay at home so long.

The letters that had seemed bland and innocuous on first reading had on a second perusal had a constant thread. Lady B had been at Mrs D's turtle dinner, Louis had sung with a Miss Stanley. Mrs C had supped at Lord and Lady K's, Louis and Miss Stanley had entertained them with a song after dinner. Mrs W had been to Sir and Lady M's soirée; amongst those called upon to perform there had been Lord Louis and Miss Stanley. After finding some six occurrences of this, Lady Sainfoin marvelled at her own blindness. She scoured the letters for more information about Miss Stanley but beyond the occasional descriptive word such as beautiful, charming, talented and elegant, Lady Sainfoin could find nothing. Equally there was no mention of her in any of Louis's letters. The girl was an enigma with no obvious family or connections. Lady Sainfoin began to understand her son's dilemma.

She spent some days trying to find a moment to talk to Lord Louis in private but there was one difference between Lord Sainfoin and Lord Campion. While neither liked to attend other people's venues, Lord Campion enjoyed having people to stay; he was forever inviting whole parties of people to shoot or to go stalking. Lord Sainfoin would retire to the east wing of the castle and let his son's guests run tame everywhere else.

It was not until there was a lull of some three days between one party leaving and the next arriving that Lady Sainfoin hoped to catch Lord Louis. Her luck it seemed had turned, on the second morning she found him alone in the breakfast parlour.

Lady Sainfoin stopped in the doorway, so great was her surprise.

'Where are your brothers?' she asked abruptly, fearful of interruption.

'Etienne and Fabien have come in from their ride and taken Campion out to the stables. I believe one of the horses came in lame, they want him to advise them,' replied her son in an offhand manner.

He had stood up from his meal on her arrival but resumed his seat almost before the footman had placed hers under her. She waited until the servant had withdrawn.

Lady Sainfoin studied him out of eyes, which were framed by the same dark lashes as his. For a moment her mind grappled with the knowledge that she had borne him. Upstairs was a tiny bundle, which, God willing, would one day match him in stature. It still filled her with wonder.

He caught her looking at him and lifted an eyebrow in inquiry. Hastily Lady Sainfoin picked up a newspaper, she was not quite ready to confront him yet.

The paper was open at the court and social page. Her eyes widened.

'Have you seen this?' she asked quietly.

Lord Louis remained unmoved. 'Seen what?'

Lady Sainfoin began to read: 'The marriage between Carmichael Winstanleigh 3rd Baron Restharrow and Davida Stanley is announced.'

'Davina,' corrected Lord Louis absently before the information sank in.

'And further down,' continued Lady Sainfoin quickly as she saw realisation smite him, 'it announces the betrothal of your friend Charles Winstanleigh to a Miss Ernestine Greenaway, daughter of a rector in Gloucestershire.'

There was silence. Lady Sainfoin put down the newspaper

with exaggerated care, folding it neatly, determined not to be the first to speak.

Lord Louis stood up, thrusting his chair backwards with a jab of anger. 'So they snared her in the end!' he said bitterly.

'Snared?' asked his mother surprised. 'What can you mean?' She put out a hand to him but he shied away from her.

'I cannot talk of it now, mother,' he said and slammed out of the room.

Lady Sainfoin did not repine at her failure to communicate with her son. She knew she had breached his defences and that when he was ready he would search her out himself.

It was later that evening when Lady Sainfoin was settling the infant Guillaume for the night, a little ritual a whole retinue of nannies and nursery maids had never persuaded her to forfeit, that Lord Louis, certain of where she would be, sought her out.

Casting a look of concern at his face, Lady Sainfoin drew the coverlet over the baby's shoulders and then shepherded her eldest son out of the nursery and into the adjoining schoolroom. In wordless harmony they lit the candles around the walls and then Lady Sainfoin, positioning herself at the governess's lectern, smiled sympathetically at her son.

'Tell me your troubles, dearest,' she said, 'for I know you are not yourself. Your brothers have never before complained of your lack of attention to them.'

Lord Louis, folding his long form in behind one of the diminutive wooden desks, sat on the adjoining chair and began to fiddle with a quill, which was resting on the desk. After a moment's thought he got out a knife from the desk and began to sharpen the nib.

Lady Sainfoin did not again prompt him; instead she studied with some pride the deep lustre on his dark waving hair and the fine line of his nose and overdefined eyes. She was proud of all her long line of sons but Louis had always demonstrated an affinity with her own aspirations that the others could not boast. She awaited his pleasure.

'I presume you have discovered in me an attachment to Miss Davina Stanley,' he began heavily.

'I believe so,' agreed his mother.

'You believe aright.' He shot her a look from under his lashes. 'From the first, you understand, I was drawn to her, she is so beautiful, so ...'

'Spare me the details of her appearance, Louis,' said Lady Sainfoin. 'I have read of that. It is her character of which I am in ignorance.'

'Her character,' the quill snapped in his hand, 'her character is flawed by too strong a sense of duty,' he growled.

'How so?' demanded the lady. 'Is not duty a virtue in a woman? In a wife?'

'Possibly,' he conceded, 'if it is directed at the right person.'

'And Miss Stanley directed it at the wrong one?'

'Oh most certainly! She had aligned herself to Charlie Winstanleigh under pressure from Lady Thistledown.' Lord Louis extracted himself from his cramped position and began to pace the area between the lectern and the half dozen desks. 'You must know that the Winstanleighs have been in debt forever,' he said, 'and that Charlie has had an understanding with Miss Greenaway.'

Lady Sainfoin nodded. 'You have told me as much in the past.'

'When he announced his engagement to Miss Stanley I tried to put him off. She may have figure and fortune but she had no history, no lineage. It was not well done in me, for she overheard and recoiled from me.'

'I am not surprised,' said his mother whimsically.

'This is no laughing matter, Mama,' responded Lord Louis, turning to brace his hands against the front of the lectern. He looked into her eyes fiercely. 'Throughout the Season, we were thrown together and I became more and more determined that the marriage would not do. Not for his sake now but for hers.' He drew an angry breath. 'She would not waver though, despite all Charlie's perfidies. You must know that I had it on good authority that he still visited Miss Greenaway regularly.'

'Did you offer for her, Louis?' asked Lady Sainfoin.

'Mama! How can you ask such a thing?' His eyes blazed at the effrontery of the question.

'And why not!' countered his mother, not in the least chastened. 'You might have offered the lady a way out of the tangle.'

'You are not listening to me,' cried her son in anguish and flung away again. 'She did not want a way out or so I thought. God knows what contrivance has forced her into the arms of Restharrow. I cannot credit it. Saving your presence Mama, the man is old enough to be her father.'

Lady Sainfoin was silenced. She thought of the unknown girl starting out in a life with a man more than twenty years her senior and shivered at the prospect.

Noticing, Lord Louis came over to her. 'You are cold, Mama, we should leave this room. No doubt dinner will soon be served.

'Let it await our pleasure,' said the lady, putting up a hand to push back a lock of her son's hair.

'Why did you not make a push to get her released, Louis? You are not telling me all. Your credit in Society would have carried it off. As your wife she would have been received whatever her background.'

'Do I not know it,' he said bitterly. 'Setting aside my duty as Charlie's friend, it was not Society I feared but my father. Would he have accepted such a girl?'

Lady Sainfoin seemed to consider for a moment. 'Yes I believe he would have,' she said slowly. 'You see he sets little store by Society and its fashions.'

'Well,' said Lord Louis as he went to hold the door for his mother to quit the room, 'it is of no account now, is it?'

27

*L*ord Louis did as his mother requested and took his brothers Patrice, Henri and Jean Luc on rides when the weather was not inclement. He suffered to play pool with them and was once again pronounced to be their favourite elder brother but he carried out these tasks with a heavy heart and the smile on his face was seen to be forced and rigid. Lady Sainfoin was in despair but she knew there was nothing further she could do but bear with his crotchets and let him vent his unhappiness on her.

Another party full of guests had gone and been replaced by a parcel of Lord Campion's contemporaries from his time at Eton. As a result they had been wont to visit Sainfoin Castle over a period of many years and were on terms of some intimacy with most of the family members. Lord Louis paid lip service to their raillery and even ventured a laugh at some of their richer jests but he was brought up short one evening after the ladies had retired from the dinner table when one, Sir Geoffrey Sythe, began to talk. He had done so as a result of a prompt from Lord Campion, who in the absence of his father was sitting commandingly at the head of the table, his square figure perfectly in tune with the baronial nature of the dining hall.

'So come now, Sythe,' had cried Lord Campion, glass of port raised in his hand, 'you are the one amongst us who has all the latest on dits. Entertain us with the current tittle-tattle.'

Sir Geoffrey Sythe, who was proud of his ability to worm out information about the upper ten thousand smirked and in Lord Louis's eyes seemed to swell with self-importance. He began to go through his repertoire of names, many known to Lord Louis but few of interest when suddenly Sythe turned in his chair and looked up the long table at his host.

'But I have saved the finest till last for you Campion,' he said. 'Do you recall Carmichael Winstanleigh from our school days?'

'Of course I do, he was our prefect when I was first there. A fair man but solemn even then. I gather he recently wed after years of withstanding the estate.'

'Ay he did and this is the nub of the matter. He has married a widowed lady, named Stanley, of unknown origin but a mystery surrounds the affair as the lady has a daughter.'

Lord Campion sipped his port and seemed unimpressed. He had not seen his brother stiffen or he would have been more avid for information.

'Oh come, come, many a widow has a daughter, what of it?'

'Well society has seen the daughter, have they not, Lord Louis?' Suddenly the unwelcome attention of the room was directed at Lord Louis.

'If you mean Miss Davina Stanley, then yes.' Louis managed, by superhuman effort, to keep his voice steady.

'There was some talk that your little brother had some interest in her, Campion,' said a Mr Walter Hill mischievously, on his lordship's right, 'but it came to nought.'

Lord Louis kept his countenance but only just. He gave a valiant and hopefully dismissive laugh.

Lord Campion's interest was caught. 'So what of this gel, Sythe? How has she caught the *ton*'s interest?'

'Why, because my lord, she has the look of Restharrow and opinion is divided. Some think she is his peccadillo, a base-born daughter, while others cite his refusal over the years to take a bride. They suggest she is his legitimate daughter.'

'And which explanation do you favour Sythe?' asked Lord Louis, a hint of derision in his tone.

Sir Geoffrey Sythe cast him a look of loathing. Trust Lord Louis to want a judgement now. Sythe was not ready to commit to either camp; that was not the way to catch all the gossip. He saw a way out.

'I would think you better placed to judge than I, Twayblade,' he said.

Lord Louis shrugged and signalled for the decanter that had passed him by the first time. He filled his glass and raised it to the opulent room. 'Touché,' was all he said.

Lady Sainfoin, who had well-trodden routes by which she became a party to the goings on in the dining hall after the ladies had retired, was in possession of some very interesting information by seven o'clock the next morning. She was thus not surprised to find her eldest son clad for a journey when she descended in search of her breakfast.

'You are not going without taking leave of your father, are you?' she said hurriedly as it appeared to her he was already impatient to be gone.

'No, of course not,' he said turning on his heel and making for the east wing. Lady Sainfoin had to lift her skirts to keep up with him.

Lord Sainfoin was not yet dressed. He was sitting in a chair swathed in a brocade dressing gown in his panelled dressing room while his valet exhibited before him a number of coats from which he might make his choice for the day. On acknowledging the deputation before him, Lord Sainfoin dismissed his manservant.

'I see you are leaving us,' he said to his son. 'This is a sudden change of heart, what brings this about?'

This mild approach rather threw Lord Louis who had long been in awe of his austere father.

'I go Sir,' he said executing a formal bow, 'by your leave, to make an offer of marriage to a young lady.'

'And is this young lady the one your mother has spoken of to me?'

Lord Louis glanced at his mother whose face was crimson. 'Very probably, my lord,' he said.

'And is it the young lady discussed at table last night?'

Lord Louis's eyes widened, wondering at his father's information. 'Yes Sir,' he said.

'And do you know her true estate?' The questions were coming at him now like volleys from a gun. Lord Louis wished he had slunk from the castle as he had intended rather than facing this interview.

Lord Sainfoin sat very straight in his chair. He wore a grey wig despite being en déshabillé but he was clean-shaven. He had been a handsome man in his youth and life had been good to him; he had rarely had to exert himself except in the field of sport. His wealth and his bearing placed him on a pedestal, which even his sons could not scale. His remoteness was legendary. Lord Louis was baffled by his interest now.

'I believe her to be of legitimate birth,' said Lord Louis with as much conviction as he could muster.

'Do you?' asked his mother 'Do you?'

'Yes, yes I do,' Lord Louis assured her. 'You know that I did not use to but over the summer those thoughts were dispelled.' He drew in a huge breath and stood his full height, 'but frankly, Sir, I do not care. I would marry her whatever her parentage.'

'This is spirited talk, Louis,' said his father, surprising him that he knew which one of his many sons he was. To Louis it seemed that Lord Sainfoin had only ever acknowledged his heir. 'What of her fortune, is that genuine?'

'There can be no doubt of it, Sir.'

'Then I will not stand in your way,' pronounced his lordship, surprising his audience still further. Lord Sainfoin gave a crack of laughter. 'Do not stand there and gawp at me,' he said to his wife and son. 'You know as I do, that at any time Campion could marry and beget an heir. Divided between you and your brothers, the unentailed funds would only result in a competence, not a flush living. A wealthy wife would be a good insurance.'

'It is not for that reason that I would marry her, Sir,' said Lord Louis.

'Good God, I know that, but this I would request of you.'

'Yes.'

'Ascertain the truth yourself before you wed her. I care not which side of the blanket Restharrow begat her but I want you to know the truth before you marry her.'

'And how Sir might I do that?' asked Lord Louis feeling suddenly deflated, fearing that his father had found an unassailable obstacle without even exercising his veto.

'I would try with the parish records at Gretna first,' said his father, waving his hand in dismissal.

Lord Louis saw no reason to take leave of his elder brother and his friends. They had left early on a day's stalking and would not think anything of his disappearance, common as it had been in the past.

He had already said his goodbyes to his young brothers but now Etienne awaited him in the hall. He was a shorter, thinner version of Lord Louis. There was the warm light of affection shining in his eyes as they settled on his brother.

'I will accompany you as far as Gretna,' he said, 'so that I can bring back the information you find there.'

'Good God, is nothing sacred?' cried Lord Louis. 'How have you come by the information about my plans?'

Etienne laughed. 'I met Mother in the corridor,' he said, slapping his brother on the back and bundling him towards the door.

Snow had fallen over the last few days but it was not thick, the horses made good progress and it was not two days later that they arrived at Gretna and viewed the parish records. There, plain for both to see, was the marriage of The Hon Carmichael Winstanleigh and Miss Davida Burdock. On request and after a handsome gratuity, the minister in charge made them a copy of it. Lord Louis took the scroll and rolled it up, placing it securely in his breast pocket.

'She is mine now,' he said to his brother as he waved his coach a fond farewell.

28

*I*t was in fact more than a fortnight later that Lord Louis's chaise drew up outside Fromeview Place. It was not that his ardour had cooled but the fickle weather had turned against him and he had been forced to take refuge at a cousin's house near Lancaster. In other years he had been wont to spend some three weeks as her guest at this season, so he could not just flee south as soon as the roads became clear. It took all the patience he could muster to wait out a week there before putting his horses to.

Now at journey's end Lord Louis was loath to put the matter to the test. He had rehearsed his speech to Davina since passing Manchester and while he had no doubt of his own feelings he could not rely on hers. She had never given him any word of encouragement and although this was understandable because she had ostensibly been betrothed to Charlie, it did not enhance his lordship's confidence in the outcome.

He stepped languidly out of the vehicle, taking in for the first time the proportions and beauty of the house. The only other time he had visited it, it had been in darkness; now it was bathed in the early afternoon sun. There was a hint of spring in the air, the birds were singing gustily and the tiny crocci were showing a touch of colour as they forced their heads out of the ground. There were even swaths of snowdrops nodding enthusiastically at him in the light breeze. He chose to take it as encouragement and knocked loudly at the door.

It took the elderly butler some time to come to the door. He had had to dispense with his afternoon naps since the arrival of the Burdocks and this was inclined to make him slower.

Lord Louis asked for Lord and Lady Restharrow and was ushered into the house. Old Mr Blackthorne saw no reason to attempt an explanation as to whom was actually the current host at Fromeview Place, thus it was that Lord Louis found himself confronted by three pairs of eyes in faces none of which he recognised, when he was shown into the morning room.

Mrs Burdock, seeing his bewildered expression, stood up from the chair from which she had been reading aloud, and came towards him.

'My dear Lord Louis, how good of you to call,' she said as though she had known him forever.

'I'm sorry,' said Lord Louis, 'I presumed I might find Lord and Lady Restharrow. There has been some mistake.'

'No mistake,' said Mrs Burdock cheerfully, 'I am Lady Restharrow's mother. May I introduce you to my husband, Mr David Burdock, and my other daughter, Miss Grace Burdock.'

Lord Louis, now that he was awake to the relationship could see the likeness. He executed a formal bow to each of the occupants of the room and had one returned punctiliously by the cheery gentleman. However Miss Grace Burdock took one look at him with wide fearful eyes and moved to cling to her mother's arm. Mrs Burdock covered her daughter's hand with her own.

'I'm afraid my daughter does not take to strangers,' she said simply and on closer inspection Lord Louis could see how she was afflicted. He smiled a warm smile at her and then directed his gaze at Mr Burdock.

'Would you be able to advise me as to where Lord Restharrow is currently residing?' he asked the man.

'Lord and Lady Restharrow are at Restharrow Hall,' he replied. 'You will find them there.'

'You look vexed, my lord,' intervened Mrs Burdock, 'but I must tell you Miss Davina Winstanleigh is here with us. You might like to have words with her about her parents' whereabouts.'

Lord Louis looked at her sharply and could see that she was gently laughing at him. She had clearly guessed his errand and it interested him that she made no attempt to pretend that Davina was anything other than Restharrow's daughter. He wondered whether she was doing it to test him or to dissuade him.

At that moment the door behind him opened and Davina stepped into the room. She looked more beautiful than ever in a simple yellow dress. She was carrying a bundle of ribbons and, not having been told of his visit, started to talk as she entered.

'Look Grace, these will trim our cushion nicely.' She halted abruptly. 'Lord Louis!' she gasped.

'Hello, Miss Stan…Winstanleigh, you were not perhaps expecting me?'

'No indeed,' she agreed rather breathlessly. The ribbons fell to the ground. He came up to her and took both her hands kissing one after the other.

Mr Burdock was heard to clear his throat. 'Would it not be opportune, my lord, if we were to have a few words in my study?' said the old man, showing how quickly he had recalled his gentlemanly ways.

Lord Louis dropped Davina's hands and wheeled round. Then with one backward glance at her, he walked through the door Mr Burdock was now holding for him on the other side of the room.

Davina could only stare after him bewildered. 'Why has he gone? What is he about?' she demanded of her grandmother.

'I think that is what your grandfather intends to find out.'

'Davida, Davida.' Grace had gone over to pick up the fallen ribbons and now brought them up to Davina. She took the girl's hand and tugged at her to go to the table where the cushions were laid out. She now understood that when her parents spoke of Davina, they meant her Davida but she still adhered to the belief that this person was her sister whatever she might now choose to be called.

Mechanically Davina did as she was bid, picked up a piece of material and began to match it to the ribbons but she could find no soothing words for her aunt, her mind was a frenzy of conjecture.

'Will he return do you think?' she asked Mrs Burdock.

'Almost certainly my dear,' replied her grandmother comfortingly.' I do not foresee your grandfather saying anything to put him off.'

Davina gave a sharp intake of breath. 'Do you think he knows what is being said?'

'Indubitably. If the gossip has reached us here it will most certainly have reached him wherever he was.'

Davina put down the material and rubbed her brow in chagrin. Her distress was communicating itself to Grace, who began to weep and rock herself backwards and forwards on her chair.

'Oh come now Grace,' cried her mother, 'there is nothing to cry about, nothing at all. Davina was just surprised to see her friend after such a space. See,' she said as Davina drew herself up straight and tidied her frock, 'she is better now, so should you be.'

Davina tried to concentrate and turned her attention back to the cushions. Gradually Grace's agitation subsided and she began to lay the ribbons out in the colours. She had nearly finished when the two men returned. Mr Burdock was looking soulful whilst Lord Louis was slightly ruffled. Mr Burdock did not come all the way into the room and flicked his head to indicate he wished his wife and daughter to withdraw.

Mrs Burdock began to cluck around and encourage Grace from the room but she had to drag her reluctantly away from Davina and Grace could still be heard sobbing gustily beyond the door once it was closed after them.

There was an uncomfortable silence as the two remaining struggled for an opening line.

'What did my grandfather want of you, my lord?' At last Davina's curiosity got the better of her.

'To ascertain what mine intentions towards you are,' he replied with aplomb.

Davina blinked in surprise. 'Your intentions towards me,' she repeated, 'but you can have none!'

'Can I not?' he asked keenly. 'Would you not consider me as a suitor?'

'A suitor,' she repeated his words back at him again.

'Yes damn it woman. I am offering for you. What is your answer to that?' He threw up his hands. 'And don't just repeat "offering for you" please.'

A smile broke from Davina's lips at his words. 'Am I being rather stupid?' she asked.

'Yes,' he said, advancing on her.

Davina stepped strategically behind the table covered with her stitchery and grasped the back of one of the wheel-backed chairs.

'Stop my lord, please,' she begged plaintively. 'I know I deserve your censure but do not tease me, I implore you.'

'Tease you.' It was his turn to repeat her words. 'What can you mean?' he asked bewildered, 'this is no jest, Miss Winstanleigh, I am offering you the protection of my name.

'But this cannot be so, my lord,' she countered. 'I have not forgotten your words at Avebury. You would not have me wed Charlie because of its consequences. You cannot now think that the consequences to yourself would be any less.'

'I do think it,' he averred, 'most certainly I believe that my credit in Society would right you in the eyes of the world.'

'Then I think you must be in error.' She fumbled rather shakily in her reticule and withdrew a crumpled letter. 'See this,' she said waving it at him, 'this is from my friend, Lady Purslane. She writes that it is fortunate that I chose not to visit her this coming season after all as I am now the subject of much speculation: am I Lord Restharrow's by-blow or his legitimate daughter? She says she does not think I would be received and does not want to pain me in attempting it. This, my lord, is to what I am reduced.

I cannot, in all honour, accept a proposal from you knowing how it may affect you.'

'I am prepared to take that risk,' he said resolutely. He came up to her gently now and removing the little bag and letter from her hands, he placed them on the table. He then drew her out from behind the table and took her over to the fireplace. 'Come, throw your lot in with me and let us flick our fingers at polite society,' he said.

'I cannot,' replied Davina, bracing herself so that she did not lean towards him, and draw comfort from his embrace. 'I cannot risk reducing you to an outcast.'

He attempted to interrupt her but she pressed on. 'I have had some experience of it now. I know what it is like to have people whispering as you pass, to have conversations stopping as you enter, to have no visitors. I cannot subject you of all people who has spent a life at ease with so many friends to such a life, please do not ask it of me.'

'But I am asking it of you, I am demanding it. Davina you are the wife I have chosen.'

She gave a snort of derisive laughter. 'You betray yourself in your ignorance of its deprivations, my lord,' she said. 'You believe you can carry everyone along with you but you cannot, so I must protect you from the consequences of that arrogance.'

He was bereft of speech. He had thought she might need some gentle persuasion, he had not expected to be confronted by this solid resistance.

'Have you not forgiven me for what happened at Avebury then?' he asked sadly.

'Of course I have,' she assured him hurriedly. 'You were far too much my friend last summer not to have forgiven you long ago.'

'Then what other consideration is preventing you from throwing caution to the wind? Is it that you have lingering feelings for Charlie? Surely you must have known soon after your engagement that he had eyes for no one but Ernestine?'

Davina was surprised into looking into his eyes.

'I always knew that, my lord,' she said. 'The betrothal was a facade to dupe the creditors, nothing more.' It felt like a weight had been lifted from her shoulders to admit it to him. She expected him to recoil in horror. Instead he smiled.

'You have relieved my mind,' he said, 'I feared you had been tricked into the engagement.'

She shook her head. 'No, not into the engagement but its consequences. I confess I do not know Ernestine as well as I thought I did.'

'I presume it was her idea?'

This time Davina nodded.

'Then you owe them nothing,' he said gently, 'so come, tell me what other bar you perceive to our union. I know that you think there is one.'

There was silence and he knew he had hit the nail on the head. There was something else holding her back. 'I think you owe me at least the knowledge of it before you reject me out of hand.'

'Perhaps I do,' Davina faltered, 'but I cannot hope to make you understand.'

'Try I beg,' he said walking away from her to the window. Outside it was still sunny, but the golden sun had reached the tops of the trees and was on the point of sinking below them.

'You are right, of course,' she acknowledged; she drew a deep breath before enlightening him. 'When my parents were rediscovered to each other but would not allow me to be known as their legitimate daughter, I demanded some compensation. I insisted that my mother attempt a reconciliation with her parents. As you have seen this has been achieved but at a price. My aunt whose mind is that of a child had never recovered from my mother's disappearance but on her reappearance did not recognise her. She took me to be my mother.' Davina paused, thinking of the irony of what had happened. 'You have already seen how I figure in her affections. I cannot be away from her for long or she becomes much distressed. I cannot abandon her, my

239

lord. Do you not see that? It was I who forced the reunion. I cannot be the one to impose another parting. I have a duty to suffer the consequences of my actions.'

'So you would sacrifice our love for the sake of a feeble-minded aunt of some two months' acquaintance?' he demanded bitterly.

There was a silence as she looked at him with sorrowful eyes. 'Yes, my lord, I must,' she said.

29

*H*e was gone. He had strode out in anger and Davina had maintained a rigid control over her emotions for fear that if he saw her cry he would break down her defences and sweep her along in the tide of his love. As she heard the front door close, Davina's body sagged. She turned on her heel and headed for her bedroom. She was not ready to deal with the enquiries of her grandparents no matter how sympathetic. She met Mrs Tulley in the hallway and beseeched her to ensure her an hour's quietude in her room. Not for a long time had Davina yearned for the bracing comfort that Nancy was used to provide her but she longed for it now. Nancy however was out of her reach having gone to Restharrow Hall to act as lady's maid to the new Lady Restharrow. Davina was left to discover what inner strength she could and draw comfort from it.

In the saloon downstairs, unaware of the result of Davina's interview with Lord Louis, Mr and Mrs Burdock were speculating on what it would be like to be aligned to such a grand family. Grace sat silently listening but only able to grasp half of what was said; her face began to look pinched and haunted. When Mrs Tulley came to report that Lord Louis had left without saying goodbye, Grace slipped out before Davina was mentioned. She ran to the morning room and finding it empty went in haste, first to the music room and then to the breakfast parlour. By the time she had visited every downstairs room in the house her worst fears were realised: Davida had left her again. Grace gave a shudder of despair, then, dressed only in her floral dress and woollen shawl, she went out into the dying embers of the evening sun in search of her sister.

It was not until Davina descended the stairs nearly an hour later that Grace was missed. Her parents assumed that she had followed Davina to her bedchamber. While they were aware that Davina had requested solitude, they had decided that Grace's need for Davina was greater. It therefore came as a shock when Davina entered the saloon a little after darkness had fallen and enquired after her aunt.

'But was she not with you?' asked Mrs Burdock in quick concern. 'We felt sure she was safely upstairs with you.'

Davina shook her head. 'I have been alone in my room,' she insisted.

Mr Burdock stood up from his chair and pulled the bell-rope vigorously. There could be no doubt in the servants' hall that it was an urgent summons. Both Mrs Tulley and Blackthorne felt the need to respond.

Having ascertained that neither knew the whereabouts of his daughter, Mr Burdock demanded the presence of all the servants and set about arranging a systematic search of the house. For some twenty minutes rooms were scoured for any sign of Grace. Every cupboard was opened and even the attics were penetrated, all to no avail. Grace was nowhere to be found.

The search was extended to the garden. Great flaming torches were lit and lanterns retrieved from all quarters. The stables and hayloft were searched, the succession houses were checked and also the antiquated carriages stored in the coach houses were entered and eliminated as possible hiding places. Mr Burdock cursed that he had not yet taken up his shooting again. Had he had a gun dog he was sure he would have found her. An hour later all the activity remained fruitless. Grace remained unfound.

'She must have escaped on to the common,' said Mrs Tulley wearily when the last of the servants returned from their luckless errand.

'No,' gasped Mrs Burdock, 'no, not my dear girl out in the dark on such a cold night, she will be terrified, terrified. We must find her, we must.'

Mr Burdock took his frantic wife in a strong embrace and tried to soothe her. 'We will rally more helpers,' he said. 'Mrs Tulley, send a man out to the Rectory and beg their assistance. I will ride to the Ragged Cot and request some help there. The others must start to walk the common.' He released his wife before continuing, 'Davina, you stay here to support your grandmother. I do not want her left alone.'

'Oh you cannot ask that of me Grandpapa,' cried Davina. 'Let Mrs Tulley bear Grandmama company. I of all people must join the search. I know the common better than anyone here present. Even in the dark, I know its hollows and hidey-holes. Please say I may go with them.'

Her grandfather looked at her wan face and knew he must let her have her way. 'Very well,' he said, 'but keep close to one of the men and dress warmly. I will have no one succumb to cold. Understand me?'

There was general assent from the gathering of servants who had not previously bothered to put on greatcoats and woollen jackets as everyone had been so sure that Miss Grace could not have strayed so far. All manner of attire was now donned. Every hat on the premises was called into service, as were a range of hand wear from mittens to gauntlets. As the evening had turned into night the temperature had taken a cruel dive and it was now bitterly cold.

Davina attired herself in two pelisses and then borrowing a vast cape from her grandfather's wardrobe put that on as well. She did not think that she would need it but she was so sure that she would find her aunt that she wanted to carry the extra clothing in which to wrap her.

Already the footman was on his way to the Rectory and Mr Burdock was mounting his horse.

'I do hope your appeal is successful.' Davina reached up and grasped his hand. 'Should you not take someone with you? The lane is very dark and lonely.'

'No, no, no one can be spared from the search. Now stand aside my dear and let me be on my way.'

The inn to which Mr Burdock intended to take his plea was a little more than three-quarters of a mile down the road. It was the haunt of yeoman farmers and Mr Burdock hoped to find a goodly crowd of these worthies to aid his search.

As he drew close in the dark, he could see that he was in luck. The Ragged Cot was clearly very busy. From every downstairs room there could be seen light blazing. They had no need to close the shutters to keep the heat in, the throng would generate its own warmth.

Handing his mount to an overworked ostler, he made his way to the taproom. As he stepped through the door he was hit by a wave of odour, which was a mix of the strong smell of tallow from the hundreds of yellow glowing candles that served the room, with acrid smoke from a chimney, which did not draw properly. There was also the smell of tobacco from several pipes. Mr Burdock made his way to the bar with some difficulty as many a burly fellow enjoying his ale impeded his path. When he eventually reached his goal the landlord was an elusive quarry, hurrying from customer to customer while ranting at two flustered serving wenches.

'Quickly, Sir, what's your tipple?' the man came to him.

'It is a service I crave, not a beverage,' said Mr Burdock in a voice suddenly hoarse from the cacophony of atmosphere.

'I can provide no service, Sir. All my rooms are taken and my only private parlour let,' the heavy-jowled man replied unhelpfully.

'It is men I need not beds,' hurried on Mr Burdock. 'I need manpower for a search of the common. My daughter has gone missing and we fear for her well being in this cold and darkness. Can you make yourself heard? Can you encourage these people to help me?'

The landlord looked sharply at Mr Burdock but before he could speak one of the wenches nudged his arm and whispered something in his ear.

'So you are from Fromeview Place,' he said his eyes narrowing.

'Yes, yes, close to the common. This is why the case is so desperate. My daughter is lost on the common.'

'What is that to me.' The landlord's voice had a penetrating quality and it carried above the hubbub to the group next to Mr Burdock. They turned and watched him in silence. The landlord continued: 'I see no reason for anyone to help those from Fromeview Place. Have not the Stanleys turned on those who have always called them friends? Miss Greenaway has been sorely treated.' There was nodding and a murmur of assent from the group and it caught the attention of the next. The silence moved like a wave throughout the crowd until Mr Burdock found himself centre stage.

'You are mistaken Sir, Miss Stanley and Miss Greenaway are lifelong friends. But what can this have to do with my poor daughter. I beg you,' he turned to confront the bulk of his audience, 'I beg you assist me in my search. My daughter must be found tonight if she is to be found alive.'

'You have no business here man, and you will get no succour either,' raged the landlord. 'Get out of here now if you want to save your whining carcass.'

'Please I implore you.' Mr Burdock could feel fear rising in him as he sensed the crowd tense into a mob but his fear for his daughter was greater. 'Will you not help me?'

'Get him out of here,' ordered the landlord and three large farmers in homespuns responded to the call. Two went to Mr Burdock's arms and the third lifted his legs clean from under him. The path was miraculously cleared to the door and a chant was set up accompanied by the banging of tankards on any hard surface available. Mr Burdock was bundled out of the door and was sent sprawling on the ground. With a nasty kick to his body and a jeering laugh, the men returned to the taproom.

For some little while Mr Burdock struggled with his breathing for they had winded him. He then rose shakily to his feet gingerly holding his ribs, and retrieved his hat. He was about to make for the stables to fetch his horse when he saw the ostler turn it out and give it a hefty whack on its backside. Normally a staid animal it came past him at a gallop and Mr Burdock had no chance of capturing its reins. He was left with no recourse but to limp homewards in the dark, unattended by even a lantern.

In the private parlour at the back of the inn, a muffled version of the events had penetrated even Lord Louis's abstraction. He had intended to put as much distance between himself and Davina as he possibly could, such had been his anger at her rejection, but once beyond the grounds of the house he had been unable to tear himself further away. He had let the reins of his horse slacken and he had meandered along with dusk falling around him. He had seen the inn and been drawn to it. Whether he planned a second visit to Fromeview on the morrow even he could not decide, but it was a comfort to be near her. He had eaten a slow supper, as much by choice as because the inn was busy and was now sampling a plate of sweetmeats. The landlord came in to replenish the wine.

'I heard a commotion,' said his lordship to the man as he attempted to quit the room. 'Have you a riot on your hands? I do trust it will not disturb my sleep!' He wondered at himself for being so frivolous when his heart ached so.

'Oh it was nothing, my lord,' the landlord assured him hastily, 'just an unwanted guest who needed to be evicted.'

'It sounded more than that, my man,' countered Lord Louis.

'Oh no, nothing serious, my lord,' the landlord repeated, keen to get away. The pointed questions were most unwelcome as the man was already suffering slightly with his conscience.

'Come, come, landlord, give me a fuller account, I pray. Otherwise I will be fearful of my own safety and pack my bags now.' He was jesting but he saw that the landlord was uncomfortable.

'Very well, my lord.' The landlord came back into the body of the room and put down the tray he had intended to remove. 'If you will have it so.'

'I will man, I want chapter and verse.'

'Well you must know the background then.' The landlord gave a heavy sigh. 'There is a large house just a way up the road with a young lady resident with her mother.'

Lord Louis stiffened, this was not what he had expected. The landlord had paused. 'Go on man, go on,' his lordship prompted.

'The young lady was mostly friendly with the Rector's daughter. Like sisters they were, a joy to set eyes on. But the girl was found to have a wicked streak. She stole the Rector's daughter's beau and although nothing has come of it, we cannot forgive.'

'I know something of this,' said Lord Louis in haste to defend his lady love. 'I can assure you that Miss Stanley acted in all honour to her friend.'

The landlord looked sceptical. 'That's as may be in your eyes, my lord, but we are simple folk, we see the matter differently.'

'Very well, but what has that to do with tonight's disturbance?'

'Well the young lady's grandparents and aunt have now moved here from the north. The aunt is a moonling.'

'I know of the aunt, I have seen her,' snapped Lord Louis.

The landlord bristled. 'Do you want me to tell this tale, my lord?'

'Yes, yes, I crave your pardon, continue.'

The landlord heaved another great sigh. 'Well, tonight the aunt has gone missing, believed to be lost on the common. The old man came for help with the search.' He faltered but Lord Louis had got the picture, and leapt to his feet.

'And you said him nay and sent him roundly on his way.'

'Yes, my lord,' acquiesced the landlord almost inaudibly.

'Good God man, how could you? That girl is more a child than a woman and you would have her perish because of some perceived wrong her relative had done. How could you man? Have you no soul?' Lord Louis grabbed his coat. 'Come, we must muster a search party. Quickly, quickly before it is too late.'

Quite without knowing how he had been carried along by his lordship, the landlord found himself standing at the peer's right arm as he addressed the taproom demanding and getting volunteers.

Soon there was a party of some twenty men with torches and lanterns aloft striding up the road towards the common. It was not long before they overtook the blown Mr Burdock. One look at his face in the lamplight told Lord Louis how badly he had been used.

'You two,' he commanded two of the tallest men. 'Make a chair for this man and carry him to the house.' It was soon done and with no demur. Mr Burdock looked on in wonder.

30

On the moor Davina did not see the reinforcements arrive but learned of it through a chain of whispers from others about her. She had stopped calling Grace's name now, knowing that if her aunt was still alive, she would be in no condition to respond. Davina heard a garbled version of Lord Louis's actions and her heart sang. It ennobled him even further in her eyes that he could forgive her so quickly and come to her aid. Once she caught a glimpse of him, his top hat silhouetted against the lamplight although she could not make out his features. She knew it had to be him as he was a good head taller than his companions.

Despite her warm clothes, Davina's hands and feet were beginning to suffer the cold. The night seemed to stretch out before her, a long yawning tunnel of anxiety and fearful anticipation. She listened to the calls of the others, longing for the shout of discovery but it would not come.

The church in Minchinhampnett struck the hour of ten, then eleven and Davina's weary body knew it would soon strike twelve when the sound she had longed for did at last come. Davina was in earshot close to the escarpment and picking up her many layers of skirts and finding energy which a minute before she would not have believed she possessed, she ran towards the noise.

'Grace, Grace, oh my darling.' She could see the crumpled form under the light from the lamp belonging to the man who had found her. 'Does she live?' she cried even before she reached him.

'I believe so, Miss, but she is very cold.'

Already a crowd was gathering. Davina stripped off the great cape and draped it over Grace's recumbent form. She found herself crouching beside her aunt, looking up at a circle of faces; all seemed incapable of action. It was with considerable relief that she saw Lord Louis make his way through the crowd. He bent down and picked up Grace as though she was as light as the child she appeared to be and began to stride back towards the road. The movement broke the spell and someone helped Davina to her feet and the weary searchers followed at differing speeds in his wake.

By the time Davina reached Fromeview Place, the hallway was filled with a motley selection of searchers. Blackthorne, the old butler who had not attempted to join the search, now came into his own and was serving hot wine and cinnamon biscuits. Leaving him to cope, Davina made her way to the saloon and discovered her grandfather and Lord Louis there. Mr Burdock was seated on the edge of a chair resting heavily on a stick. He was ashen faced and beads of perspiration were evident on his brow. Davina ran to him and sank at his feet.

'Grandpapa, pray tell, what has happened to you? You look most unwell. Let me call the doctor.'

'The doctor is here, Miss Winstanleigh,' said Lord Louis evenly from his place by the fire. 'Mrs Tulley called him when she saw your grandfather's condition but he has subordinated his claim to your aunt. The doctor is with her now.'

'But what has caused you to be in such pain?' Davina cried.

Before he could answer, they were interrupted by the sound of someone coming quickly towards the saloon door. The door was flung open and the Rector was seen to enter the room. He made a striking figure in his black cloth.

'My lord, Mr Burdock, Miss Stanley.' His piercing blue eyes took them all in with a sweeping glance. 'I came as soon as I heard. You must let me be of service to you in this time of trial. Your daughter, Mr Burdock, what news of her?'

Mr Burdock sucked in a painful breath and seemed unable to speak. Lord Louis spoke for him.

'We await the doctor's verdict, Rector. She became very chilled, we do not know whether it will have lasting consequences.'

'Then I will wait with you in your vigil until you have news, if you will permit it.'

Here Lord Louis deferred to Mr Burdock with his eyes.

'Yes by all means,' he said, finding his voice between gasps of breath. 'We would be grateful for your solace.'

It became clear to the Rector that Mr Burdock was injured.

'My dear Sir, what ails you? You are in considerable discomfort, are you not?'

'What indeed?' cried Davina. 'Tell us I beg.'

'I'm afraid your grandfather is in no condition for lengthy explanations, Miss Winstanleigh,' said Lord Louis as he came over and extended his hand to help her up from her position on the floor, 'but I believe I know the background.' Having led Davina to a chair, he turned to the visitor. 'I'm afraid his injuries are to be laid at your daughter's door, Rector,' he said. 'It seems your flock perceives Miss Winstanleigh as wronging your daughter in some way. When he went to the Ragged Cot to beg assistance for Miss Grace, he was summarily removed and viciously attacked.'

'But how can this be!' cried Mr Greenaway. 'I saw the landlord from the inn out in the hallway enjoying Mr Burdock's hospitality as I came in.'

'My lord prevailed on him to change his mind,' said Davina, having heard this from her fellow searchers.

'Yes,' confirmed Mr Burdock whose voice was now a hoarse whisper, 'we have his lordship to thank that my daughter was found so quickly.'

'Then I am grateful to you Twayblade,' said the Rector in some embarrassment. 'I can only apologise to you all for my daughter's conduct. Her wilfulness has tainted us all and I am sorry for it.'

Davina could not bear his discomfiture, she had so long revered and respected him. She stood up and came to him. 'Please, Sir,' she said, 'do not torture yourself, there is little you could have done.'

'You are too kind, my dear, I am grateful for your solicitude but I am gravely at fault. Once I knew what my daughter had done I should have righted the situation immediately. I have been tardy in re-establishing you in the eyes of our neighbours and have brought more misery on your family.' His gaze flickered to Mr Burdock and away again. What he saw stiffened his resolve. 'Come,' he said, drawing Davina's hand through his arm, 'you and I must go and thank all those who turned out tonight. We will present a united front.'

Davina went with him unresistingly and while she was away, Mrs Tulley returned to the room with the doctor.

'What news of Miss Grace, doctor?' demanded Lord Louis on his entrance.

'There is little to tell, my lord,' the middle-aged doctor responded but there was a calmness about him which gave reassurance. 'Miss Grace sleeps and we can only wait to see if her lungs are affected but I have high hopes that she will escape anything too serious.'

He turned his attention to Mr Burdock and with infinite care he helped the old man to his feet and escorted him from the room attended by the ever-loyal Mrs Tulley. Lord Louis was left to await the return of the Rector and Miss Winstanleigh.

He did not have to wait long. They soon appeared with Davina leaning heavily on the arm of her mentor. The long day had taken its toll and she was feeling weak and shaky. The Rector drew her to the fire, which Lord Louis had had the forethought to replenish.

'I think I will not stay after all,' said the Rector. 'I hope to hear comfortable tidings of both your grandfather and your aunt in the morning, I shall be over after morning prayers to get news of them.'

'You are very kind Sir,' said Davina but her brow was furrowed.

'You must not be anxious for them, my dear,' said the Rector, seeing it, 'they are in the best hands.'

'I know,' she agreed, 'it was not of them I was thinking.' She drew a deep breath. 'I fear for Ernestine and Charlie. How will they maintain themselves?'

'You need lose no sleep over them,' snapped Lord Louis, anger throbbing in his voice. 'They have been fickle friends to you, they do not deserve for you to suffer a moment's further discomfort on their behalf.'

Davina turned her head away and bit her lip. Taking pity on her the Rector braved Lord Louis's wrath.

'I believe Lord and Lady Restharrow have offered them the Dower House at Restharrow,' he said. 'It is in poor condition and they will have little more than two hundred pounds a year but it will be a lesson to them to manage on it. I feel sure they will learn in time.'

'Pshaw.' Lord Louis turned away in disgust. 'I believe you to be too sanguine, Rector,' he said, perceptibly grinding his teeth. 'They will spend many a week at house parties where others will frank them. They will see no need to live out their lives frugally at Restharrow.'

'Oh please, please,' Davina made a beseeching gesture with her hand, 'do not malign them so. I would wish them every happiness. I cannot begrudge it them. I have made other truer friends.' There she looked directly at the Rector. 'Your daughter, Lady Purslane, earns my deepest gratitude and Miss Amelia too.' Then she paused as though seeking the courage, before coming up behind Lord Louis and placing her hand on his upper arm. He turned slowly to look down into her dark eyes, which were sparkling with tears. 'And you,' she said, 'have been the truest friend of all.'

The Rector cleared his throat and made a move to the door but Lord Louis stopped him.

'Before you go, Sir,' he said, 'will you not assure Miss

Winstanleigh that she need no longer feel apart from the society hereabouts.'

'Most certainly I will and gladly,' he said, coming back to shake Lord Louis's outstretched hand. 'And I take it you will be adding your might to ensuring her entrée into polite society.'

'And my name, Rector, and my name. This time I will not let her say me nay.'

'Good man; then I leave you now and will see you again on the morrow. Goodnight to you both.'

With that he was gone. The two he left behind remained in silence as his firm footfall faded away down the corridor and was eventually cessated by the thud of the front door.

'There,' said Lord Louis on a long outlet of breath, 'you now have your trustee's and your grandfather's consent. What other obstacles will you find to keep us apart?'

'There is still my aunt, my lord,' she responded, desperately fighting for self-control.

Lord Louis pulled her to him and held her in the circle of his arms. 'Your aunt is no impediment, Davina,' he said gently as he raised her chin so she had to look into his face. 'I have no objection to living here with your grandparents and her. I, after all, have no other place to call my own.'

'Oh but that is not true, you have Castle Sainfoin.'

'My father's, then my brother Campion's, it's not likely ever to be mine.'

'But surely your family has other estates, other houses which are yours?'

'None as pleasant or contained of company capable of holding me there for more than two sennights together.' She was silenced and he saw that he must jolly her out of her woes if he was to gain her acceptance of this simple solution. 'And don't suggest, I beg you, that we should take up residence with your parents at Restharrow for I have no taste to be associated with Charlie and Ernestine yet awhile.'

'No, of course not. I would never suggest such a thing.' She looked so anxious to reassure him that he could no longer resist temptation and he brushed his lips across hers. He felt her quiver in response and tightened his hold, his face so near to hers that his strong features were now almost a blur.

'Come Davina, tell me yea.'

She tried to pull away from him and chivalry dictated that he had to let her go.

'What now?' he demanded, exasperated.

'You forget Lady Purslane's letter,' she said on a dry sob. 'Society is divided, my parents are unwilling to acknowledge my true state, I cannot accept you while all this uncertainty surrounds me.'

'There is no uncertainty, Davina,' he said emphatically and drew out the copy of the marriage lines from his breast pocket and showed it to her. 'No uncertainty at all. I confess I do not understand your parents' reasoning for the denying of you.'

'They fear the gossip will persuade the creditors that they will flee abroad. They fear being hounded to pay all immediately.'

Lord Louis threw back his head and laughed while Davina stared at him in wide-eyed wonder.

'Oh come, you foolish girl,' he said, casting aside the document and once more advancing on her, 'marrying me can only confound the creditors, not incite them.'

Davina found she had to agree.

'You are determined then to wed me?' she said. 'To remain closeted here in rural Gloucestershire?' She shook her head. 'No, you would soon feel trapped.'

'Oh call a halt now, Davina,' growled Lord Louis as he swept her into his arms. 'I am sure I shall be allowed away on visits now and then.'

'Oh I don't think so,' said Davina dulcetly. Finally dropping her resistance, she grasped the lapel of his coat, 'because now have you for mine own, I do not think I am ever going to let you go.'